For my family; you are my world.

The Ingredients for Happiness

LUCY KNOTT

ONE PLACE. MANY STORIES

HQ
An imprint of HarperCollins*Publishers* Ltd
1 London Bridge Street
London SE1 9GF

This edition 2019

First published in Great Britain by
HQ, an imprint of HarperCollins*Publishers* Ltd 2019

ISBN: 978-0-00-834866-3

MIX
Paper from
responsible sources
FSC™ C007454

This book is produced from independently certified FSC™ paper
to ensure responsible forest management.

For more information visit: www.harpercollins.co.uk/green

Typeset by Palimpsest Book Production Ltd, Falkirk, Stirlingshire

Printed and bound in Great Britain by
CPI Group (UK) Ltd, Croydon, CR0 4YY

Chapter 1

Rum Baba

Ingredients:

Flour
Sugar
Eggs
Baking powder
One of those vanilla/baking powder packets with the angel
on the front

What to do:

Mix all ingredients together and pour into crème caramel ramekins.
(Wait, what about the rum? Nanna didn't say rum; she laughed when I
mentioned it. Is there no rum in rum baba? Maybe I soak it at the end
— I'm certain the one Grandpa made me was soaked in rum.)
Figure out rum.
(Hang on, I think Nanna missed out a few ingredients when she told me.
Yeast! Doesn't Rum Baba have yeast in it?)
Figure out missing ingredients.

The sun was trying with all its might to cast warm rays down on Manchester, but January was having none of it. With every hint of a glow came a grey cloud that swooped in to steal the spotlight. The dreary sky would not be affecting Amanda's mood today though, she was absolutely not going to let it. She was sure that

1

today they would find her café and her positive energy would make it so. That, and they had to. She was all too aware that Dan needed to get back to LA for label meetings and to discuss the future of *San Francisco Beat* with Sabrina and his bandmates, but his opinion on her new place was paramount. She clutched his hand tighter; her body had an automatic reflex to her brain thinking about his departure – it did not want to let him go either.

As if reading her mind, and her body, Dan suddenly pulled Amanda into a little side street they were passing and within seconds his hands were in her long, wavy hair and his lips were on hers. Amanda kissed him back with a smile permanently playing at her lips. Since they had both admitted to their feelings for each other in Italy over the holidays, Amanda had come to find out that moments like this happened often when she was 'more than just friends' with Dan. His reasoning behind his grand public displays of affection was simple; he couldn't get enough of her and he told her so. With Amanda not being so great at relationships and her last one being a total wrecking ball, Dan's ways of showing he clearly only had eyes for her were a welcome change and soothed old rumbling insecurities.

Dan pulled back slowly, biting Amanda's bottom lip gently as he did so. He had one hand up against the wall and his other still entangled in her hair. When his chocolate eyes met hers, they smiled as bright as his lips, causing dimples to appear in his cheeks. If the kiss hadn't made her knees buckle, just looking at him would have. As casually as it had started, Dan took her hand and they were back on the pavement heading to their eighth possible café of the day.

Chills surged through Amanda's body and goose bumps rose on her arms as they neared the building on the corner of the street. One look at Dan and she knew he felt it too; he looked at her and nodded. Past the book shop and next to the tattoo shop was the perfect-shaped building. The worn-down door stood side

2

by side with the tattoo shop to give way to a beautiful bay window that wrapped around the corner of the street.

'Dan!' Amanda gasped, clasping her hands together. She wasn't one to get giddy but then again, she hadn't believed she would ever be looking to purchase her own café, and here she was.

'Let's look inside,' Dan replied. His face was joyful, but he would not get ahead of himself like Amanda. He was the calm to her storm. He opened the rusty door with a creak and gestured for her to go first.

Amanda's eyes grew wide as she took in the open square space. Tucked into the left-hand corner at the rear was a built-in bar area. Next to this, two swinging double doors led to the kitchen. Amanda spun around on the spot, catching the estate agent's eye as she did so.

'I do apologize for being so rude. Hi, I'm Amanda,' Amanda said, sticking out a hand. The estate agent took it without making eye contact, and gave her a one-sided smile. He was clearly not too bothered by her rudeness; he seemed quite happy with the other half of her party and couldn't take his eyes off Dan. Of course, Dan would never be so ignorant as to ignore a person and had not missed a figure in the room upon entering. But Amanda had been sucked into the charm of the building. She didn't wish to be rude by not joining in the conversation Dan and the estate agent were currently engaged in, but she made her way to the double doors, unable to wait for them to finish talking. She knew that the estate agent would be lost to Dan's raspy voice for a good fifteen minutes, or for life, and that was a seriously long time to wait when the kitchen was calling her name.

Another gasp escaped Amanda's lips when she walked through the 'enter' side of the double doors. The kitchen, too, was square and in the centre stood a considerable island. It was Amanda's dream kitchen. Immediately her mind began bursting with visions of where each piece of machinery would go, where Grandpa's special knick-knacks and tools would be stored. Amanda wondered for a moment why the previous owners had had to give the place up and her stomach gave an uncomfortable lurch. *This is not the time for doubts Amanda*, she thought to herself. *You've come this far.* Just then Dan walked through the door, very, very closely followed by the estate agent. Amanda watched him as he looked around the room and did a double take at the island before giving her his all-encompassing grin. The worry lines on her forehead smoothed out.

'I love it,' they said in unison. Amanda walked over to Dan and tip-toed to give him a kiss on the cheek. 'It's beautiful,' she added. From the corner of her eye she could see the estate agent eyeing her up and down and longingly glancing back to Dan.

'If you love it, it's yours,' Dan said softly, giving her a disarming smile and bowing to kiss the top of her head. The estate agent practically melted before them. If Dan knew he had this effect on people, he never let it show. His ego was still very much non-existent and the attention and kindness he gave to everyone never faltered, even after three years of the media being infatuated with him and his every move.

'I really love it,' Amanda said softly, staring into Dan's soulful eyes, before turning on her buckled boots and scanning the kitchen once more. There was an enormous amount of work to be done, but she felt in her bones that this was her place; this was where she was going to build her café. She greatly appreciated Dan's generous gesture and she would let him do what he wanted for now, because arguing with him over this matter would be like drawing blood from a stone. But she had her own money saved for this such occasion – she had simply been too frightened to use it before now. But with her former sous-chef Jeff, ruining her reputation and giving her the kick up the backside she needed to finally walk away from Rusk, and with the death last year of her grandpa – her role model and the man that inspired her cooking – she had known it was time to take a giant leap of faith and make her and her grandpa's dream a reality.

She walked in a circle around the island and back through the swinging doors. A single tear rolled down her cheek as she willed her happy thoughts to get to her grandpa, hoping he could see her now, finally going after the dream that had eluded her and scared her silly for years. She had been secretly squirreling away every bit of pocket money he had given her since she was eight years old, ready for this moment. Her heart squeezed in her chest at the thought that this was as much her grandpa's as it was hers. Taking a deep breath and wiping at her face, she drew her shoulders back and pulled out her phone. She hadn't had time to think about the time difference; she just hoped that both her sisters were available.

*

After a brief, but positive FaceTime with both Sabrina and Louisa, who both saw the place's potential and encouraged Amanda to follow her gut, and an excited phone call with her parents, Amanda was ready to give Dan the go-ahead. She would of course email the estate agent and make an appointment to go over the payment plan, but for now Dan could be in charge. If he wanted to read through long pages of contracts, Amanda was more than happy to let him. She had never been one for the fine print and Dan had experience where this was concerned. She more than appreciated his help. He too had shared in this vision with her during the course of their four-year friendship. Besides her family, Dan was her biggest supporter.

With a nod of her head and a pep in her step, Amanda walked over to the estate agent and Dan, who had followed her back out through the double doors, and expressed her keen interest in the vacant café. She saw a twinkle in Dan's eyes, and he beamed with pride at her.

'We'll take it,' Dan said to the estate agent. The estate agent puffed out his chest and his smile widened. He shuffled through some papers and had Amanda sign a few, just as a security deposit, then reached out to shake their hands. His handshake with Dan was far more enthusiastic than hers, Amanda noted.

It seemed the sky was trying to celebrate with her as they stepped back outside into the January chill; there were a few scattered sun rays lighting up the little establishment overhead and Amanda felt her grandpa's approval. In her wave of happiness, she hugged the estate agent in thanks, which garnered an actual smile and eye contact. Then Dan handed him his card and told him to message if he ever fancied coming to one of the boys' shows when they were next in town. With the giddy, slightly unprofessional handshake that followed, Amanda worried for a moment that the estate agent was not going to let go.

The knot in her stomach that had been there all morning had finally untangled and as they walked back to Amanda's house, she felt a thrill of excitement for this new beginning. The past few months had been tough on her family, with the sudden passing of Grandpa. Louisa had opted to stay in Italy with Nanna and Sabrina was preparing to move back to Manchester after four years of living the high life in LA, now that San Francisco Beat had parted ways with their record label. Life had changed quite drastically for them all. But the decisions had been made and now they had to rise to the challenges they now faced.

With this thought, her excitement faded to fear and she gripped Dan's hand a little tighter. He would be leaving tomorrow and that wasn't quite the challenge she wanted to face, which was silly really. She and Dan had spent plenty of time apart over the years – months and months away from each other – and their friendship remained strong. A twinge of the hurt she had felt after Jason tried to shadow and dampen her good vibes. It felt different now. Before, she never cared about the tabloids, the girlfriends and the crazy life thrust into the hands of rock stars; now, the ever-present groupies and parties to attend made her insides squirm, but she was determined not to let those negative thoughts weigh her down. Dan had never given her any reason to worry.

She was not about to let her mind play tricks on her. Dan was her best friend first and rock star second.

She wasn't the jealous type, but whatever was causing her unease definitely felt like jealousy. Years of being relaxed with her ex-boyfriend Jason had only meant that he had cheated on her more times than she cared to remember, and she always forgave him; would Dan do the same? The idea of girls throwing themselves at him no longer made her want to roll her eyes and punch Dan in the arm in playful jest, but instead curl up into a ball and cry. But they were together now and Dan knew that. Dan had wanted that too. And he would be back soon. This jealousy was an imposter and had no place in her heart.

'Should I be Team Cap or Team Iron Man?' Dan piped up as they turned onto Amanda's street. They had been walking in a comfortable silence hand in hand, though it hadn't been all that silent in Amanda's head.

'Huh?' said Amanda, glancing up at Dan. His wavy hair was getting caught in the breeze and falling in his face. She automatically reached up to brush it behind his ear. He caught her hand when she did so and kissed her palm, sending tingles through her entire body. A teasing smirk appeared on Dan's handsome face. 'There seems to be a civil war going on in that brain of yours, baby girl.'

Amanda laughed at Dan's superhero reference. It was difficult to stay worried and anxious when looking into Dan's rich brown eyes. They did something to her; they melted away her fears and replaced them with a sense of calm and contentment – as though his own demeanour transferred over to her when she needed it most.

'No, I'm okay. I can't believe how perfect the café is. I think Grandpa would have loved it. Thank you for staying with me and helping me look for a place,' Amanda said, brushing the hand that Dan was still holding close to his lips, over Dan's cheeks. He was supporting a five o'clock shadow; she enjoyed the feel of his

7

stubble against her fingers and the softness of his skin. He looked edible in his chunky black knit cardigan, jeans and white tee. What was it with men and never getting cold? She herself was wearing her oversized pink teddy coat that kept in all the heat, over a grey woolly jumper, with a scarf for good measure.

'Of course; I could never deny my best girl when she offers me a proposition,' Dan replied, referring to New Year's Eve when they were standing on her zia's balcony overlooking the Amalfi Coast and she had told Dan that she would only be his 'sexy' Manchester tour guide if he helped her search for a café. He'd had the same confident glint in his eye back then at the word 'proposition' as he did now. 'Speaking of which, I have a proposition for you,' he added, letting go of her hands to allow her to rummage through her bag in search of her keys.

'You do? I have a feeling this proposition is more suited to that dangerously sexy mind of yours,' Amanda replied as she unlocked her front door. She was no longer battling with her insecurities. Instead she was just focused on Dan, the moment she was in and what he was going to say.

Dan laughed, a low laugh that made her stomach flip over as they entered the house.

'I was going to suggest we spend the rest of the day baking together, but if you had other things in mind ... I was just thinking rum baba.' He gave her a sly grin, before kissing the base of her neck along her collarbone as she shimmied out of her coat.

Would she ever not be phased by that voice? Amanda playfully pushed him away.

'Isn't a proposition supposed to have something in it for both parties? I somehow only see that being beneficial to you and your budding appetite,' Amanda said teasingly before shoving Dan towards the kitchen.

'Argh, but you need practice for the café; I saw it on your list, and I am happy to be a guinea pig to make sure everything is up to standard.' Amanda laughed as she walked behind him, watching him casually brush a hand through his wind-styled hair, which of course looked dreamy on him. Amanda wished the wind had that effect on her own locks. They entered the kitchen and she busied herself in the fridge, keeping Dan in her peripheral vision. It was hard to take her eyes off him. She watched as he took off his cardigan, his white tee taught against his muscles. He'd put on a few extra pounds over Christmas and while staying with her these past three weeks. It suited him – filling out his muscles, making his tall frame broader. She loved wrapping her arms around him.

Speaking of arms, she felt his thick biceps wrap around her shoulders as she collected the ingredients for rum baba. 'You make a cute guinea pig,' Amanda said, putting down a pot of cream and reaching up to grab his forearms. She felt safe snuggled up in Dan's arms.

'Speaking of lists and recipes, how do you know how much of each ingredient to use, my love? There are no measurements for this recipe,' Dan whispered into her ear, peering over her shoulder at the tatty piece of paper Amanda had scrawled on. Amanda chuckled and squeezed his forearms. Then she shrugged, a smile spreading across her lips and goosebumps tickling her arms.

'Erm, I don't really know. I guess I just know. When I read it, I see Grandpa and I just do what he did.' Her smile widened as her words made her think of him. Dan squeezed her back. 'Your mind is my favourite,' he said, lovingly, making Amanda's grin reach her ears.

'Let's celebrate.' She reached into the still-open fridge to get the red wine.

'What? My making a cute guinea pig?' Dan chuckled, making her shiver. Amanda rolled her eyes and wriggled out of his grasp to retrieve two wine glasses. She handed a glass to Dan – who nodded, watching her adoringly from under his long lashes – and filled up both of their glasses.

'To *Torta per Tutti*,' Dan said, raising his glass to hers. Amanda's knees immediately buckled, and she went to sit down at the kitchen table, floored that Dan had remembered the name she and her grandpa had come up with for their dream café, years ago. She had only shared this with Dan on one occasion. Hearing him say it out loud made it more real. She wasn't just doing this for her, she was doing it for Grandpa too. Dan took a step closer to her, so she had to look up and meet his gaze.

'And to us,' he added, clinking her glass. They each took a sip, before Dan set about getting the rest of the ingredients for the rum baba out of the fridge. The niggling insecurities she had about her being bad at relationships were the last thing on her mind. She felt every doubt she had ever had about life vanish as she watched him move confidently around her kitchen. If she thought Dan couldn't get any sexier, she had been very wrong. She stared at him as he put on her apron, pursed his lips and creased his eyebrows in concentration while he read through an Italian recipe, and her heart exploded with happiness.

Their relationship had been going strong for four years. They had faced loss, fame and distance together. Dan and his forever chilled persona had found solutions to problems without drama; he centred Amanda, they knew each other inside out. Nothing could tear them apart.

Chapter 2

Vanilla Tea Cupcake

Ingredients:

For the cake:

4oz sugar
4oz butter
All-purpose flour
1 tbsp vanilla – infused with a few drops of Earl Grey tea
2 eggs
1 tsp baking powder
1-2 tbsp milk

For the frosting:

Butter
Icing sugar
2 tbsp tea
1 tsp vanilla

What to do:

Cream butter and sugar together.
Add eggs slowly, then milk.
Combine baking powder and flour and sift into mixture.
Add tea and vanilla.

Sabrina glanced around the overcrowded coffee shop. In every direction she looked there were people staring at laptops and phone screens; headphones bobbing along to music. Occasionally she had a rare glimpse of people communicating, looking at each other, fully engaged in conversation as they sipped on their vegan chai tea. She had loved LA for its vibrant culture and colourful mix of inhabitants. She didn't regret her time here for a second but having spent Christmas in Italy with her family she knew going home was the right thing for her. She'd learnt so much during her time in LA, from both the highs and the lows. She had immersed herself in her work, given Lydia and Jones Records her all, but now it was time to really show the music industry what she was made of.

Since arriving back in LA after the New Year, her phone had been buzzing continuously. The news was out that San Francisco Beat were free agents and that Sabrina was no longer working for Jones Records either. Her first point of call had been to address the situation and so she had made a statement that she was still very much the manager for San Francisco Beat and that yes, they were on the market for a new record deal.

She sipped her Earl Grey, longing for an Italian espresso, but knowing that over Christmas she had been well and truly spoilt by the fresh Italian coffee her zias made and that here in LA, no matter what Italian brand they used, it just wouldn't quite be the same. On the other hand, the Earl Grey did satisfy her needs and made her stomach bubble with excitement about getting back to Manchester. She eyed her list of emails, a swarm of potential record labels flooding her brain. When Levi and Dan had asked her to remain their manager she had been thrilled. She had leapt up and down, grateful that she still had a job and overwhelmed and touched that they believed in her. Of course she still felt all those things, but now there was a niggle of nerves partying in her stomach that she was having trouble evicting. This was a huge decision. In this business it was a trying task to stay true to who you were. Record labels could suck the soul right out of a band with the temptation of making millions and making you a star – after all, they knew exactly how to do that. But Sabrina was smart. San Francisco Beat were already a huge success across the USA and were making waves across the pond too, thanks to their last song 'Need a Little You' being popular with radio DJ's. Sabrina had been able to converse with the band's music publisher on a few occasions without Lydia breathing down her neck. She'd snuck in a few mentions as to what UK radio stations she believed would be a good fit for the band and her moments of bravery had paid off. Sabrina had done her utmost over the last three years to fight for the band and what they represented, despite Jones Records' best attempts at getting them to strip down to their boxers and create their own perfume; that was wonderful for some acts, but it just wasn't them. Being their manager, due to her big sister's meddling, meant Sabrina had a lot of say in their careers. However, with her attachment to Jones Records and working so closely with Lydia as her assistant, Lydia had certainly made this hard for her.

So now she needed to find a label that would complement her vision and best suit the boys and their sound. Her palms were sweaty as she tapped away at her keyboard, opening proposals and reading through offers. They all sounded good, many highlighting the big clientele that already worked for them and discussing the fame and fortune they could deliver. Sabrina 'umm'ed and 'ahh'ed, nothing special leaping out at her. Yes, the boys wanted to be successful. Their lives had changed dramatically over the last three years. They were no longer playing dive bars and small clubs in San Francisco, working part-time jobs to get by; they were playing arenas across America and had all been able to buy houses and pay off their parents' mortgages. For that they were incredibly grateful, but money did not drive them. Sabrina loved that about them. She kept them grounded and they kept her grounded in this crazy world of showbiz.

It was vital to her that the label understood who San Francisco Beat were; artists whose music came first. To them it was all about performing and connecting with their audiences, putting on shows that gave people a sense of belonging, checking their egos at the door and providing for their families.

Thinking of family reminded Sabrina that she had a few texts from her sisters that she needed to reply to. As she picked up her phone to do so, it started ringing – a number flashing across the screen that she didn't recognize. She hastily accepted the call, keen to stay on top of the requests for San Francisco Beat. Her pulse quickened and the nerves raved on in her belly.

'Hello, is that Sabrina Collins?' a man's voice asked rather loudly and forcefully, causing Sabrina to pull the phone away from her ear. She cleared her throat, wanting to sound confident and professional.

'Yes, yes, it is. How can I help you?' she replied, as she played with the string from the teabag that dangled out of her little teapot.

'I'm Kyle Jennings with *Music Life* magazine. We'd like to run an article on San Francisco Beat and I want to get the boys in for an interview as soon as possible. They're in high demand and we want them. You need to be aggressive, love. The boys are hot commodity right now and where are they? Looking at cafés in Manchester and hanging out in skate parks when they should be riding the free-agent wave.'

Sabrina opened her mouth, then closed it, then opened it again. She didn't know what to say. The man's abrupt tone threw her off. While she wanted to appreciate his advice, she was stunned at his rudeness. Then again, she shouldn't have been. This was LA – where there was money to be made everyone wanted a piece of the action. She sat up straighter in her chair. She currently didn't have anyone helping her with San Francisco Beat. She couldn't hide behind publicists or label execs when conflict got too much – she was now the first line of defense where the band were concerned. She certainly didn't have Lydia's brazen approach when it came to dealing with people, but she knew she needed to be tougher. She rolled her shoulders back and cleared her throat once more.

'San Francisco Beat are currently on a break. They have families and lives to live, just like the rest of us, and at this time they are not available for interviews,' Sabrina said as she tugged at her lip, brows furrowed, not wanting the man to get nasty with her, but well aware of how journalists could talk. After the peace and anonymity that Italy had offered, it unnerved Sabrina that the paparazzi were now hounding the boys. They must have spotted Dan in England with Amanda and caught on to both Dylan and James being back at home in San Francisco spending time with their families before the whirlwind of a new record deal had them on the road again.

'Suit yourself, sweetheart, but people don't want to see the boys on playdates with their other halves. They're rock stars, they best start acting like it. And they're talented at that. I just hope you don't run them into the ground.' With that he hung up and left Sabrina aggressively stabbing at her vanilla cupcake that donned far too much frosting.

She put her phone down next to her barely touched cupcake, suddenly having lost her appetite. *Come on, Sabrina*, she urged herself. *You need to pick one.* Though she didn't care for the man's patronizing tone, he was right. Sabrina couldn't dawdle forever and stall this next step. She needed to believe in herself and follow her gut. The band's fans would be waiting for a new album and a new tour; she had to deliver. She drew her eyes back to the screen before remembering her sisters' texts. She picked up her phone to reply quickly just as Tyler Wall's name filled the screen.

She had to answer. It was Tyler Wall, international rock god and one of her dearest friends.

'Bri, how's it going hon?' Tyler's chirpy voice sang down the line.

Sabrina eased back into her chair, happy to hear a friendly voice. 'It's going wonderfully Ty, how are things with you?' she answered, dipping the lid of her laptop so her screen would stop judging her. *All isn't one hundred per cent wonderful* the screen shouted at her from its display of never-ending emails.

'Good good, flower. I need a favour,' Tyler said, causing Sabrina to sit up. She would do anything for Tyler, he had done so much for her – giving her her first big break all those years ago during the Leeds music festival and keeping her sane while working for Jones Records.

'Of course, anything,' she replied enthusiastically, covering her phone-free ear with her hand so she could hear him better.

'There's this band currently on the market for a record deal and well, my label wants to snap them up. I would be their golden boy if by chance I was able to sweeten up their manager and get them in for a meeting,' Tyler said.

Sabrina suddenly felt deflated that without her contacts at Jones Records, she might not be able to help her friend. She didn't reply straight away but let out a small sigh, trying to think of a plan.

A few moments passed by as Sabrina racked her brain, ready to break the news to Tyler that she was unable to take her contact list with her.

'Bri, are you still there? Bri, I'm talking about you!!' Tyler exclaimed with a bark of a laugh which Sabrina could see in her mind. He often threw his head back when something tickled him. She palmed her forehead and blinked back to reality.

'Gosh Tyler, my brain is totally frazzled going through all these emails and phone calls, not to mention packing up my apartment. I was away with the fairies,' she said and let out an embarrassed laugh. 'Forgive me.'

'Nothing to forgive hon. You're a doll. So, what do you say?' The excitement in Tyler's voice picked up again, laughter still light in his words.

Sabrina sat on the edge of her seat, going over what Tyler had offered and trying to compute it. When her brain clicked, she gasped, almost knocking her cupcake to the floor with her knee and getting a few strange looks and the odd smile from the other occupants of the café.

'Yes, Tyler. Oh wow, that would be incredible. Yes, thank you,' she expressed, with sheer surprise and delight in her tone. Tyler's record label, City Heights Records, had done a fantastic job with Tyler's career thus far and more importantly than that, Tyler was extremely happy there, which spoke volumes for them in Sabrina's eyes.

'Amazing Bri. So, when can you round up the troops?' Tyler queried, making Sabrina gulp.

'How soon are we talking?' she asked, a slight wobble in her voice. She picked up her pen and tapped it anxiously against her notebook.

'They were thinking the day after tomorrow. You know what it's like hon, the ride never stops.'

'Okay, I'll see what I can do. Thank you so much for this Ty. I owe you one. In fact, I probably owe you like three now,' she said, making Tyler guffaw again.

They said their goodbyes and Sabrina immediately looked to her calendar, having promised to send Tyler a time for the meeting. It shouldn't be too difficult, she hoped. Dan was due back from England late tomorrow evening anyway, and she would just have to message Dylan and James and hope she wasn't interrupting any important family events and that they could fly back tomorrow too. And Levi, well she could just tell Levi the great news when she got home later that day. The excitement bubbling in her stomach tripled with that thought.

Chapter 3

Almond Torta

Ingredients:

Flour
Ground almonds
Butter
Slivered almonds
Eggs
Sugar
Pretty sure Nanna adds a dash of some liquor
(ask her what it is)

What to do:

Next time write it down, might be a nice one for blog, and not everyone can read your mind.

The smell of almond *crema pasticcera* lingered in the air, mixing with the rich espresso that Louisa and Giulia had indulged in over lunch. Louisa could eat one after another and she didn't think she would ever tire of the sweet and crunchy pastry filled with the most flavourful crema she had ever tasted. Compared to her often-rushed lunches when working back in England as a receptionist, lunchtimes with Giulia here in Italy were like a long weekend. All work was put aside while the focus was placed on the meal they were about to enjoy.

Sometimes they ventured out for lunch, other times Luca, Louisa's boyfriend and Giulia's brother, would whisk Louisa away for a lunchtime adventure, and then other times Giulia and Louisa would set up a picnic in the office, concocting an array of antipasti with fresh meats and breads they picked up from Giulia's family *pasticceria* in the morning before their ten-to-fifteen-minute commute to Amalfi from Orzoro. It could take longer when the summer season kicked in, due to the coaches and buses carrying tourists from town to town and fighting over the narrow spaces on the mountain sides. It was one of Louisa's favourite times of the day and made her love her job even more.

It had been a month since her sisters and parents had gone back to England after the holidays and staying in Italy had been a dream thus far; though she had to admit there were days when she missed her sisters terribly. She couldn't help but think of Amanda as the thought of what tomorrow's lunch would bring danced around in her mind. Right now her big sister would no doubt be mulling over menus for her café. There was scarcely a time when Amanda wasn't thinking of food; she'd been dreaming up menus since she was a child. Louisa shook her head. She shouldn't be thinking about food right now; she had actual work to do, if she could call it that.

Giulia's boutique was an honest-to-goodness fairytale. Louisa knew she had made the right decision in accepting Giulia's job offer, upon meeting her and the rest of Luca's family over Christmas, when she had first laid eyes on the exquisite shop. Gold and pink lettering glazed the shopfront with mannequins dressed in such eye-catching bespoke pieces that they made Louisa's sketching hand itch. Every day brought a new challenge, be it repairing clothes, working on her own designs or serving customers in the shop and helping them pick out the perfect outfit.

More recently came the added challenge of preparing five impeccable outfits for Italy's Young Designers Fashion Showcase that was now only a few months away. Giulia had worked her magic and Louisa was the youngest designer on the bill, not to mention the newest. No pressure. Louisa hadn't been expecting this. Giulia had brought her on board initially to help her with Milan Fashion Week in the autumn but when Louisa had shown Giulia her sketches, Giulia had waved her hands dramatically in the air in typical passionate Italian fashion while shouting 'Bellissima, bellissima!' Giulia then proceeded to busy herself with phone calls that Louisa was not to overhear – she would receive a wagging finger if she was caught earwigging – for a few days before she announced the news about the showcase to Louisa. It had all been extremely hush hush with the showcase being a prestigious event and difficult to get a spot at. Louisa felt eternally blessed to have Giulia on her side.

Now Louisa stood with pins in her mouth, eyes like slits, concentrating on getting the perfect fold to the hem of one of the pieces she was making for the showcase – a beautiful crochet-covered, contrasting-collared black and pearl dress – when her phone vibrated in her pocket. She gave a slight jerk as it tickled her thigh and plunged her hand into her cardigan pocket desperate for it not to cut off.

Prodding the mannequin with the pins she was holding, careful not to prick herself, she quickly swiped the green answer button.

'Amanda, hey,' she said, loudly, excitement in her voice at being able to speak with her big sister. It had felt like forever, when truthfully it had only been two days, but with Amanda being busy at the café and Sabrina still in LA trying to get the boys a record deal, she hadn't been hearing from them much.

'Hey Lou, how's it going? How's galivanting around Italy with a drop-dead gorgeous Italian and eating cake the size of a football going?' Amanda asked. Louisa could almost see her sister playfully smirking down the line.

'It's going swimmingly,' Louisa noted, a smile creeping up on her face as she leaned back, resting against her office chair and eyeing up the dress in front of her. It seemed Amanda had been checking her Instagram – that was at least a good sign where her sister's blog was concerned. Hopefully Amanda had actually started to understand how to use it.

'Happy to hear it. So, what's new?' Amanda asked. Louisa hopped up on her chair, turning away from the dress that was distracting her from being one hundred per cent present with her sister. She had been waiting patiently to talk to Amanda over the past couple of days, excited to share the showcase news with her. The difficult hem on the dress could wait.

'I've got an incredible opportunity coming up actually that I've been dying to tell you about,' Louisa started, absentmindedly picking up a red pencil crayon and shading in a flared skirt on another design she was working on.

'Oh yeah, me too, but you first. Tell me, tell me,' Amanda sang. Louisa smiled; she sure did miss her sister – even the sarcasm and teasing she so often dished out.

'So, Giulia got me this amazing opportunity to take part in Italy's Young Designers Fashion Showcase, I still can't believe it to be honest, but being here, well … I've been designing nonstop, it's like all my passion has coming flooding back, inspiration is everywhere,' Louisa gushed, pausing in her drawing to gaze out of the office window and into the pretty shop glittering with stunning fabrics and extraordinary pieces. She could just make out the edge of the Pasticceria Pansa sign to the right across the way from their shop. How was this her life now?

'Lou that's awesome. Oh, I'm so proud of you. Wow,' Amanda said, a little breathless, which made Louisa's smile grow wider. It meant the world to have her sister's support. She hadn't realized how much she had needed Amanda's words to give her that extra boost of confidence. The dress she had been working on today had been bugging her, she just couldn't get it right. Amanda's words encouraged her. 'Maybe if things are going according to schedule here, I can come and watch,' Amanda added. Louisa shrieked at the thought of her sister coming back again soon.

She knew Italy wasn't far but understood work could get in the way. They had been used to Sabrina living across the world for four years and accepted each other's dreams. Though Louisa's cheeks flushed at remembering the times she hadn't been so understanding of Sabrina being so far from home.

'Thanks Amanda, that would be lovely. I'd really like that,' Louisa replied, twirling her crayon between her fingers. 'So, go on, tell me your news?'

'Well ...' Amanda paused. If Louisa knew her sister this would be for dramatic effect. 'I think everything should be set for March 23rd – our opening day, can you believe it?' Louisa could have sworn her big sister actually squealed. 'I mean the place is still a mess and I don't have electricity yet, but you know, that's the plan.'

'That's amazing Amanda, wow. This is a great day for good news. Wait ...' Louisa suddenly felt sweaty as she reached out for her desk calendar. *March 23rd, March 23rd, why did it ring a bell?*

'Is everything okay Lou?' Amanda questioned, her voice holding a hint of concern.

'Yes, everything's fine. Just one second,' Louisa said hastily, flicking through the sheets on the calendar to a month from now. She cast her eyes on March 23rd. Staring back at her, written in bright pink marker and circled with stars either side, was 'Italy's Young Designers Fashion Showcase'. Her heart sank.

The showcase was everything her heart desired, but she hadn't accounted for missing Amanda's opening day. Just like Amanda had been dreaming of the day, so had Louisa. She couldn't wait to witness her sister make her dreams come true and honour their grandpa's dreams too. But she had been working on the pieces for the showcase day and night for a month now and had eagerly, and nervously, been counting down the days to make her entrance into the fashion industry. An opportunity like this was like gold dust. She was an unknown in the fashion world, but with Giulia's help her designs had slowly been making their rounds within Giulia's well-connected circle. She couldn't possibly blow this opportunity and skip out on the showcase and nor did she want to – well, maybe just a little bit now that she had heard Amanda's news.

'Lou?' Amanda's concerned voice asked again.

'I'm so sorry Amanda, but I won't be able to make it. March 23rd is the day of the showcase,' Louisa informed her big sister, feeling deflated, not only because she wanted to be at Amanda's grand opening but because she had well and truly been floating on cloud nine at the thought of having her sisters at the showcase with her.

'That's okay, Lou,' Amanda said, though her voice lacked the same enthusiasm as before. 'You'll just have to take lots of pictures and we'll Facetime so neither of us miss out.'

'Yeah, I guess,' Louisa replied, shuffling off her stool and tugging the pins from out of the mannequin.

'Sorry Lou, but come on, you're going to kick butt at the showcase and my café will hopefully still be here when you're able to come and visit,' Amanda said. Louisa noted the slight wobble in her voice though Amanda tried to keep her voice strong. Louisa imagined her sister had plenty to be anxious about with opening her café so she didn't want to sulk too much or burden her sister with feeling bad about not being able to get to Italy as soon as she had hoped.

'Sounds good, Amanda. I'm certain it will be. They will be queuing for miles to get a taste of your food,' Louisa said, a touch spritelier.

'Thank you, Lou. Right, give my love to that Italian god of yours and I'll catch you soon.' They hung up after a chorus of *love yous* and Louisa willed herself to focus on the task of the disobedient hemline instead of the pity party her brain was conjuring up over not being able to be in two places at once.

*

'*Amore*, you are tired no?' Giulia's perfectly shaped brows were creased in concern as she took in Louisa. Louisa had spent the past few hours trying to get the correct hemline on her lace piece, but she couldn't shake the feeling that she was going to be missing out on a big day in her sister's life.

In comparison to Giulia, who rivaled Sophia Loren with today's choice of updo and fitted black dress with blood-red kitten heels, Louisa's eyes were now dreary, her concealer creased from squinting and wiping at her eyes too much. She had kicked off her heels two hours ago and the chill that ran through her bones over what she was feeling had lent itself to her grabbing one of Luca's giant hoodies that now hid her demure blouse.

'*Si, ma* I'll be okay,' Louisa smiled at Giulia. Giulia wandered over to the dress Louisa had been working on and allowed her hands to caress the material as she studied Louisa's work.

'*E bella*. These judges at the showcase are going to be blown away by your pieces,' Giulia breathed, in admiration of the outfit. Louisa felt inspired by Giulia; everything from her Italian fashion, the way her words came out like a song when she spoke and her girl boss attitude, made Louisa love her that little bit more. She could see so much of Luca in her and was starting to understand their family traits. Since starting work with Giulia a month ago, she had been taken aback with her kindness, her relaxed yet businesslike manner and how much passion she had for her work. It was contagious and something she also caught when spending time with Luca. Their upbeat attitudes and joy of both life and work had been rubbing off on Louisa. Compared to the stress of her old nine-to-five reception job – the harassed looks on her co-workers faces and the constant countdown for the weekend – working with Giulia was complete bliss. Every day was cause for a celebration of amazing food and adventure. Louisa felt calmer than she had ever felt and truly more motivated with her creations.

Giulia stepped back from the garment Louisa had been working on and looked up at the clock.

'We must get going,' Giulia said with a sweet smile, the clock having moved to ten past four. It was family time now or time to grab a coffee with friends or prepare the dinner. Work for the day was done, if Louisa could call it work; she loved what she did. As Giulia stepped back, Louisa noticed the pins on her hem had moved. She did a double take as she watched Giulia move towards the door and she herself grabbed her bag. Casting another look at her dress before she followed Giulia's shouts of '*Viene, viene*, come, come,' she shook her head. The woman was like her guardian angel sent down by Grandpa to guide Louisa and put her on the right path.

With the hemline now perfect and ready to be sewn in the morning, it gave Louisa a sense of purpose. She appreciated this opportunity that Giulia had given her; she needed to focus on what she was doing and the passion she had inside her and not what she was missing back home. She had given up too easily last time on her fashion dreams at university; now she needed to face the fears of being away from her family and not run back home the minute it got tough.

Chapter 4

Grandpa's Focaccia

Ingredients:

1 sachet of yeast
1 cup warm water
1 tsp salt
1 tsp sugar
Sprinkle of fennel seeds
1/3 cup of olive oil
3 ½ cups of Tipo 00 flour

What to do:

Place warm water, salt, sugar and yeast in a bowl. Mix and allow to sit for fifteen minutes.

Add your flour, fennel and olive oil and another dash of salt for more flavour.

Allow to rise for at least an hour, covered under a tea towel and in a warm spot. (Grandpa sometimes placed near radiator.)

Roll out. (You can use a rolling pin or just manipulate it with your hands to make your rectangle shape and prod with your fingers to flatten it. No harm getting stuck in and it makes it more rustic.)

Cover with tea towel on baking sheet for twenty minutes, drizzle with a touch more olive oil, then bake at 180 degrees for 20–25 minutes, until crisp and golden.

When they had returned from Italy in the New Year, Amanda had been a ball of energy – a woman on a mission and a force to be reckoned with. She and Dan had buried themselves in newspapers and estate agent windows, as well as tirelessly wandering the streets of Manchester looking for the perfect location for her café. She was now standing in front of that perfect location, terrified of going inside.

The paperwork had been straightforward, though Amanda had certainly been glad of Dan's presence. As was the case with her blog and social media, she wasn't one for reading the fine print, editing, or patience – she just wanted to get in and create her vision. But once the paperwork had cleared, Dan had joined Sabrina and the boys back in LA and Amanda was left to face the task of building a café from the ground up, with no previous experience, knowledge, or known skills when it came to flooring, shop-fitting or that of plumbing or electrical matters. Her dream had quickly turned into a shambles.

The door creaked open and she made a mental note to remember to get WD40 on it sooner rather than later. She stepped over the threshold with her eyes closed and breathed in the smell of plastic and a subtle burning scent. 'Oh god, what's that?' she said out loud. She flicked the light switch and opened her eyes, but nothing happened. When she flicked it again, she heard a click and a hiss and the wire that was dangling from the ceiling sent out a spark. She quickly pulled her phone from her pocket and turned on its flashlight. Newspaper covered the floor in addition to a layer of dust, and the plastic-covered tables and chairs were piled high to one side. The newly painted walls were splotchy, with paint having made its way onto the skirting boards and light fixtures. The place was a mess.

'Okay Amanda,' she told herself, 'you have to fix this. When the electrician comes today, he needs to know that this won't do, and that you need your kitchen up and running this week.' She carefully treaded over the newspapers to put her bag down on the bar, still using her phone for light when it started ringing. Her dad's name appeared on the screen.

'Hi Dad,' Amanda answered, as chirpily as she could. 'How are you?' She went to lean on the counter but thought better of it with the dust and grime present in a thick layer, so instead hovered by it awkwardly.

'Hi sweetheart. I wanted to check in on the work at your café. How's it looking? Do you need any help today?' he asked. Amanda could hear the pride in his voice when he said, 'your café' and she didn't want to let him down. The girls had been lucky, growing up with parents who supported them in all they wanted to do. Amanda wouldn't have travelled the world, exploring exotic cuisine or completed her strenuous placements in restaurants over the years if it wasn't for their encouragement and belief in her that she could do it. Now, with no job and Jeff having tainted her reputation, this café had to work. She wasn't just doing this for herself and her career, she was doing this for her family.

'Everything's fine thanks, Dad. I've got it all under control,' she gulped, looking into the gloomy abyss. He had already helped unload the furniture earlier this week, which he had done with a smile on his face, but Amanda hadn't missed his occasional pauses where his hands rested on his lower back, while he took in deep breaths, pain crinkling his eyes. He wasn't as young as he looked and when Amanda had rung her parents' house at 7 p.m. that evening to thank him once more, her mum had answered and told Amanda she would pass on her message in the morning when her dad woke up. The day had wiped him out. She couldn't do that to him again. 'Have a good day, Dad, and I'll keep you posted,' she said, ending the call. She glanced around at the dark and dreary shell of a café and then down at her watch.

'Okay, so the electrician will be here any minute and I'll just text the decorators and ask when they'll be coming back to do another coat and final touch ups and clean the sockets and skirtings, then everything really will be fine,' she said. She walked over to the bay window and rolled up the matte gold blinds that had recently been put in, just enough to let some light in but not enough for onlookers or paparazzi to get a good look. San Francisco Beat were a big deal – the media had already sniffed out Dan's scent while he was visiting and helping her look for a place.

Thinking of Dan made her pulse quicken but her stomach sink. She missed him like she'd never missed anyone before, and she wished he were with her, making this task feel less daunting than it was. But she understood his work; she knew his life was his band and it made her happy to know that he was living his dream. She had to admit that it felt different now though. He'd been gone three weeks and the distance and time difference had thrown her for a loop. Had it been this difficult to stay in touch when they were just friends? Anyway, she couldn't think about that right now. She had to get her own dream back on track. Another crackle and spark jolted her from daydreaming of Dan, and she turned abruptly to see that it came from one of the plug sockets by the bar. 'Any minute now, the electrician will be here,' she repeated to herself. 'Any minute now.'

*

The minutes turned into hours. It was now three in the afternoon and thankfully the day was still bright; the sun high above the houses, enough to cast a glow on her café, so she didn't have to sit in the dark. Amanda was sprawled out on the cold unfinished floor, covered in dust and muck, feeling pretty useless and no longer caring about the state of her clothes. She had been waiting for the electrician since eight o'clock this morning and he still hadn't turned up. She had received no reply from the decorators, and they were not answering their phone. She was feeling sorry for herself, missing Sabrina's efficiency in a situation like this and replaying her conversation with Louisa from weeks ago, still feeling gutted that her little sister wasn't going to make it to her café opening.

This wasn't like her at all and she hated herself for acting even remotely defeated. Grandpa would be having none of this. If he was here, he would be busy bustling around, making sure everything was done exactly the way he wanted, even if that meant doing it himself. Nothing would interrupt his vision, Amanda thought. With opening day looming in a little over two weeks, she could simply not afford to be sitting on a dirty floor when there was food to be ordered, staff to hire and 'Electricity for Dummies' to purchase. By the end of the day she would know how to rewire a light fixture; just because she was a chef, didn't mean she could not or should not teach herself a bit of electrical DIY. Knowledge was power, her Grandpa would say, and she wasn't going to let anything stand in her way of whipping up plates upon plates of rich sea salt focaccia to get the neighbours talking.

She jumped up and headed to the door.

*

'How's the café coming along?' Amanda's face beamed as Nikki's voice came down the line sounding cheerful. It helped to keep Amanda's spirits high – either that or she had inhaled more paint fumes than one should. At this point she couldn't be quite sure, she had been painting all afternoon, having dared to roll up the blinds and let the sunlight illuminate the café. She didn't quite have Louisa's creative streak or flare for design, so she had prayed to the painting gods that the walls would not be a complete tragedy when she was done.

But at least the paint was pretty, Amanda thought to herself, as she gazed at the white walls that glittered with gold specs in the flickers of the fading sunlight. She considered Nikki's question. It felt good to hear Nikki's voice. Amanda had met Nikki in San Francisco; she had been the one to officially introduce Dan to Amanda and the one to take Amanda under her wing during her time there. They had kept in touch over the years and Amanda hoped to visit her again one day. She had loved San Francisco and Nikki's feisty attitude, big heart and love of cooking.

'Oh Nikki, I know it's come a long way since we started the whole process a few weeks ago; to think we have floors and furniture, a kitted-out kitchen and no holes in the walls now! But I'll be totally and completely not a monster anymore if we can just get this electricity sorted,' Amanda said, with a squint of her eyes as she wiped at her brow. She hadn't meant to be naïve, but she hadn't accounted for the hiccups. Amanda often saw the big picture and that big picture ninety-nine per cent of the time revolved around the food; thinking about the recipes, when could she go buy the food, when she could start cooking the food, when she could start eating the food and when she could start serving the food. Stopping the process to take pictures or deal with shoddy painters and unequipped electricians was not part of her game plan.

'I get it hon,' Nikki started, 'I'm insanely proud of you, you know,' she finished with a thoughtful sigh. Amanda plonked herself down on the floor, for fear of leaning on anything and breaking it or smudging it. 'Thanks Nikki,' she whispered, feeling grateful to have Nikki on the line. She missed her terribly.

'How are things over there? How's the café doing?' Amanda asked. She thought about Nikki standing behind the counter at Bruno's, the café that her dad owned and that had been in her family for generations. Amanda's mind flashed back to the day she first laid eyes on her. Nikki was standing behind the very same counter she was right now at the other end of the phone, with her gorgeous mauve lips, perfect eyebrows and a welcoming beam, and Amanda's world was forever changed. Nikki became an instant best friend, with their matching passionate attitudes and love of early mornings in the kitchen. She introduced Amanda to all the best food spots Frisco had to offer, allowed her to help at Bruno's and bake alongside her in their famous kitchen. Amanda had to admit that Nikki got the most brownie points for having introduced her to Dan. Thank you Nikki. *Thank you, thank you, thank you,* Amanda's brain sung to itself in a quiet tune. Amanda couldn't help the smile that curved her lips and reached her eyes when she thought about meeting Dan.

Dan had been playing in Nikki's café that day, his voice having stopped Amanda in her tracks when she walked into Bruno's. When he had taken a break from his set, he had made his way over to the counter and after overhearing Amanda rave about the hot chocolate Nikki had served up for her, Dan had requested one of the same. He had then proceeded to talk to Amanda and the moment he did so there had been an invisible string that tied itself around each of their hearts, deeming them inseparable. Granted, him being from San Francisco and Amanda from Manchester, they had of course been physically separated over the years, but that hadn't stopped them talking on the phone every single day thereafter; bar a couple of months last year when she broke that record when trying to understand her feelings for him. She had eventually figured out those feelings and now her relationship with Dan was more than she ever could have dreamed. Nikki's voice interrupted her thoughts.

'Everything's great thanks, babe. Busy as ever and four years later, your Biscoff cupcakes are still flying off the counter. I still get people asking about you. They want to know where our boy has got to, too,' Nikki said, a hint of mischief in her tone. 'Speaking of which, are you keeping him out of trouble?'

Brushing her forefinger over the layer of dust that covered the floor, Amanda hadn't realized she had absentmindedly been drawing hearts as Nikki spoke. She cleared her throat.

'He's great ...' Amanda's voice sounded wistful; it often did this where Dan was concerned. It was never intended, but without warning her independent bravado turned to mush while her heart melted at his name. It was worse when she missed him too. No matter how hard she fought it, she pined for him when he was away. She was missing a piece of herself and had to keep her mind active and focused, so it didn't drift off, always thinking and searching for its missing piece. It hadn't helped that since he went back to LA, they hadn't been able to speak much. She understood that being free agents meant a lot of work and pressure for the boys, though it was odd for Dan not to reply to messages within ten minutes or for them not to catch up on the phone before bed. She tried to put a stop to her worries and getting the café up and running had been a wonderful, if not stressful, distraction. She didn't want to burden Nikki with her unwarranted thoughts. She didn't want to sound ungrateful. Dan had spent Christmas with her, and they had enjoyed an amazing few weeks here in Manchester together, but she knew he would have to get back to work and that things would be extra busy with San Francisco Beat as they prepared to sign a new record deal. Her brain needed to cut him some slack. Thankfully Nikki pulled her out of her thoughts.

'All this time, I still can't believe it. You do know I called it that day in the kitchen? You do remember, don't you? I think your exact words were 'ewww',' Nikki said. Her attempt at a British 'ewww' and the memory itself caused them both to howl with laughter. Amanda had indeed said 'ewww' when Nikki suggested her and Dan being something more than just friends.

'Don't you start!' Amanda managed through chuckles. 'I get told "we told you so" at least twice a day from my sisters, I don't want to hear it from you too,' she finished, mock-serious.

At that moment there was a loud bang on the door that scared the life out of Amanda. She jumped and very nearly sent her phone flying across the room. She shot to her feet and spun round, squinting to try and make out the figure behind the blinds. It was 5 p.m. – who could be knocking at 5 p.m.?

'I bloody hope that's the electrician,' she said, trepidation in her voice as she tip-toed ever so carefully to the door. It had been a few days now since any reporters had come knocking, but the week that followed her and Dan's initial visit saw paparazzi hovering nearby, some even knocking on her door and bombarding her with questions. Amanda had kindly sent them away. She hadn't wanted people to see inside her café. The pressure of making everything perfect was enough without the hassle of flash photography and nosey parkers, and she could do without the likes of her old work partner, Jeff, knowing the ins and outs of what she was up to. He had already tried to sabotage her once before.

'I'll stay with you until you see who it is, hon,' Nikki said gently.

Amanda rubbed at a smudge on the glass before she heard her dad's voice chatting with what could only be an electrician – if his bold red van that had 'Frank's Electrical' scrawled across the side, was anything to go by. Amanda let out a breath and removed the latch on the door before turning the key in the lock to let them in, while Nikki remained on the line.

'Hi Dad,' she said, giving him a kiss on the cheek as he came through the door. She very nearly repeated the process with the electrician, before remembering she had never met him before. No matter how Italian she was, she somehow didn't think Frank would appreciate that. She felt her cheeks burn red as she stepped away from him, just slightly awkwardly. Catching his eye, he smiled a handsome smile. He didn't look like a Frank. His face was young, bearing some fluff. His hair was black, longish and his hands were strong as he shook hers. Amanda felt like she was hallucinating. What was her dad doing here and who was this electrician?

'I take it you haven't been kidnapped? The café been ransacked? Or have the cameras just turned up for your new reality TV show?' Nikki's voice almost gave Amanda whiplash, as she quickly snapped back into the present, turning her head away from Frank.

'Just taking this call,' she shouted to her dad as she stepped into the chilly February evening. *How long should one stay in a newly painted room?* she asked herself, wafting the breeze in her face with her hand.

'Sorry Nikki, it was just Dad and Frank. Sorry, an electrician, Frank. Though he doesn't look like a Frank or an electrician, mind you. He looks like, well, I don't know what he looks like.'

'I don't believe it, you're swooning over this Frank?' Nikki said, with a comical, flabbergasted laugh, that made Amanda roll her eyes.

'I was absolutely not swooning over Frank,' Amanda said defiantly, mock-offended, but taking in a deep breath as she did so. She hadn't realized just how antsy she was when it came to the thought of reporters and paparazzi hovering at her door. Amanda wasn't usually phased when it came to speaking to new people, but even her strong nature could take a beating from reporters trying to stir rumours, asking about Dan's whereabouts, exes and who she was to him. In addition, they could make you feel quite vulnerable when they sprung up on you unannounced when you were on your own, and *that* she didn't care for. She had been grateful to see a kind, friendly, and, okay, handsome face following her dad. Heck she had been grateful to see her dad after being alone all day.

Nikki's laugh rang down the phone once more. 'I'm kidding,' she started. 'Right, I love you, but I need to get back to my customers and make sure my own café is still afloat.'

'Oh god, sorry, yes. Thanks for being there for me. I bloody miss you,' Amanda replied, walking back and forth past her bay window.

'I bloody miss you too. Be sure to send me a picture of Frank,' Nikki teased, and Amanda could practically see her winking down the line. Nikki's injection of British words into her American vocabulary never failed to make Amanda grin.

'I am not taking pictures of random electricians,' she replied, stopping in front of the door and nodding at a curious passerby.

'Why not? It's not exactly like your one-in-a-million, delicious rock god with a perfectly chiseled jawline and a ridiculously sexy pout boyfriend could possibly get jealous,' Nikki said. Amanda let out a howl of a laugh as she wiped at her tired eyes. She loved her best friend.

'I am one hundred per cent going to tell Dan you just said all those nice things about him,' Amanda noted.

'Oh, don't do that, you'll only go and pump up his ego more,' Nikki responded with a fake whine in her voice.

'If Dan had an ego,' Amanda sighed wistfully. She played with the door handle and looked around at her surroundings. There didn't seem to be anyone hiding behind telephone poles today.

'We can create a bad boy rock star out of him yet,' Nikki replied, making Amanda chuckle once more. 'In all seriousness, you should take some before and after pictures for your blog. I'm sure that will get some interest and create a buzz before opening day.'

'Oh shoot, my blog. Nikki I'm going to be completely honest, I've not posted at all in the past two months. Everything just got so busy and crazy.'

'You know, it's quite comical how much you suck at social media yet run a successful food blog. Well, it might not be successful now you've abandoned it and run it into the ground, but …'

'Are you quite done?' Amanda interrupted, laughing. 'I thought you had a café to run two minutes ago?' She turned the handle on the front door, pushing it open and blinking a few times to adjust her eyes to the darker indoors. 'And I get your point, thank you for the idea.'

'You're welcome. Keep me posted. Love you,' Nikki said, before Amanda heard the line go dead.

Putting her phone in her pocket, she made her way over to her dad to ask what was going on. When she tapped him on the shoulder, he turned around and answered her question before she had time to ask it.

'Sweetheart, I appreciate you trying to do this by yourself, but I'm your dad, it's my job to help. How long were you going to try and work in darkness this evening, with no electricity?' he asked. Amanda shrugged, for lack of a sensible response. 'Your mum and I drove past earlier and saw you pottering around in the dark and cold. Really Amanda, it's okay to ask for help.' All Amanda could do was hug him. 'Thank you,' she whispered.

Then, trying to push Nikki's words out of her head – she would not ogle Frank – she tried to act casual, like she hadn't just been told off by her dad in front of him.

'So, Frank, do you think you will be able to fix this mess?' she asked, waving her arms around at the room. Frank had produced a battery-powered wall of spotlights that were now directed at the wiring spewing out of the ceiling.

'It's Liam. Frank is my dad's name, and I think I can,' Frank replied, with a dashing smile that caused Amanda's cheeks to flame. Dammit Nikki, she thought to herself.

Saving her from further embarrassment, her phone beeped in her pocket. Amanda returned a smile to Liam and quickly turned away. She found a cooler spot a safe distance away, dug her phone out of her pocket and sat herself back down on the dusty floor. Embarrassment aside, at least she now had one less thing to worry about. Of course Amanda wanted the place to have lights and look pretty, but more than anything she wanted her kitchen up and running so she could begin preparing food for her customers and get the neighbourhood talking about the delicious smells arising from her little corner of the world.

'Don't be running off with electricians – if it's sparks you're after, I'm watt you're looking for.' It took her a minute to understand Dan's text, but once it registered, Amanda was hunched over in stitches – she had definitely inhaled too many paint fumes today. Her laughter was becoming delirious. The small knot in her stomach at not hearing from Dan as much over the last few days untangled. She breathed a little easier. Before she could tap out her reply her phone beeped again.

'Too cheesy?' read Dan's second text. She quickly replied, 'Way too cheesy. Xx' before then firing a text off to Nikki, 'I thought you had to go and be an adult and run a café? Xx'.

Chapter 5

Grandpa's Pasta Ciotti

Ingredients:

For the dough:

(A bit of this and a bit of that as Grandpa would say, until dough forms.)
Flour
Sugar
Unsalted butter
Milk
Egg
Baking powder
Salt
Vegetable shortening
Vanilla

For the filling:

3 tbsp cornstarch
½ cup sugar
1–1 ½ cups whole milk
2 egg yolks
1 tbsp butter
1 tsp almond extract

39

What to do:

For the dough:

Combine dry ingredients then add in butter and shortening like you're making a crumble.
Mix together wet ingredients then add to dry and make a dough.

For the filling:

Like Nanna's custard, make a roux with cornstarch and sugar. Add milk and eggs and almond extract and keep whisking until thick.
Roll out dough and make shells that fit a cupcake tin.
Spoon in two tbsp custard. Then layer a circle on top.
Refrigerate for 30 mins.
After 30 mins sprinkle with a splash of egg wash and bake for 12–15 mins at 22 degrees.
Once golden, remove and leave to cool.
Serve with a dusting of powdered sugar.

Sabrina began to stir. The golden rays of sunshine had no respect for the current time of 4.30 a.m.; it barged its way in through the curtains without any apologies. Sabrina stretched out her arms and legs so she resembled a starfish, and jumped at a sudden cry of 'ouch' as the blanket next to her started to shuffle.

She let out a laugh and a feeble 'sorry' as Levi reached under the blanket and grabbed at her daisy print pajama shorts. She tried to smack his hand away, but it was no use – even in his sleepy state she couldn't match his strength. He pulled her on top of him and snuggled into her sandy blonde hair, breathing her in.

'How do you smell so good in the morning?' he asked, playing with her locks as they fell around his fingers. 'You smell like sunshine and flowers.'

Sabrina laughed. 'Why thank you,' she replied, kissing his nose. 'I see your charm is never switched off, even at four-thirty in the morning.'

'You're the one that woke me at four-thirty in the morning to have your way with me! And I'd be a fool to say no to that.' Levi's cheeky tone made Sabrina laugh even more. She actually giggled as he smothered her with kisses. She loved the way he made her feel.

'No,' she cried through her laughter. 'The sun was too bright, it woke me.' She paused as Levi sat up, causing her to move with him so that she ended up sitting on his lap as he leaned his head against the head rest. 'And I must admit, I'm nervous about today. Are you nervous?'

Levi touched the tip of her nose and traced her jaw with his thumb. 'I wouldn't say I'm not nervous,' he said, with a soft shrug. Levi was the most laidback of the group. He and James were like double trouble, always the life and soul of the party, never taking anything too seriously. It was no surprise. Levi's older brother had taken the more conventional route in life; good at school, left to get a great job, married by twenty-five, two kids. Levi's mum had never had to worry about Chase, but Levi had certainly made up for that. Dan wasn't exactly a troublemaker but put him and Levi in a class together and they never got any work done. Records were constantly spinning in both their brains and if they weren't whispering to each other about guitar riffs or band names they were doodling on desks or in the back of their schoolbooks. Levi's mum had to deal with her fair share of meetings in the principal's office and grounding Levi whenever him and Dan snuck out of the house to see a gig. Dan had mellowed out the older he got, Levi not so much, especially when side by side with James.

When Sabrina had first met Levi's mum, Joanne, while the boys were on tour in San Francisco for their first album, the first thing Joanne had said to her was, 'Thank you for giving him focus sweetheart. It makes a mother's heart happy to see her baby living his dream.' Then she'd added with a chuckle, 'That and I thought he'd be sleeping on my couch until he was forty.' Sabrina had instantly warmed to Joanne and though back then her relationship with Levi was strictly professional, she'd felt a kindred spirit in Joanne. They had Skyped often over the years. Joanne liked to check in on the boys, but would always spend an extra ten minutes catching up on Sabrina's news, asking if there was anyone special in her life yet, dropping hints about Levi being single and 'that boy would be too daft to notice if love was right under his nose' then telling Sabrina to keep a close watch on him. Of course, Sabrina had never told Joanne about the time she had kissed her son or how much she wanted to be with him, but she always sensed Joanne knew. Sabrina guessed it was a mum superpower.

It had been a pure delight to inform Joanne via Skype over the holidays, that they had finally taken the risk and become an item. Joanne had rolled her eyes noting, 'It took you both long enough. What did I tell you? Right under his nose.' Though Joanne often teased Levi for his goofy manner, Sabrina could see where he got it from. Levi's dad hadn't been around much when he was growing up, so while Joanne had had to step it up and look after her two boys on her own – keeping them in line and out of trouble as best she could – where Levi was concerned, there was definitely an element of fun to her. She always added a touch of lightness to any situation, having never wanted her sons to grow up in a miserable environment just because their dad wasn't around. Sabrina had never experienced Levi feeling sorry for himself; it was rare that he mentioned his dad, but he doted on his mum. Sabrina sensed that his humorous nature was a way of keeping that sparkle in his mum's eyes. Whenever the two of them were together you could bet there would be laughter.

As she gazed at Levi now, his face lit up by a sliver of sunrise coming through a crack in the curtain, his chestnut brown eyes flittered over her face, his jaw relaxed and a slight curve to his red lips teased a playful smile. 'How about you take my nerves and look after them for a bit?' Sabrina said sweetly, pulling the duvet up over her shoulders to ward off the chill.

'Baby, nerves are for wimps. Today is going to be epic. We have the best manager there is and Dylan's one hell of a bass player – he makes the rest of us look good. And if they want us to find a new lead, we can just replace Dan with another mysterious San Francisco hippie, and no one would know the difference,' Levi stated, trying to keep his lips straight but his eyes were glinting with cheek. Sabrina burst out laughing and shoved him in his bicep.

'Do you ever behave?' she asked through her laughter. In reply he yanked the duvet up and over both of their heads and tickled her until she was screaming, tears of laughter soaking her face.

In that moment, Sabrina felt eternally grateful that they had found their way back to each other and that their book of love had been reopened ready for a rewrite. Yes, she thought, borrowing some of Levi's confidence, today would be epic.

*

The office was spacious, clean-cut and very LA, but with a refreshing pop of colour that pleased Sabrina. Anyone that cared for bright yellows and pastel pinks was sure to be someone that Sabrina would get along with. Sabrina sat on the chair directly opposite the solid mahogany desk while Dan, Levi, Dylan and James sat behind her on the couch. Levi and James sat back against the cushions and Dan and Dylan sat on the edge, elbows on their knees, hands clasped. Dan, Sabrina could see, was ready to talk business. He would have her back if she needed him to step in. Sabrina cared greatly for Dan, and not just because he was her big sister's boyfriend, but because they shared a similar mind for business and, ninety-nine per cent of the time, were on the same page and had been since the day San Francisco Beat had walked in to Lydia's office over three years ago. Dan challenged her to be her best and she loved him for that.

A rustle at the door signalled the start of the meeting as a tall lady with shoulder-length black hair, red-rimmed glasses and Chanel ballet slippers bounced in. The lady was elegant and screamed retro chic and those shoes – seriously, Sabrina was having trouble tearing her eyes away.

'Hello all, how are we doing today? My names Keira and I'm thrilled to meet with you,' Keira said as she walked over to the couch to shake hands with each of the boys, all of whom stood up to greet her. 'It's a pleasure to meet with you too,' Dan said, speaking on behalf of the band, his husky voice confident.

Sabrina stood to greet Keira when she made her way over to shake her hand. Both women paused for a moment as Sabrina got a close-up of Keira's Chanel shoes and flashed her Chanel bag that she had splurged on last summer – much to Louisa's delight and Amanda's disapproval. 'Think of how many truffles you could have bought with that,' Amanda had said, to Sabrina's amusement. She hadn't wanted truffles, she had wanted the pastel pink Chanel bag with a gold clasp.

Sabrina beamed. 'Thank you for meeting with us. We're interested to hear the marketing strategies you would propose for a band like San Francisco Beat and we have heard nothing but wonderful things from Tyler,' she said, as both ladies took their seats. Keira was a sharp contrast to what Sabrina had been used to in Lydia. Whereas Lydia was icy and poker-faced, Keira was warm and had a smile permanently at her lips. Her mascaraed lashes fluttered when she spoke and she spoke with such passion, that Sabrina finally felt like this could be 'the one'; the record label she had been searching for when scouring her emails each day.

'Your work speaks for itself. You've been doing a stellar job so far and we don't wish to barge our way into an image and sound that has clearly been working for you all – that, and I can sense there would not be much use in me trying to persuade such creative and smart minds into my way of thinking.' Sabrina noticed Keira give Dan a small smirk as she said this. 'The way we would like to move forward is to allow you the platform to continue as you wish and give you our full support and encouragement to create an album you want to create. We want to see what it is you are all truly capable of and then, should we see room for changes once the first year is up, we can possibly renegotiate terms and market accordingly. For now, there is a rapid fan base waiting on your next move, and I have full confidence in you, Sabrina, that you know exactly what you want that next move to be.' Keira finished with a bright smile that made Sabrina sit up straighter and feel like she could take on the world. This woman could be a motivational speaker.

'I appreciate your confidence not only in myself but in the band too. Your offer is the best one we have received so far.' Sabrina smiled, then turned to Dan for confirmation to make sure he was happy with what he had heard too. Dan rubbed his hand over his chiseled jaw and gave Sabrina a small nod. This day was certainly shaping up to be epic.

Keira stood. 'That's what I like to hear. I should expect you will want to talk over the offer in private. All I ask is that you get back to me this afternoon. You'll understand this business moves at a rapid rate and we don't wish to be kept in the dark. The offer will only stand for a short period,' Keira noted as Sabrina and the boys followed suit in standing.

As they each took a step closer together to thank Keira, Levi casually placed his arm around Sabrina's waist. Sabrina felt her palms grow sweaty instantly. She never wanted to hide or deny her relationship with Levi, especially not after the years they'd wasted due to Lydia putting the fear of god into her. She loved Levi and was proud of their relationship. However, that didn't stop a flurry of butterflies exploding in her stomach as Keira spotted this intimate movement.

Keira opened the door and one by one the boys filed out, with nods, handshakes and sincere thanks. Before Sabrina could shake Keira's hand and step out of the office, Keira half closed the door and gently placed a hand on Sabrina's elbow. Sabrina turned to face her, grateful to see that her face was still rosy and friendly.

'I have to ask. Are you and Levi an item?' Keira queried, one hand resting on the door, the other still on Sabrina's arm. Sabrina took in a deep breath to steady her nerves and remind herself that she could be both a professional and in love and if the record label didn't like it, well … well, she wasn't quite sure what she would do. All she knew for certain was that she was not giving up on Levi again.

'We are, yes, and you have my word that it does not get in the way of our business. I do what is right by every member of the band – he receives no special treatment when it comes to work,' Sabrina said boldly, then cringed at the last bit. That was way too much information, Keira did not need to know what special treatment she gave Levi outside of work. She bravely attempted a smile when Keira's brows furrowed. After what felt like an eternity Keira's features relaxed, her pink-stained lips curved upwards.

'I will warn you – the label as a whole doesn't think too fondly of talent and managers mixing. There's been trouble with it in the past.' Keira shook her head and waved her hand away as if it had all been a silly mix-up and shouldn't have been a big deal. 'I like you and I'd really love to work together with these guys and take them to the next level – not with fame, I can see that's not a priority for them, but with their music and the reach it can achieve. However, I'm not going to sugarcoat it. Our publicists are tough and I like to keep everyone working together on the same page and running like clockwork. There will be compromises for all parties involved. So, think about it and get back to me as soon as you can.' Keira squeezed Sabrina's arm and opened the door once more. Sabrina thanked her again and took a step into the corridor where Levi and Dan were waiting. James and Dylan had walked further up the corridor. Sabrina appreciated them looking out for her.

She glanced back at Keira when she heard a small chuckle. 'I can see it,' Keira started. 'You make a cute couple, but be smart,' she said with a wink before waving them off. Sabrina ignored the prickle in her throat. This was the offer that they couldn't resist; freedom when it came to recording and writing. It was time to celebrate. Sabrina was certain that if she could handle Lydia Jones for all those years at Jones Records that she could handle whatever the publicists would throw her way here at City Heights Records.

Chapter 6

Torta Caprese

Ingredients:

Farina
Zucchero
Uova
Polvere di cacao
Burro
Mandorle macinate
Rum
Cioccolato

What to do:

Sciogliere il burro e il cioccolato insieme a fuoco basso.
Sbatti gli albumi in una ciotola separata. Mescolare gli ingredienti secchi insieme.
Aggiungi rum.
Infornare in forno per un'ora.

The small balcony off the kitchen was home to the most magnificent view of the Tyrrhenian sea. Louisa had the brown double doors propped open so she could feel the night's breeze on her skin and smell the perfumed air. She couldn't quite put her finger on the scent of Italy. Yes, there was the hint of salt from the sea, but it was more flavourful, more powerful than just that. It was mixed with the lightness of the elegant flowers that blossomed in every garden, the lingering aromas of the day's food that swirled through kitchen windows and the ever-present smell of coffee being brewed somewhere, accompanied by the sweet scent of pastry. She breathed it in, allowing her body to relax at the smell of home. She made herself comfy in one of her zia's wicker chairs. The navy-blue hue of the night sky was mesmerizing; a vast ocean of sparkling dots caught her attention as her eyes flickered in search of the brightest one.

'Ciao Grandpa,' Louisa whispered before casting her eyes over the sketch she had been working on.

She had her sketchbook propped up against her knee and the arm of the chair and a few pencils tucked away at one side of her legs. She never went far without it these days. Since being in Italy she had been drawing nonstop. Everywhere she looked she found inspiration and that passion she had lost during her stint in London, trapped in her most recent nine-to-five, had come roaring back.

The current piece she was working on had been inspired by the ceramic shops she passed daily on her way to work. For every Costa coffee that Manchester had, here in Orzoro there was a shop selling limoncello soap and ceramic pottery that drew Louisa in every time.

The extra special shops were those where no two pieces were the same, where you would often find the owners hunched over a table in the back of the tiny store painting, each brush stroke working its way purposefully over the pot. Louisa especially loved when the artist mixed the blues and yellows and greens together; something about those colours screamed Italia to her.

Her blank paper was now alive with a deep cobalt A-line pencil dress with a square neck, a yellow patterned trim around the neck, waist and hem. Louisa could picture Sabrina wearing it for an important day at her new office with the boys. The thought made her smile. She was proud of her sister for taking

49

Dan and Levi up on their offer of continuing to represent them and helping them navigate the next part of their journey in finding a new record deal. Louisa knew Sabrina was more than capable. She was pleased too that Sabrina would no longer have to work under Lydia at Jones Records. Louisa had apologized to Sabrina for always assuming her life was that of a glamourous celebrity manager, attending flashy parties, red carpets and dining with the rich and famous; she hadn't accounted for Sabrina missing her as much as she had missed Sabrina. Her millions of Instagram followers and her band's international success hadn't exactly signaled lonely to Louisa, but they had talked over Christmas and her snipes and moody remarks were water under the bridge. Louisa now understood the workload behind the social media and album sales, and she couldn't be more in awe of Sabrina.

Louisa felt that having some space over the past month and a half in Italy had helped her understand her sisters. She had always been the one to stay home, to be there for her parents and grandparents. She had felt angry at Amanda and Sabrina for leaving the family, and her, behind. But she was realizing that finding that balance between family and pursuing your own dreams was important. Being in Italy, doing something for herself, made her feel invigorated. As though she had finally stepped out of her older sisters' shadows and found some sunshine of her own. Though she had to admit that going after her own dreams here in Italy meant that she missed her sisters more than ever.

There was a small part of her that truly believed she could make something of herself in the fashion industry and this was one of the things that was keeping her going. Another thing was Luca.

Growing up, Louisa had been surrounded by love; her parents had been happily married for over thirty years and her nonni had been sweethearts for sixty. It was this love that had squashed any doubt about giving the Italian man she met in Alfonso's pasticceria, before Christmas, a chance. Luca had been a kind stranger at a time when she had needed it most. Though it all happened quickly, Louisa had felt a certain pull of magic, like Luca was her own Prince Charming.

Luca had spoilt her with picnics overlooking the mountainside, candlelit lunches in the cozy confines of her office and the finest tables at Orzoro's best-kept secrets; to which Louisa had made mental notes to take Amanda to next time she visited. In addition to their extraordinary dates, Louisa had also spent time getting to know Luca's family more, while Luca too often visited with her nanna and zias. The qualms about it being just a holiday romance were dissolving as fast as Luca's *sfogliatelle* melted in her mouth.

Louisa wished more than anything she could tell her grandpa all about Luca, his family and the pasticceria, but somehow, she thought he already knew. Taking her eyes off her new favourite design, she looked out across the peaceful night sky and smiled as the brightest star flickered as she watched.

Suddenly her phone buzzed in her pocket. She grabbed it eagerly in hopes that it was a text from Amanda or Sabrina, but Luca's name flashed across the screen. She smiled as she read his text wishing her a *buona notte* but couldn't shift the loneliness she felt from her sisters having not responded to her for the third day in a row. She slumped down in her chair, a pout playing at her lips.

'*Cara mia, cosa c'è che non va?*' Nanna's voice came out of the shadows in the kitchen doorway. Louisa sat up right away, not wanting to give cause for Nanna to worry. She was being silly. She loved her sisters and she knew they loved her too. They were simply busy, and so was she. Life in Italy was wonderful and not just because of Luca and work, but because she got to see Nanna getting to spend time with her own sisters after eighteen years apart. Unlike Grandpa, Nanna had not been able to travel back and forth from England to her home in Italy over the years.

51

Ailments and illnesses had kept her grounded. She had become terrified of flying because of this. But last year after Grandpa passed, she had wanted to see that he got home and had inspired the girls when she agreed to come with them for his funeral. Nanna was strong and had put on a brave face. That face bore wise wrinkles, her skin a still-glowing olive tone and her eyes glistened brighter than ever before when she pottered about her childhood home. Now she shuffled along the tiled floor in her navy slipper sandals, concern making the creases around her eyes more prominent.

'Nothing's wrong Nanna, I'm fine thank you,' Louisa said softly, getting up out of her chair to hug her. That always made her feel better.

'You miss your sisters, no?' Nanna questioned. Nothing could ever get past a nonna, Louisa mused, better luck next time.

'Yes, I do. I'm so excited about the fashion show Nanna, but I can't help thinking about how fabulous the opening of *Torta per Tutti* is going to be. I know she can be a stubborn pain sometimes but when it comes to cooking, Amanda knows her stuff. I was looking forward to seeing it come to life, you know, just being there for her and being a guinea pig, making sure the menu was perfect. But I know she will have everyone else,' Louisa confessed, her arms wrapped tight around her nanna who she could have sworn had shrunk a couple more inches since arriving in Italy.

'I understand *cara*. I know of this problem. Life is balance. What can we do?' Nanna said, her voice an airy whisper. She, more than anyone, knew the heartache of years away from loved ones, yet she had always remained so strong and happy with what surrounded her, her sisters always sending cards and parcels.

'That's it! *Grazie* Nanna. *Grazie*,' Louisa cried after a few moments passed. She kissed her nanna on the cheek, an idea having sprung to her mind. 'You take a seat and you teach me,' she added, guiding Nanna to the kitchen table but grabbing a yellow cushion to make the seat more comfortable. Just then Zia Sofia walked into the kitchen waving a torn piece of paper in the air as if she had read Louisa's mind. Zia Sofia was the youngest of her three zias and the one always bouncing around after everyone; taking the lead in the kitchen and reminding Louisa fiercefully of Amanda.

'*Aspetta, aspetta,*' she said, before reaching Louisa's side and pinching her cheeks with her paper-free hand. 'You need this. We make it now,' her zia announced, turning on her heel and collecting up pots and pans. Louisa gazed at the browning paper now in her palm and blinked back tears. It was Grandpa's hand-writing and read '*Torta caprese*'.

She looked to Nanna, unable to speak. Nanna's eyes twinkled, a spark of happiness followed by a gleam of pain. Louisa missed him every day; she couldn't imagine how Nanna felt.

'Family recipes, they are the treasure of the life,' Nanna noted, as Zia Sofia carefully pulled the recipe out of Louisa's hand, handing her bowls and spoons and shouting instructions in fast Italian. Louisa would do well to remind her that it was Amanda that was the chef of the family and not her, but she had been the one to want to learn, so she did as she was told, following the instructions as best she could, feeling content that her zia had read her mind and agreed that food was always the answer, espe-cially when made with love.

*

Rest had not been on the cards last night, Louisa was too excit-able. At 6 a.m. she crept into the kitchen, grabbed her coat from the coat rack, picked up her bag from where she'd left it next to the wicker chair, collected the brown parcel from the kitchen counter and tip-toed in her black ballet pumps out onto the balcony. The soft morning breeze cooled her warm bones.

Louisa walked in silence down the cobbled path, past the blocks

53

of apartments whose shutters were all closed. She almost wanted to tip-toe, scared to make even the smallest of noises and disturb the tranquility of the sleeping village. The street looked like a rainbow, as each window bore a different shade of turquoise, pink and yellow. As she made her way further down the mountain, closer to the village square, lights illuminated bakeries where Louisa could see little old nonnas preparing the doughs for the day. Louisa's thoughts drifted again to Amanda and how she would soon be doing the same thing in her café back home and it gave her an extra pep in her step. She wanted to stop and give the nonnas a hand, knowing how tiring the process was, after years of watching Amanda beat herself up over loaf after loaf, trying to perfect them and get them exactly like Grandpa's. But she knew this was what the Italians lived for – waking up to cook with love, to feed the world. She knew the nonnas would be just fine and kept on walking.

Disturbing the silence up the street were the fisherman delivering their catch to the market stalls and restaurants. The salty fragrance of freshly caught squid reminded Louisa of her childhood summers spent fishing with her grandpa. The girls had promised they would be back to fish in the summer; Louisa hoped that with both her sisters being so busy that they would somehow still be able to stick to this promise. She would try and understand if not.

Arriving at her first destination, she snuck in to the back of the bakery and was immediately greeted by Luca's mamma. 'Buongiorno cara,' she said, hugging Louisa and then holding her back at arm's length, her hands still on Louisa's shoulders. Louisa was accustomed to this behavior. Luca's mamma was assessing her up and down, finally resting on Louisa's eyes. It was the kind of evaluation she received daily from her nanna and zias, usually to check that she had eaten enough and that there was happiness behind her eyes. But before the interrogation began, Luca appeared, and Louisa's stomach turned into a swarm of butterflies.

'*Ciao bella*,' he said, his eyebrows raised and surprise in his tone. Then he walked over to her and kissed her sweetly on each cheek.

'*Buongiorno*,' Louisa replied, merrily. She then turned to Luca's mamma, hoping to be excused so she could go and cuddle Luca before she needed to head off.

'Come, we have coffee,' Luca said, reaching around Louisa's waist and guiding her out of the kitchen.

He pulled down two chairs from a small table at the front of the café and gestured for Louisa to sit while he went around the counter and brought the coffee machine to life. Louisa contemplated the street through the gold lettering on the giant window. Only the food vendors were bustling about in their stalls and cafés, getting ready for the morning rush. The other shops remained vacant, void of light and life. Orzoro sure was beautiful at sunrise.

With a whistle and a gurgle, the robust smell of Italy's finest espresso wafted her way, along with a tall, dark and equally robust Italian man. Louisa took him in once more, smiling when he placed her tiny coffee in front of her.

'Everything is okay?' Luca asked, as he sat down opposite her.

Louisa took a sip of the strong coffee and looked Luca straight in his ocean-blue eyes. These eyes had a way of drawing out her fears since the days she had first gazed into them, but today she was full of positivity and exuberant energy, her fears having melted away along with the bowl of butter and chocolate she had mixed together last night.

'Can I get some of your cinnamon biscuits to add to my box, please?' she said enthusiastically. For the first time since they sat down Luca took his eyes off hers and looked to the box.

'What it is?' Luca asked, touching the box and toying with the lid, sniffing the air as he did so. Louisa chuckled.

'My family's secret *torta caprese*, for Amanda,' she answered,

55

allowing him to lift the lid and peak inside. Luca's eyes lit up. He leaned forward to get a better look, eyeing up the cake in the same fashion Louisa had witnessed Amanda doing when they had first stepped into Alfonso's bakery last year and Luca had given them a box of cakes. It was like he was trying to figure out its secrets just by looking at it. 'I know I can't make it to the café opening, but I can still be part of it in some way. Amanda is probably busy and stressing about it all right now, so I think this will make her smile and remember what it's all about,' Louisa added, placing the lid carefully back on the box, making sure it was snug against the cake so it wouldn't break in transit. She would get a bigger box to protect it further once she got to the post office and filled it with more goodies from Luca.

'You can tell me the recipe, no?' Luca asked, wiggling his eyebrows, a sweet smile turning up at the corner of his lips as he picked up Louisa's hand and planted a kiss on her palm.

'Not a chance,' Louisa said playfully, though she meant it and he knew this too. Family recipes were sacred in Italy; she couldn't go giving them away no matter how handsome Luca's smile was or how mesmerizing his eyes were.

'Eh, what can I do?' he said with a laugh. Louisa jumped up, moving to his side of the table to hug him. When Luca wrapped his strong arms around her, she didn't want to be anywhere else. He already smelt like pastries and vanilla; she wanted to stay in his embrace all day, but she had work to do. She dropped a kiss on his soft locks and stood up, checking her watch to see if the town's only post office would be open yet.

Ten minutes later, Louisa walked out of Alfonso's with a flush in her cheeks and a much heavier parcel. Walking towards Orzoro's town centre, she thought about Luca and his dream of travelling that he had shared with her during a special beach date over the holidays and hoped that one day they could maybe deliver a similar parcel in person, together, to Amanda's café. The thought made her grin as she headed to the post office. With the smell of rum and chocolate occasionally wafting up from the box, she couldn't wait to get to work today, feeling inspired by her family and the love in her heart.

Chapter 7

Garlic Bruschetta

Ingredients:

Whip up Grandpa's bread mixture
Garlic
Parsley
Butter
Olive oil
Plum tomatoes

What to do:

Slice bread and lightly toast.
Blend butter (a fork will do to squash, the mix with spoon) with diced garlic and parsley. Add a dash of salt and pepper.
Spread butter onto bread and layer with chunky pieces of garlic and baby plum tomatoes.

Amanda was doing her best to drown out the hammering and the clatter that was coming from the kitchen by squinting really hard at her clipboard to try and absorb the words that were staring back at her. Sabrina had been the one to suggest she get a clipboard. If Amanda could focus on the words, she wouldn't even notice the noise. It was 7.30 a.m. and Manchester was just beginning to wake, a faint orange glow appearing above the tree tops and houses across the road. Liam had fixed the electrical work a few days ago but there was a problem with the pipes that he was currently attempting to fix, being the handy man that he was. Amanda was ninety-nine per cent sure the initial plumber had made it worse than it was before he arrived. She was getting antsy not being able to cook, but thankfully Liam had proved to be a knight in shining armour with the electricals and she prayed he could save the day again.

'Kate, how's everything looking with the register?' Amanda asked her recent recruit. Kate was Louisa's age, twenty-four, polite and quiet. She had been doing a great job tailing Amanda and doing what was asked of her over the past few days. Amanda wasn't quite sure her head would still be screwed on if it wasn't for Kate. So far, she had organized Amanda's scraps of paper that held shopping lists and menu ideas and replaced them with colour coordinated notebooks and pens for each such occasion. She had cleaned a small area at the back of the café and set up a table and chairs so Amanda could actually sit down and go through the business plans and have a place to conduct interviews and speak with her team. She had plugged up the register and saw to it that Amanda had Wi-Fi and a landline installed. Amanda was impressed by this woman's efficiency. It rivalled that of Sabrina's, yet Amanda still wished her sister were here.

'It's all linked up to the Wi-Fi, as is the card machine and your phone. It should be ready to go, boss,' Kate replied, with a confidence that made Amanda look up from her 'to-do' list (which had been Kate's doing too). She saw Kate smiling in her direction and couldn't help smiling back. Kate was coming out of her shell and starting to relax in Amanda's craziness.

'Thank you. I appreciate that. Once the rest of the team arrive within the next hour, we'll go through kitchen protocol and get the dining area set up, I should think,' Amanda said, eyeing up the plastic-covered furniture and dusty floorboards. Better yet, she might make a start on it before the others arrived; she didn't want to put them off by having them cleaning on their first day, though she had mentioned this in the interviews. With the café being brand new, she had expressed her need for staff to aid in the final preparations and seating plan. No one had pulled a face, so she had taken that as a good sign.

Suddenly a loud crash came from the kitchen causing Amanda's clipboard to fall to the floor, her hands flying up to her chest to keep her heart in its cage. She took a few steps towards the double doors when there came a loud banging on the front door. She had the blinds down so no one could see inside, and she could not see out. With her heart still beating painfully, she waved Kate in the direction of the kitchen. Kate nodded in understanding, and Amanda made for the front door.

She peeked through the blinds and was pleasantly surprised to see that it was in fact her two new hires; that would teach her to be a pessimist she thought. Then Amanda noticed a third woman that she didn't recognize. She was hesitant to open the door, her fingers hovering over the lock, but she couldn't exactly leave her new staff standing in the cold – what kind of impression would that give them of their new boss? She forced a smile with pursed lips, welcoming the staff inside, but wasn't quick enough to hold off the other woman.

Immediately the lady started snapping photos on her phone, before turning to Amanda and shoving the phone in her face. The new trainees looked at this interaction with mouths wide opens, their brows low in confusion. The boy was bouncing at his knees unsure whether he should step forward and interfere, yet ready to do so if Amanda gave him the go-ahead.

Amanda waved him off, with a fake closed-mouth smile and pointed for them to go and sit at the sole table in the dining area. Then she turned to the lady to speak, but the lady beat her to it.

'So, this is what San Francisco Beat are retiring for? Might I ask your name? The lucky lady who snapped up one of the hottest lead singers in the world right now.' The lady was a picture of confidence and casual, with one arm crossed over her black blazer and untucked blouse, and the other arm holding her recording device aloft. As she spoke her wrist waved from side to side, in an air of arrogance Amanda was not a fan of.

'Excuse me, but you cannot be on this premises, we are not open yet,' Amanda said as politely as she could, opening the door a little wider now. But the lady was eyeing up the room, her recording device still in the air. A loud grunt came from the kitchen followed by a slur of swear words and Kate shouting, 'It's okay!'. Amanda shook her head; she didn't have time for this. 'I asked you to leave, please,' she said, slightly louder, her voice wobbling. The lady sauntered over to Amanda, ignoring the open door and concentrating on Amanda's face. Amanda could feel the judgement in the lady's glare.

'Tell me, what've you got that all those models and actresses don't? Me and the rest of the world deserve to know, so we can bag our own rock star. It's only fair us ladies help each other out,' the lady said with a wiggle of her eyebrows and an attempt at a friendly laugh that only sounded cold and creepy to Amanda's ears.

Amanda remained silent. She wanted to shove the lady out of the door, but thought better of it, not wanting to be sued for harming a so-called 'journalist'. 'Go on, I know there's a voice in there somewhere. We know Dan likes them feisty; he's always being snapped with the troubled starlets and harlots after all.'

Amanda felt as though David Beckham had just taken a penalty and it had hit her square in the stomach knocking the wind out of her. She steadied herself with one hand holding the door frame and the other on her hip. Why was she letting this lady get to her? She knew Dan better than anyone. He had been with her six weeks ago. Life had been pretty magical since Christmas. Yes, Dan had dated his fair share of women, but this lady knew nothing and was simply stirring the pot – that didn't stop Amanda's lungs grasping for air though. But she would not let this show; she kept her mouth closed, her eyes still looking out of the door and into the grey Manchester morning. 'Garlic, olive oil, salt and pepper. Garlic, olive oil, salt and pepper.' She tried to conjure up the smell in her mind to take the edge off the lady's words.

'Cat got your tongue, hey? Afraid you might not match up to the throng of women succumbing to that irresistible voice of his? Or are you just so sure of yourself that you're his soul mate, that he's not like all the other rock stars before him tempted by the high life, that you don't feel the need to talk to people like me?' The lady's voice was vicious in its assault, dripping with spite and jealousy. Amanda wanted to retaliate, but she couldn't. This lady had somehow gotten under her skin; she wasn't sure if it was the clouds that were fuzzy or just the tears threatening to spill over. This was not like her, she didn't get emotional like this. She needed this lady gone. Amanda knew better than anyone not to overthink the media, because it would eat away at you if you let it. She had caught a glimpse of the gossip magazines recently and knew San Francisco Beat having just signed with City Heights Records was a huge deal, but Amanda had felt better when she kept her focus on the café. Not that she wasn't proud of the boys and Sabrina for this amazing achievement, but the music business was not her world. Dan was Dan. He was not a celebrity to her.

She turned to look at the woman and edged closer to her, not giving her any alternative other than to take a step back. A few more steps forward from Amanda, and the woman and her conceited smirk were out the door. Amanda snapped it shut as quick as she could and exhaled a shaky breath.

'Everything okay, boss?' Kate asked, forcing Amanda to snap out of her wayward thoughts and focus on today's agenda; getting the café up and running, and clean.

'I think I should be the one asking you that question,' Amanda said, brushing a hand through the loose strands of hair that had escaped from her messy bun and shrugging off the encounter with the rude journalist. 'So?' She raised her eyebrows at Kate as they started walking towards the waiting staff.

'So, it's not looking too bad. Give him a couple more hours and Liam says we'll be right as rain,' Kate replied, stopping on the way to greet the others to pick up Amanda's clipboard that she had dropped earlier.

Amanda reached the table and clapped her hands together, offering a cheery hello to make the two new hires forget about the odd conversation that had just ensued.

'Having trouble with your boyfriend's ex?' the boy queried, swiveling around on his chair, casually draping his arm over the back of it. Amanda couldn't help but chuckle at his innocence. It felt refreshing to relax back into her anonymity. It was a sharp contrast to how over-exposed she had felt just moments ago.

'Something like that,' she said. The boy offered her a sympathetic smile. 'Right …' Amanda started, before there was another loud knock at the door. Three sets of eyes bore into her as though she were running a mad house.

Amanda turned on her black trainers and rushed to the window to get a peek at who was knocking. Looking through a gap in the blinds again, she saw a tall man with a clipboard in his arm and a briefcase in the other. He didn't scream paparazzi – he was standing rather tall for a sneaky journalist. In Amanda's experience they hid in bushes or dressed far more unassumingly, like the demon lady from before, but this man was in a full-on suit.

'Do you think I should answer it?' Amanda tilted her head towards the back of the café at Kate and her other potential staff. She feared she looked like a madwoman. Why was she asking them? They had no idea of the skeletons that lurked in Amanda's closet. *Really?* Amanda thought to herself. *Skeletons? That's a touch too dramatic, don't you think?* It wasn't like she had to hide the fact that her sister was a manager to a famous rock band from potential hires, they would soon find out on opening day. So why did she feel the need to keep it from them a while longer?

'What kind of café is this?' Amanda heard the girl whisper to Kate. A side glance and Amanda saw Kate shrug in lieu of a response. She didn't blame her. The place was a mess, she had no running water, no food, but a healthy slew of random people knocking down her door. She had to get a grip and probably come clean after this.

Despite the unpleasant ache sitting on her stomach she unlatched the door. At the first sound of life, the man sprang into action, raising up his laminated badge and making to step forward. Amanda gripped the door tighter.

'Excuse me, we are not open yet, this is private property,' Amanda said loudly, not exactly sure that was true or not, but right away she didn't care for this man. He took a step back and sighed at the confrontation.

'The badge, ma'am, look at the badge. I'm Tom Bennett, it is not in my job description to announce my title, but I suggest you don't get on my bad side. Now, please move aside. I do not stand for idle chit chat, bribes of any kind or immaturity,' Tom said, stepping forward once more, trying to push himself inside. Was this guy having a bad day or was he always like this? Was he a health inspector? A reviewer? Were they all this mean? She hadn't met a critic before on her travels that was this patronizing. Was he hangry?

Amanda's grip on the door grew tighter, she looked at his badge and noticed the pen on his clip board was from Rusk. Was this her ex-sous-chef Jeff's, plan to sabotage her? Did she really have to deal with this now? She hadn't had to think about her conniving, women-hating, weasel-like former colleague since she'd quit her job as head chef at Rusk just before New Year, and her life was much more pleasant because of it.

'Mr Bennett, I have no intention of bribing an official, but you simply cannot force yourself into my café when I don't know who you are. I find that terribly unprofessional and I would ask that I have the number for your boss or whoever it is you work for,' Amanda said sternly, trying to figure out who this man was. She didn't want to be uncooperative if this man was someone important, but she was done with feeling like a fool in front of her new staff.

'I don't feel like you are comprehending what it is I do or who I am. I do not go around announcing myself. We make surprise visits to truly see how a place is being taken care of, how the food is being cooked and how the kitchen is being kept. But your ...' he paused, looking down his nose at Amanda's scruffy attire and then taking in the dirty windows. 'Your establishment seems to be quite secretive, causing me to have to knock and deal with this needless conversation.'

Amanda couldn't help the small grin that began to creep up on her face. This had to be Jeff's doing, surely? He could have got his timing a little better, but if it was a tour the man wanted, then fine.

'Please forgive me Tom. Do come on in,' she said, stepping aside and waving him in.

Tom certainly was doing his best to uphold Jeff's plan. Clearly, he didn't want to give up too soon in needing to put the fear of god into Amanda, but by the confused look on his face at the sight of the indoors, he knew he had messed up.

'So, here is where our customers like to dine,' Amanda started, waving her hands over the plastic covered seating area. 'I find it so much easier for my staff to clean up at the end of the day with our usage of the plastic wrap. Any food or drink spills simply wipe up with a wet cloth. And the customers don't seem to mind it, it's a new kind of chic. Again, we're doing things a little differently here, taking rustic to a whole new level. The newspapers on the floor make for an exciting game of stepping stones on your way to the bathroom, the kids love it.' Amanda couldn't help smiling and batting her eyelashes.

'Oh my god, just wait till you see the kitchen. It comes with our onsite fixer-upper, he works tirelessly day and night to keep this place running smoothly. Even the kids know him by name and he's a firm favourite with our customers.' Amanda used her butt to open the swinging door into the kitchen. Give him credit, Tom had yet to give her an eye roll and he was sticking it out. Amanda was intrigued as to what he would come up with to try and scare her off when her whole dramatic act was over. Her staff remained huddled around the table, each wearing a bewildered expression as they watched their new boss in action.

Tom remained quiet throughout Amanda's charade and she wondered how he could possibly remain professional in a situation like this. Would he admit his mistake? Would he laugh it off? Were Jeff's steeds even allowed to laugh? If he hadn't been such an ass upon meeting, Amanda might have felt a tad sorry for him, but then she remembered he was in cahoots with her ex sous-chef and all sympathy vanished. Jeff had sabotaged her last job, he was not about to stomp on her dreams. She felt her cheeks begin to redden with anger at the thought of Jeff, and without waiting for Tom's review of her clearly not-finished café, she marched him through the café and swung open the front door and gently shoved him through.

'Thanks for stopping by. Do say hello to Jeff for me. It's a shame your timing was a little off, but I'll be sure to have everything in absolutely fabulous condition by the time you come again, and you know, I will actually be open and shall be welcoming health inspectors and reviewers with open arms.'

Amanda slammed the door; her fists were curled into balls and she could feel her heart thudding uncomfortably in her chest. It hit her all at once that this café was her baby and that she would not take kindly to people trying to destroy it. This had been her dream for so long; it was for her and for Grandpa and she would fight to make it a success.

With her fingers against the bridge of her nose, she glanced down at her watch, a scoff escaping her lips. It was only 9 a.m. It was going to be a long day.

Chapter 8

Nanna's Zabaglione

Ingredients:

½ cup white wine
½ cup Marsala
1 tsp sugar
2 egg yolks

What to do:

Whisk together egg yolks and sugar over a medium heat.
(Careful not to scramble.)
Pour in wine and Marsala and whisk until thick and fluffy.

The skylight above was letting in the soft morning sun, rendering the kitchen in a yellow glow. From the glass sliding patio doors Sabrina could see the silhouette of Santa Monica pier and the rows of palm trees along the paths bristling in the breeze. Spring was just beginning to bloom with March in full swing; LA boasted an orange sun and warm air at six in the morning.

For four years, her view from her tiny apartment had been that of brick walls and dumpsters decorating the sidewalk. She smiled inwardly that her view upon getting ready to leave LA better represented what she had set out to do all those years ago, and what she had accomplished. Nestled high up in the Santa Monica hills overlooking the ocean, the sunlight causing the white kitchen to gleam and the clear-blue water of the swimming pool to glisten under its rays; yes, it was certainly a step up from her previous living quarters and a far cry from the life she had led when she had first moved to LA. She had been fortunate that her move to LA had come with a job at Jones Records, but she had never been so nervous putting down a deposit on that rusty apartment, especially since the weeks that followed felt like a painful initiation into Lydia's world and Sabrina had been tempted to give up more than a handful of times. Being an assistant, she had started at minimum wage – getting a raise was dependent on passing Lydia's tests. For a year that raise alluded her, even after the 4 a.m. coffee runs, 2 a.m. dry cleaning emergencies and brilliant idea after brilliant idea that Lydia stole from her.

It was only when San Francisco Beat came along that she was able to start saving, with high hopes for the future, and occasionally purchase a sparkly dress here and there for fancy events instead of simply renting them. The home she was currently residing in might not exactly belong to her, but she allowed herself to feel proud that she'd had a hand in San Francisco Beat's success and in turn them being able to afford such a luxurious home.

With the money Sabrina had saved from sticking out her hole-in-the-wall lease and with their new deal with City Heights Records, she was looking forward to buying her first property in Manchester. She helped herself to a mug of coffee, wishing that she was like Amanda and could whip up a small batch of *zabaglione* to dollop inside it. She triple-checked the flight details that lay on the kitchen counter, allowing herself to breathe in the fragrant aroma, and patted herself on the back for getting the year off to a great start with the boys. Granted, Tyler had been the brains behind this record deal, so he deserved most of the credit, but she was proud of herself for handling the meeting and negotiations with Keira that had followed, before they signed the dotted line.

Her phone rang with a loud shuffle across the kitchen table.

She leant forward, careful not to spill her giant mug of coffee, and pulled the phone to her ear.

'Morning,' Sabrina greeted Keira in a chirpy whisper, though she was certain that the boys could not hear her from upstairs; the house might be modest in comparison to the mansions on *Cribs* but it could still fit her apartment inside it twenty-fold.

'Morning Sabrina! So, amazing news, I wanted to catch you before you got to the airport. The recording studio in the UK is all booked. I think the guys will love this one. There's no time restraint on it yet, I want to see how the boys get on. If you just keep me posted on where we're at along the way – how the songs are coming together and such – and then we can get a better idea of our marketing strategy and radio promotion as we go,' Keira said, the coffee and her words waking Sabrina right up. Sabrina was getting used to Keira's fast-talking and straight-to-the-point ways.

'Sounds good,' Sabrina said, moving to sit at her desk and grabbing her notebook to jot down things to remember.

'March 30th is when the band is due in the studio and I'll most likely be heading over to pay you all a visit during that week too.'

'Okay, yes. I've got it all written down. March 30th. I'm sure they will be eager to get started. Thank you,' Sabrina said, circling March 30th a few times in her notebook.

Keira chuckled down the phone. 'I'll send over an email with all the details – just confirm when you've received it and we'll be good to go.'

Sabrina put her pen down, but then picked it up again out of habit. She didn't always trust emails – she liked to write things down and would only be transferring important bits of information from the email into her notebook anyway. 'I will do.'

'Great. Safe travels, and Sabrina – be smart and keep your wits about you. See you soon,' Keira said before hanging up. Sabrina gnawed on the end of her pen, staring deeply into the coffee pot across the kitchen. She watched the still, black pool of liquid, pondering her next moves and how she was going to make them.

*

It was Thursday morning so naturally LAX was rammed with people. Normally crowds would fill Sabrina with nerves, but today she was glad of it. With the traffic getting here and the constant bumping into fellow passengers there had been barely any time to stand around or for the boys to stand out. In other words, less opportunity for her and Levi to get cosy, hold hands or cuddle up to each other and less opportunity for someone to catch them in the act and snap a shot.

Sabrina was marching forward, all business, as she made her way up to the kiosk. She checked them all in; it helped keep the process smooth and flowing. If she let the boys do it they would be there for hours as James and Levi would charm the men and women behind the desk, leading them to request pictures, causing more people to catch on and draw attention to them. It had happened on more than one occasion and Sabrina could do without it today.

The lady smiled at Sabrina and handed her back her passport. As she opened each one of the boys, she sent them each a coy glance, her mouth slightly parted. She knew who they were, but Sabrina was prepared, answering each important question and stepping in to ensure the boys gave short answers when the lady wouldn't accept her response. Sabrina understood that the boys were grown men, but if anything happened to them it would be her head on the line.

Sabrina knew the boys were more than capable of appeasing a group of screaming girls, men, and women. They would flash their dazzling smiles, answer questions and bid them farewell in a manner that made people thank them and give them their space. She'd witnessed it thousands of times before. However,

70

grown men just looking to give them a hard time and women wanting inappropriate body parts signed were a different story, and, right now, not a story Sabrina wanted to have to explain to Keira on her first week on the job.

The minute they were handed their boarding passes – for first class thanks to Keira – Sabrina ushered them towards their gate, with ten minutes to spare. She was certainly not going to miss the LA rush.

As Levi walked up behind her to take the seat next to her, she stopped abruptly, turning into him and putting a hand up to his chest to stop him.

'Is it okay if Dan sits with me? I have a bunch of emails to go over with him. I might as well get a head start with all these hours ahead of us.' Sabrina tried to keep her voice level and airy, not wanting to give Levi reason to overthink her request, but that didn't stop him looking crestfallen. It took all she had not to reach out and hug him, but she didn't know who might see them.

'Sure,' he said after a moment's hesitation.

'Great, thank you baby,' Sabrina said with a bright smile as big as she could muster, turning to take her seat before Levi could kiss her.

Chapter 9

Mozzarella in Carrozza

Ingredients:

Bread
Mozzarella (drained – use kitchen roll to soak up moisture)
Butter
2 eggs, beaten
Splash of milk
Salt
Pepper

What to do:

Make up mozzarella sandwiches.
Add splash of milk to beaten and seasoned eggs. Dip sandwiches
into the mixture.
Coat bottom of a saucepan with butter and allow to heat up.
When the pan is hot, fry sandwiches on either side until golden brown.

Louisa heard the cockerel before her eyes had even opened. This had become her morning ritual; she no longer required an alarm clock or had to rely on her phone. Her trusty cockerel friend had her back, whether she liked it or not; her requests for keeping the noise down on weekends had gone unanswered. It took all of two minutes for her bleary eyes to snap wide awake and her stomach to grumble to attention. Nowhere in the world did she believe one could wake up to the sweet and mouthwatering aromas that were wafting from her zias' kitchen. Nothing could compare to Italian food, especially when her zias made it and to give her big sister credit where credit was due, anyone would be hard pressed to find a better Italian chef than Amanda. She did their zias' and Nanna and Grandpa's food justice.

Louisa sprung out of bed, throwing one of Luca's hoodies over her pajamas. She shoved her feet into her boots and followed the delicious scent of vanilla *cornetti* and frying *mozzarella in carrozza*. There was a definite chill seeping in through the cracks in the walls and under the door frames; if the allure of food wasn't enough to wake her, her body had snapped to attention with the crisp air that made the hairs on her arms stand to attention. She rubbed at her biceps as she walked through the dark corridor. Passing through the hall, she often got distracted by the photos on display. Tealights lit up the frames that bore the departed, black and white family photos decorated the peeling white walls and dotted between them were stunning pictures of Orzoro throughout the years. Not much had changed bar the shop signs and more tourists packing onto the beaches each year. The shelf up ahead, just before the kitchen, held her grandpa's picture and fresh roses that Nanna replaced every few days. Louisa paused as she walked past it, like she had come to do every morning, and greeted her grandpa – '*Buongiorno*, Grandpa'. He was never far from her thoughts.

The kitchen was a sharp contrast to the rest of the house; the heat from the oven and the stove top immediately wrapped Louisa in a warm hug and she loosened her arms that were tightly crossed over her chest.

'*Buongiorno a tutti*,' she spoke loudly, announcing herself above the chatter of Nanna and her three zias. There was rarely a quiet moment in an Italian household; she knew this from growing up with her mum and grandparents back in Manchester and from the visits she'd made to Orzoro when she was younger. She and her sisters would run around with the village kids and numerous cousins while the elders cooked, drank wine and debated in raised voices over which region of Italy produced the best olive oil. Living with her nanna and zias over the last two months had confirmed this Italian trait; the sisters always had something to discuss – chatting over each other, getting in each other's business. The only time they were quiet was when watching the quiz shows on *Rai Uno*. Louisa chuckled to herself at the memories while she greeted each inhabitant of the kitchen with a hug and kiss to the cheek.

Within a matter of seconds shouts of, '*Mangia, mangia*,' erupted from every mouth and Louisa was guided to the dining table where a breakfast feast awaited her. She did what she was told – saying no to food was never an option, nor was it in her repertoire – with her own cries of, '*Grazie, grazie*'.

Louisa loaded her plate with fruit, a fresh vanilla *cornetto* and *mozzarella in carrozza* and sipped the coffee that had been poured for her. Today she needed her energy. With two days before she was set to display her designs and work at Italy's Young Designers Fashion Showcase, it was crunch time and there couldn't be a stitch out of place. Warm butter cascaded onto her plate and trickled down her fingers as the first bite of the smooth, velvety, eggy bread passed her lips. The day had officially begun.

The bustle of four moving bodies ceased by Louisa's third bite; her zias and her nanna joined her at the table. Nanna took to her right, sitting at the head of the table. As she eased into her chair, she surveyed Louisa in that way that told Louisa she was on to her. It was that Italian look – lips pursed, eyes slightly squinting, a subtle tilt of the head and fire behind the eyes that dared your soul – a look that would make you think something was wrong with you even if it wasn't and you were perfectly okay and weren't harbouring any anxiety or worries or keeping any secrets. Of course, Louisa was harbouring plenty of anxiety over the showcase and a chunk of sadness that she still hadn't heard much from her sisters. It wasn't like Amanda to not message her about the parcel and Louisa was eager to know what her sister thought of the incredibly special treat. Nanna knew all this. Nothing got past a nonna.

'*Cara*, what is the problem, or do you keep it from your nanna?' Nanna asked, her blue eyes now wide, eyelashes fluttering, lips pursued innocently. In typical nonna style, she had been kind in her question while also guilt-tripping Louisa, leaving no room for her to tell a white lie and pretend everything was alright because, if she did, that would make her a horrible, horrible person.

She choked on a delicate flake of pastry and cleared her throat. 'I am okay, Nanna, but yes the fashion show is in two days and I'm nervous, but there should hopefully be no problems. Giulia and I have been working non-stop; she is the most magnificent seamstress. I can't wait for you to see the pieces,' Louisa said, reaching out and resting a hand on top of Nanna's.

Nanna twisted her hand, so her palm was now facing Louisa's and gave Louisa's hand a squeeze. 'I cannot wait to see them, *cara*.' Nanna's gaze never faltered, but Louisa's smile wavered as she contemplated if she was in the all clear and could return safely back to her *cornetto*.

'And Amanda, she receives the parcel?' Ooh, Nanna was good; the Don of the family for a reason. Louisa squeezed her hand back and smiled broadly in defeat.

'Nanna,' she sighed. 'I have heard nothing, maybe it hasn't arrived yet? Maybe they've both just forgotten about me.' Louisa pushed a piece of orange around on her plate with her free hand, her eyes watching its slippery movements. Nanna leaned forward and Louisa bent closer to better hear her words of wisdom.

'They do not forget you. They forget themselves, maybe. They will know soon. Your sisters they are good girls,' Nanna expressed. Louisa believed her to be right. Family was important to all three

75

of them. Right now, Louisa had to be patient and understand that her sisters had a lot going on in their lives. She had faith that they would remember the importance of family and answer her calls sooner rather than later. Even when Sabrina had lived in LA and when Amanda had been travelling, they had been better at keeping in touch, so Louisa knew their new roles had everything to do with their lack of communication and she respected her sisters' work ethic.

She devoured the rest of her *cornetto*, knowing exactly where she wanted to go before work this morning to cheer herself up.

After freshening up and putting together today's ensemble of a short pink skirt, sheer polka-dot pink tights and a chunky cream knit, Louisa kissed Nanna, Zia Rosa, Zia Emilia and Zia Sofia goodbye, grabbed her favourite teddy coat and made her way down the steep stairs onto the streets of Orzoro.

The thrill and excitement of the fashion show and living out her dream, had taken a backseat to the negativity she had built up over missing her sisters and her fear of missing out. She was the baby of the family, the one that took care of everyone; she told Amanda when she was being too stubborn, kept Sabrina in the loop when she had lived in LA, was a phone call away from her mum and dad if they needed anything and spent most evenings and weekends with her grandparents. When she thought about it, she had very little time to herself. And that had been the way she liked it. It scared her to think that she was no longer needed. Yet she had decided upon this change; to stay in Italy and do something for herself.

She walked along the path, taking in the mismatched stone walls along one side of her – the sprouts of green peeking out of the cracks in the pavement – and the vast blue of the twinkling sea to the other. Louisa didn't think she'd ever grow weary of this view.

She was grateful that the sun lit up the blue sky today; even in the early hours it had made its appearance known and she hoped they were in for a glorious March day. The cemetery was open when she arrived, having just taken a quick detour to pick up some stunning pink roses for Grandpa. They were his and Nanna's favourites.

'*Buongiorno* Grandpa,' she said, smiling at his picture attached to his white and grey marbled headstone. This, on the other hand, was not a view Louisa ever thought she would get used to. There were days when it took all the courage she could muster to come here, her brain sometimes playing tricks on her thinking that going to visit her Grandpa would mean actually getting to see him and wrap her arms around him. She placed the sweet fragrant roses in the vase next to where he lay and squatted down, tracing her hand over the cold marble.

'Amanda's finally doing it, Grandpa. She's opening *Torta per Tutti*. I can't wait to see it. I know you'd be so proud of her. And Sabrina, she's doing really well too, she's just signed the boys up to a new label and they're recording their next album in Manchester, so she gets to be closer to everyone. I think you'd be proud of her too.' Louisa reached into her coat pocket and pulled out a tissue; she wasn't sure when the tears had started, but it was rare for her to leave without tear-stained smudges in her makeup. She patted softly at her face, spreading the flowers out in the vase so they looked pretty and had room to fully bloom, for distraction.

'Nanna laughs every day with her sisters. I know you'd be happy to hear that. She misses you too of course and she misses Mum, but I think she's really missed this place and is content to be home. And Mum and Dad are well too. I know Mum talks to you every day, so you probably already know that,' Louisa chuckled. She spoke to her mum every day on the phone and they shared fond family memories daily.

'I think you'd be proud of me too, Grandpa. I have my first showcase on Saturday. You'd never guess that I've been back behind a sewing machine and I think I might even be getting good at it. I hope you can see me.' Louisa paused, looking away from the headstone and towards the morning's bright sky. 'I made one of our designs, that lace one you told me to draw after watching *La Vita in Diretta* that day when the presenter was wearing that gorgeous lace suit. I love it – you had a keen eye for fashion, hey.' She let out another small chuckle and stood to stretch her legs. 'I miss you every day, you know, and I love you even more than that.' Louisa tapped his headstone in attempt at a chirpy exit and made her way out of the cemetery. She dabbed once more at her face, inhaled a deep breath, filling her lungs with fresh air and determination. She wanted to enjoy every moment of designing the dresses and working alongside Giulia for this showcase. It was a gift and one that she was grateful for. What had Dan said last Christmas? Something about being allowed to miss people but making sure not to forget what you have around you. He had been right, of course. Louisa had Italy, she had Luca, Nanna, her zias and a wonderful opportunity on the horizon. She just needed to find the right balance and stop her self-sabotaging pity parties.

*

The morning had zoomed by in a blur of helping customers in the shop find their perfect outfit for a christening, blogger event, best friend's wedding and wine-tasting party, and measuring two of her models for Saturday.

Amidst the numbers, the modifications and Instagrammable outfits floating around in her brain, Louisa failed to hear the shouts from the front of the shop.

'Louisa, Louisa!' Louisa jerked her attention away from her calculator at the sudden realization that someone was shouting her name and rushed to the front of the store. Giulia was stood with a customer over by the bespoke wedding dresses, waving a mobile phone in Louisa's direction. Louisa stopped at the register not wanting to interrupt Giulia and her customer or get in their space when she suddenly recognized the ring tone and her brain clicked as to the reason behind Giulia waving the phone frantically her way. She must have dropped it in the pile of unworthy blogger outfits when she was seeing to an influencer earlier.

Taking two giant strides she took the phone from Giulia's outstretched arm, muttering 'Sorry,' profusely and bowing apologetically all the way to the back. Phones were to be kept in the office, but this morning Louisa had gone against the rules in a bid to keep her customer happy; the blogger had been distraught when her phone notified her that her picture memory was full, and she couldn't take pictures of each outfit she tried on, so Louisa had come to the rescue using hers. In putting the outfits away, and rushing back to her work in the office, she hadn't noticed it falling out of her pocket.

Shutting off the wailing ringtone by sliding the green answer button, she quickly dived into the back.

'Did you really bake that?' Amanda shouted down the phone. 'I don't believe you! No really, did you bake it?'

Louisa's heart soared as she let out a laugh. 'You got my parcel?' she asked, though she already knew the answer.

'More like I've nearly eaten your entire parcel. I'm trying hard to leave some for Dan, but Lou … Lou it's out of this world. Where did you find it?' Amanda asked, excitement evident in her rapid speech. Louisa could hear her munching as she spoke. She couldn't wipe the grin off her face.

'Have you not opened the card?' Louisa said, pacing her little office, feeling a bundle of nerves and sheer excitement that she was getting to share this moment with Amanda even if she couldn't see her. 'Wait, switch to FaceTime.' She heard Amanda cough and hoped she wasn't choking on cake crumbs, then hung up and promptly started calling her through her Facetime app.

She was right. Amanda was sat her kitchen table, the cake and biscuits surrounding her, her doe eyes clearly high on rum and chocolate. 'Open the card,' Louisa urged.

Amanda put down a cinnamon biscuit she was about to bite, and Louisa watched as she flicked open the envelope and wiggled the card out. The delicate, browned, paper slipped out from the folded paper and Amanda's eyes grew wide.

'Zia Sofia has kept it safe all these years. Grandpa cooked a lot in their kitchen. It was one of the things he used to win over Nanna's mum and dad. He would join in, help the family and often cook for them all. This was one of Zia Sofia's favourite recipes he made, and she thought it was time you had it,' Louisa said, softly and slowly, not wanting to overwhelm Amanda. Amanda's hand shot over her mouth as Louisa watched her take in the recipe; Grandpa's scruffy scrawl. Her eyes shimmered through her tears. Louisa tried to catch her own, remembering she was at work.

'I don't know what to say. Louisa, thank you,' Amanda said, in short breaths a few moments later. 'I only hope I can make it as well as you.' Amanda then laughed. 'I can't stop eating it, Lou.'

The girls conversed for a few more minutes before Louisa left Amanda to eat some more cake and rush to Tesco to collect the ingredients she would need to practise it that night if she was going to make it for opening day. Louisa then placed her phone on the pile of calculations and notes of alterations and wiped away a stray tear on her chunky knit, feeling full of joy to play a part in Amanda's café opening having shared that recipe. She stood up, wandering over to the outfit she was working on. She fingered the sheer white fabric that wrapped around the skirt, letting it drape over her fingertips, the multi-coloured patterns and fabrics underneath it vibrant and visible. Fashion was to her what food was to Amanda. It was a place where her imagination could be brought to life, where she felt she had a handle on life, like she knew what she was doing.

This design in particular had been inspired by her grandpa; the colour that he added to her life and the light that he encouraged her to be. She sent up a special prayer to ask him to look after Amanda and for her opening day to be a success. Then Louisa got to work.

Chapter 10

Nanna's Custard

Ingredients:

2 pints of milk
Vanilla
Orange and lemon rind
4 tbsp flour
4 egg yolks

What to do:

Over low heat whisk together flour and egg yolks to make a roux.
Pour in milk and vanilla and add orange and lemon rind.
Don't stop whisking until custard becomes thick.
You will know when its cooked, but you can check by making sure it covers the back of a spoon.

Taking a step back to survey her café, Amanda exhaled. It was everything she had dreamed it would be and more. The golden specks in the pearly-white painted walls sparkled under the lights from the open bulbs. The wooden frames bearing the most stunning pictures of Orzoro made Amanda's heart hum a happy tune each time she looked at them. The no-filter shots were captivating and added that special touch of home, especially as Amanda had taken them herself.

The light oak furnishings reminded Amanda of the place she,

San Francisco Beat and Nikki had eaten at on her last night in San Francisco. It gave her café a hip rustic vibe, while the yellow and blue chairs that sat in the bay window added that warmth and Italian texture. She couldn't quite believe it had all come together.

She kept the matte gold blinds down still, wanting to keep her café to herself for a while longer and embrace all that she and her family had achieved. She also couldn't be sure of who would be lurking in the bushes and didn't want the paparazzi to welcome her café to the world before she did, now that San Francisco Beat were in town. She wanted that honour and felt she deserved it. Tomorrow there would hopefully be a crowd of hungry customers lining the streets; a buzz in the air of excited anticipation when she finally revealed the delicacies behind the blinds.

Kate bustled about in the kitchen while Liam triple-checked the plumbing and all the electrical outlets. He had been popping in regularly over the last few weeks, not only to keep Amanda sane when she heard a slight rumbling from a drain pipe or when she couldn't figure out how to use the coffee machine, but also to test out her food and aid her in deciding the menu for opening day. Liam had turned out to be an awesome guy to have around and Amanda greatly appreciated his dropping by whenever she needed a hand in securing light bulbs and shelving units; his witty banter and his ability to be blunt with her and snap her out of her negative thoughts as opening day drew closer had been welcomed too. She had been grateful of Louisa's parcel, understood Sabrina's manic job and Dan's hectic schedule, but it was safe to say she had missed them all terribly in preparing her café.

It had meant a lot to her to have Liam and Kate by her side, cheering her on during the stages when she had lost hope; loose floorboards and no sign of light could do that to a person.

Feeling confident that Liam and Kate knew what they were doing in the back, she continued collecting shots of her beautiful café for her blog – of the oak tables, yellow and blue ceramic napkin holders and tiled coasters. A small pang of guilt over having neglected her blog in recent months toyed with her gut. Amanda had never dreamed of being a blogger, but the more uninspired she had become at her previous job at Rusk and the more frustrated she felt with her ex sous-chef, Jeff, the more she had the urge to share her thoughts and recipes with the world. She had located her Instagram from the depths of her phone and taken to scrolling through it a few times a week. She had noticed that food pictures were very popular, and that Sabrina was really holding out on her and Louisa. Every other picture on her feed was her with the likes of Ed Sheeran and Liam Payne – she'd tut as she pressed the 'like' button.

Often these food pictures linked to a person's blog. This piqued Amanda's interest and curiosity and she found herself getting lost in reading blog after blog with her morning coffee. One day she decided to go for it and from the comfort of her own kitchen she began taking pictures of the food that truly inspired her. It was a welcome break from the mundane food she was cooking at Rusk.

As her enjoyment for writing up recipes and sharing her stash of her family favourites grew, and with the confidence from the few hundred likes on Instagram she was getting, she set up her blog 'Mangia'. Amanda didn't really feel like a blogger and her pictures were no way near themed or perfect, but they were real and that's what she wanted to be.

She couldn't pretend to be any good at blogging, but she did know that her recipes were second to none – her grandpa had told her so. Therefore, she confidently put them out into the world. It was mostly her own experiments and tweaked family recipes from over the years; there were a few sacred family treasures that she kept guarded and couldn't part with on her blog. She hadn't the foggiest about brands and didn't understand sponsored posts or getting advertising offers. It was the one or two positive comments she had received from readers and fellow food enthusiasts that were always more satisfying and Amanda had liked the idea of growing a following and creating an inspired community, over trying to sell products. This community would now include her café. She hoped people who liked her recipes on her blog would be inspired to come and visit her when she opened.

That thought motivated her as she bent down over the table to get a more artistic shot of the table sets and flowers.

'Boy, have I missed that view.' Dan's raspy voice caused fireworks to explode in Amanda's stomach, sending her body into complete overdrive, while also scaring the bejesus out of her. She spun around with lighting speed, which caused her to catch her ankle on the nearest table leg and promptly fall back with a thud on the wooden floor. Dan's perfect lips curved into a small smirk as his brows creased with at least some concern, she noted. He had arrived last night, Sabrina and the rest of the band in tow, but jetlag had got to him before Amanda and by the time she got home, after a busy evening perfecting her custard tarts, he was fast asleep. She had woken at the crack of dawn this morning to get to the café and hadn't wanted to disturb his slumber, content in the knowledge that he was with her once more.

'That's going to leave a bruise,' he said, his voice sending an electric current through Amanda's body. Dan took a giant step towards her, but instead of taking her hand and helping her up, he sat down in front of her and with his broad physique and strong biceps, pulled her onto his lap. His lips were on hers before Amanda had a chance to say hello.

Amanda kissed him back like he was the only thing keeping her alive, her heart beating erratically. She had missed the taste of him, she had missed his soft wavy hair that her hands were all over, and she had missed the feel of their bodies entwined.

Amanda pulled away and took pleasure in watching Dan's features for a moment. His eyes remained closed, his eyelashes long, his cheeks flushed, and those lips pressed into the sexiest pout. She couldn't resist him. As she traced a finger over his lips, he opened his eyes, causing her breath to become ragged once more. She would forever be lost to those soulful rich eyes.

'Hi,' she whispered, before gently kissing his nose. The kiss on the nose became a kiss on the lips, before once again they were locked in a make-out session, oblivious to the world around them. This time, after a good five minutes, it was Dan that paused.

'Do you need me to check on that bruise?' he asked, his hand grabbing a handful of her bum. Before Amanda could respond Kate and Liam burst through the double doors.

'Is everything okay out here Amanda?' Liam shouted, looking around the café before noticing her on the floor sat ever so professionally on Dan's knee. Her face burnt a rosy hue.

'Yes, yes, everything is fine,' she said, trying to get to her feet. A casual innocent laugh escaped Dan's lips. A laugh that made Amanda's insides dance. Every now and again Dan had a moment of utter cuteness that stopped Amanda in her tracks. Amanda grabbed his face and planted a kiss on his forehead before turning back to her staff-cum-friends.

Dan rose to his feet, standing a head taller than Liam. His tight black jeans, light-brown knit jumper and shaggy hair made Amanda swoon. By the look on Kate's face – she was gawping, her mouth wide open – Dan had her spellbound too.

Liam stepped forward, slightly dubious, and held out his hand in greeting. 'Liam, nice to meet you mate,' he said. Dan wavered uncharacteristically before shaking Liam's outstretched hand, but Amanda was too focused on Kate mouthing 'Oh my gosh,' to her to notice.

'Dan, the pleasure's all mine. What is it that you do here?' Dan asked. Kate suddenly sprung to life, stepping forward to say hello to Dan and shake his hand before Liam could answer.

'Hi, I'm Kate. I oversee proceedings out front, serving customers and seeing to it that this one is organized,' Kate said, her voice an octave higher than normal. Amanda chuckled.

'Rather you than me,' Dan replied in reference to Kate's last comment, resulting in a prod to his ribs from Amanda. He caught her hand and pulled her close to him, still keeping his eyes trained on Kate. 'It's lovely to meet you, Kate. I'm sure you will do a wonderful job; the place looks impeccable already.'

'Thanks, I did most of it myself,' Liam said in jest, making both Kate and Amanda laugh.

Amanda wrapped her arms around Dan. He must still be shattered. she thought. His usual calm exterior seeming suddenly rigid. 'He's not kidding,' Amanda noted, regarding Liam's comment. 'Come on, let me show you around. I tell you, they need to make a simplified version of "Electricity for Dummies" because all those wires are no joke. Liam's been a godsend. Liam got the electrical outlets working within minutes, the lights are hung to perfection and don't get me started on the shelves.' Amanda filled Dan in on every nook and cranny of the café, pointing out special photos, Grandpa's kitchen equipment and giving him a detailed rundown of the contents of the fridge and the pantry.

Dan listened to her every word. Kate and Liam had waved their goodbyes halfway through the pantry tour, while Amanda was explaining in great detail why the Italian Pernigotti cocoa powder was second to none.

Now Amanda pulled out the focaccia she had made that morning, along with leftover rum cake from the other night from the pantry, and placed them on the kitchen island in front of Dan. Food would wake him up for sure, Amanda thought. She set out olives and sundried tomatoes from the fridge and pulled up the lone kitchen stool for Dan to sit down on and eat. She had missed cooking for him, and she didn't doubt he'd missed her food. His brown eyes moved adoringly from her to the picnic she had placed before him. He sat on the stool and pulled her in between his legs so she was sandwiched between him and the island, his legs either side of her hips.

Amanda used her hands to layer the rosemary focaccia with sundried tomatoes and a sprinkle of shriveled tiny black olives as Dan's hands moved towards the cake.

'Hey, that's dessert, don't spoil your palette – you've got to try this first,' she said, whacking his hand away and handing him the focaccia. Dan nibbled on her ear before taking the focaccia and turning slightly so he could take a bite of the bread and not Amanda's messy bun. Amanda twisted to her side and leant back a touch on her elbow so she could give Dan space to eat and gauge his reaction. She valued his opinion on her cooking.

'You are an angel,' he said licking his lips once he'd swallowed the last bite. 'This place is beyond stunning, baby girl. You've outdone yourself.'

Amanda smiled, drinking him in – the dimples in his cheeks and the crinkle in his nose when he looked at her as though she were a precious petal. Only Dan could make her feel so strong when seeing through to her vulnerabilities.

'So, who's Liam?' Dan asked nonchalantly, reaching around her and helping himself to another bite of focaccia, shrugging off his question. Amanda picked at the olives, savouring their rich and bitter taste.

'Oh, he's the electrician my dad hired. I wasn't kidding when I said he's been a godsend. You wouldn't believe I couldn't even get the coffee machine working the other day – the man can do everything. I don't know how I'd have got this place fixed up without him.'

There was a moment's silence as Dan shuffled on his chair while Amanda removed the clingfilm from around the cake, filling the room with the most desirable nutty, marzipan scent. She picked at a few crumbs, allowing the soft and gooey dark chocolate to melt on her tongue. Dan rested his hand on the small of her back.

'I'm happy that he was here for you. But I'm here now if you need anything doing,' Dan noted. Amanda caught the dark flicker in his eyes as he spoke, how his shoulders appeared more rounded, his usual charm wavering for a split second. But with the familiar woodsy smell of him mixed with the syrupy cake-induced high, his insecurity was lost on her as she mistook it once more for the grueling schedule of a musician.

'I appreciate that,' she said merrily, thrilled with the idea that she could call on him, that he'd be happy to help her, and she would get to live out her dream with him by her side. Dan's eyes moved around the kitchen, and his chiseled features relaxed as he swept a hand through his messy yet stylish locks.

'I dig this place, my love. The vibe is all you, all love and warmth. It feels like home.' Dan's words hit every corner of Amanda's soul, making her feel as light as a feather. She scooped up a piece of *torta* and teased it near his lips. He felt like home to her. It hadn't been easy being away from him these past two months, she couldn't deny that, but with Dan's touch, his hands currently on her hips and his chocolate eyes piercing into hers, being away from him didn't seem so bad as long as he always came back. Waiting for him would always be worth it.

Dan parted his full lips to take a bite when Amanda pulled the piece of *torta* away and popped it into her own mouth with a cry of 'Mmm' and a wiggle of her eyebrows.

'Dangerous move, Miss Collins,' Dan said, jumping off the chair and easily moving Amanda out of the way before rounding the table, picking up the plate that held the *torta* and swiftly exiting the kitchen. Amanda threw her head back with laughter. Dan couldn't exactly go far but she admired his need for getting a piece of this cake.

'Where do you think the other half of that cake has got to, Mister? I'm not chasing you, I've already eaten my fair share,' she shouted through the double doors, her voice still rich with laughter and her heart knowing full well that that wouldn't stop her eating more if she reached Dan.

'It's all mine then,' Dan shouted back from a cosy table for two opposite the bay window.

'Well, I wouldn't say that,' Amanda said, running over to catch him. Dan took a bit a big chunk of the rich torta and flopped into the nearest chair.

'What do you do to me, woman?' he said, closing his eyes to ignite his sense of taste, ridding distractions around him and heightening the pleasure of the cake as it hit his taste buds.

'Have I told you before that you are my favourite person to cook for?' Amanda asked. She bent down and wrapping her arms around his neck as he relaxed further into the chair, knowing that she had told him many times before.

Chapter 11

Struffoli

Ingredients:

Gosh, I can't place Grandpa's recipe. Think, Amanda, think.
He made it up on the spot, it looked kind of similar to zeppole
at first.
Flour
An egg (50/50, yes egg, no egg, go with your gut)
Sugar
Lemon and orange zest

What to do:

Form a dough and roll into small balls and fry. That's all we did, right?
Right, then drain and dust in powdered sugar and more lemon zest and
orange zest and a drizzle of honey.

'*Mamma mia,*' Louisa expressed, fanning herself with her itinerary and the papers of notes she had made for each of her models and their outfits. 'Giulia, it's hot in here, right? I can't breathe. It's not just me? Tell me it's not just me. I'm sweating too much.'

Giulia was concentrating on hand-stitching the final sequin onto a stunning, sparkling bodysuit with a blue-sequined bandeau, over a pearlized white lace, that fell into a chiffon deep-navy skirt. '*Che bellissima,*' she marveled to herself, before

91

caving and giving attention to Louisa's performance. Louisa had learnt over the past twenty-four hours that Giulia was not interested in feeding Louisa's self-doubt and nerves, she didn't want to hear them and give them room to breathe. She had made it abundantly clear with every stern blue-eyed glare she sent in Louisa's direction, followed by a swift change of subject. Today, an hour before Louisa's outfits were set to hit the runway, was no different.

'*Cara*, take this,' Giulia said, waving a pin cushion, needle, thread and scissors in front of Louisa. Louisa snapped to attention, trying to balance the tools with her buddle of paper, pulling her thoughts away from how sweaty she felt to making sure she didn't knock over any coffee cups on the makeup counters as she put the tools down.

Once the tools hit the worktop, Louisa was back to frantic pacing and her babble. Her pink kitten heels clicked along the tiled floor of the dressing room, the papers causing a draft and making her hair static as she waved them dramatically once more.

'It's just, I know everyone texted this morning – Mum, Dad, Brina and Amanda. I know they're thinking of me. Gosh, even Dan, Levi, James and Dylan have texted, but they're not here. Can I really do this without them? Should I have just waited for a time when they could all have been here? I mean, those people out there are really high up in the fashion world and I couldn't even get through university. I'm way out of my league.' Louisa was rambling and Giulia was still ignoring her.

Enthusiastic, energetic and bubbly were all words Louisa would have normally used to describe herself. Frazzled, jittery and flustered better described Sabrina, on occasion, but even Sabrina managed to get her ducks in a row and keep it together enough to manage one of the world's hottest bands.

Louisa glanced over at the beautiful models wearing her creations. They were hardly rock divas with a penchant for tantrums and drama, and this wasn't exactly One Direction at Madison Square Garden that she was overseeing. She had done the hard part – designing her pieces and choosing what best represented her work, working tirelessly into the night with Giulia to make sure every stitch was perfect. Now, it was her chance to truly bring her vision to life. What was she doing pacing up and down? She was backstage at a runway show, her dream was unfolding right before her eyes and she was watching it in a panicked haze, rather than revelling in every second of it. *Get it together*, she told herself.

Suddenly Giulia's hands were on Louisa's biceps, gently pushing her in the direction of the curtain. Without saying a word Giulia nodded, which Louisa took to mean, 'Take a look,' or at least she hoped Giulia was encouraging her to take a peek at the crowd and not suggesting she leave.

Her eyes wandered over the gathering fashionistas and top designers, her heartrate picking up at the thought of being moments away from introducing herself to the world she dreamed to belong to, then it positively exploded when she saw her nanna, zias, Luca, and his mamma and papa, sat amongst the elite. In that moment she recognized Giulia's lesson without even the need for spoken words. It would not do to dwell on what she was missing and miss out on what was in front of her. If she remembered correctly, this was something Dan had told her last year whilst standing on her zia's balcony too. Of course, to have experienced this with her sisters would have meant the world and to have her grandpa by her side giving his two cents on colour swatches and patterns would have been everything, but, as she touched her fingers to the delicate white gold star around her neck, the one Sabrina had bought her last Christmas, she knew that those you loved were always with you and that life was all about appreciating the present.

Being present in this moment, she was surrounded by people

who cared about her and supported her, and she wanted to make them proud. She was also lucky enough to have people back in Manchester who loved her and were cheering her on through the airwaves. Back home, she hoped Amanda was having the time of her life, that *Torta per Tutti* was overflowing with satisfied customers, and that Sabrina was taking the music business by storm with *San Francisco Beat*'s new endeavour. She was damn proud of her sisters, whether she was standing right beside them or a plane ride away. Her eyes glistened as she held back tears and sighed at the joy in her heart at seeing her family in the crowd. There really was no need to be getting herself so worked up – she could do this.

She turned back to Giulia and offered her a grateful smile. Giulia and her gorgeous vixen-red lips returned her smile and tapped at her watch. Smoothing down her bold-pink pencil skirt and fluffing up her white and black polka dot blouse, Louisa stepped up to the model that had been awaiting her attention. She allowed her hand to glide over the chiffon skirt of her sophisticated yet flirty, with that touch of Italian sexy, skirt and crop combo, making sure it was layered over her model just right. This was a design she had fallen in love with as every stitch of it came to life with Giulia's touch. She hoped onlookers and fashion bloggers the world over would love it too.

Louisa then checked on Mia, a model with poker-straight blonde hair that rested sharply against the high neck of the white and gold Seventies-inspired crochet skater dress, that had been designed by both Giulia and Louisa. Louisa was in awe of the delicate crochet work on the top that Giulia suggested the dress needed. It added the most exquisite vintage Italian feel to the dress and had to be one of Louisa's favourites.

Caterina, a woman with long, black hair in bouncy curls and still reaching her elbows, looked striking in the red lace-trimmed dress that touched just below her knees with deep-red rose silhouettes around the rim. Louisa could picture Sofia Loren wearing this one. It screamed classic demure meets don't mess with me. Seeing her work on real people and not just the mannequins at the back of the shop made Louisa's breath catch. She was really doing this.

'*Dieci minuti!*' a lady with a clipboard announced around Giulia and Louisa's cubicle.

Giulia stepped away from the five models and clasped her hands together. '*Bellissima. Brava amore, brava,*' she expressed, giving Louisa a quick hug before noticing a few flyaway hairs on Caterina's glossy mane. Louisa was momentarily frozen to the spot. Reminding herself of her little pep talk moments ago, she too clasped her hands together, inhaled a massive breath, swallowed forcefully to get rid of the nervous lump in her throat, and prepared to take one giant leap out of her comfort zone.

*

Three hours later and Louisa was certain all her carefully applied makeup had melted off her face in a puddle of sweat. She felt exhilarated yet drained – like she had just run a marathon, when in fact she had barely moved a muscle as she watched her models take the stage. Now she was being handed back her garments, placing them delicately back into the bags and hanging them on a rack. The models had been stunning; a beautiful mix of elegance and fire, all different shapes and sizes and all representing her work in fine form. She couldn't have felt more thankful for each one of them.

'I can keep the dress, no?' Bianca asked, a small smile curving up at the edge of her rosy-pink lips, as she ever so gently handed Louisa back the black dress with a black collar, baring a sparkling silver stitched feather on each side of the neck and a pearl-trimmed waistband, that all came just above the knee. Bianca had long brown hair that glistened. Giulia had straightened it to the point where Louisa couldn't remotely hide her hair envy.

Rapunzel, eat your heart out, she thought, unable to hide the longing look she gave Bianca's tresses as she received the dress. Her cheekbones were starting to sting with the beaming smile that appeared on her face after hearing Bianca's words and that she hadn't been able to wipe off her face as her models and her clothes hit the catwalk amongst some of Italy's top up-and-coming fashion designers.

Of course, the judges had remained poker-faced throughout the entire event, so she had no idea if her work had been well received or not, but she had done it. In a matter of two and a half months she had designed and created, alongside Giulia, five bespoke pieces that she truly adored, and had gotten them ready for a catwalk.

She shook her head, suddenly aware that she was staring at the bagged-up dress in her hand and had not responded to Bianca. '*Grazie mille*,' Louisa said softly and Bianca smiled up at her sweetly, Rapunzel eyes to match her hair. 'Your work *e bella*. The detail *e magnifico e delicate. Brava*,' Bianca added, before turning her attention back to getting dressed. The backstage area had already started to disperse, makeup artists were finishing packing up their colourful trays of blushes and shadows, and the models were slipping into more comfortable attire. Louisa couldn't believe it was all over. She wanted to do it all over again; she'd take the sweat and all the anxiety just to see her pieces floating along the runway once more.

'*Sei pronto*?' Louisa heard Giulia ask from behind the boutique's clothing rack. Giulia was experienced in this field; her models were already fully clothed – coats, scarves and all – to meet the March chill, her outfits all zipped up, makeup gear and hair tools away, which left her stood waiting for Louisa, giving her a mock impatient flutter of her wispy lashes.

'*Aspetta, aspetta*, wait,' Louisa sang, quickly taking her garment bags off the back of the makeup chairs and adding them to the rack. 'Is everyone okay? Have you all got everything?'

'*Si, signora,*' they all echoed, making their way out of the cubicle, waving at the other makeup artists, models and designers on their way out.

There had been a relatively short thank you speech from the judges when the show finished, but there would be no winner announced today. They would receive a call in a few weeks on Palm Sunday. So now, Louisa could put her worries to one side and simply relax and enjoy the rest of her Saturday, right? She wouldn't think about winning the opportunity to have her pieces spread out in *Vanity Fair Italia*. It wasn't a big deal. Her cheeks stung once more from the grin stuck on her face.

'*Amore mio,*' Luca shouted as the Italian breeze met Louisa's neck, sending a shiver down her spine. It had been so warm in the building that she hadn't yet put on her coat. Luca widened his strides and was quick to greet her, immediately wrapping her up in his tall frame, warming her with his touch. 'Wow, you blow me away. You did it, *amore,*' he said, bending slightly so his piercing blue eyes met her brown ones. He held her out at arm's reach so she could see the excitement in his face – his mouth open, his eyebrows raised with such amazement and pride. Louisa reached up to his face, her coat balancing over her forearm, cupped his cheeks and kissed his cool lips.

'*Grazie*, for believing in me,' she whispered, pulling away from the kiss and planting a gentle one on his nose. Luca's eyes sparkled with her words. He stood up a little straighter, kissed her on her forehead and then seemed to take her in again, his brows drawing in with concern. 'What do you do, *amore*? You will catch a cold,' Luca said, nodding at her coat and then quickly shifting his focus to the clothes rack, giving Giulia a congratulatory hug and steering the clothes towards the car. Louisa whipped her coat around her and hugged herself tight to ward off the chill, hooked arms with Giulia and raced after Luca to the car.

The tiny towns whizzed by in a blur of colourful tapestries, beautiful almond blossoms and iron gates, as Louisa shuffled in her seat trying to get warm. Giulia had closed the boutique for the day, so they were heading to Alfonso's for afternoon coffee and cake. Louisa was ready to devour all the cake, give her Nanna a giant bear hug and see what she thought of the whole fashion show thing. It wasn't too far from the showroom in Positano back to Orzoro; with her nerves having settled a touch, Louisa sat back and enjoyed the views Italy blessed her with every day.

Once they had pulled up in the square and made the short walk to Alfonso's, Luca guided them through the hot and busy kitchen, the smell of freshly baked *sfogliatelle* and *ricotta torte* making Louisa lick her lips. She hadn't eaten much all day because of the nerves taking up most of the room in her stomach. She greeted the pastry chefs and kitchen staff with cheery waves and grateful hellos before stepping into the café.

If the dizziness from the lack of food hadn't floored her, the sight she walked into was incredibly close to doing just that; her legs suddenly felt like frail twigs that might snap at any moment.

Her zias and nanna were gathered together, along with Matilde – Guilia's little daughter – and Luca and Giulia's mamma and papa, in the alcove at the back of the shop that was usually reserved for small parties or meetings. There was a sign above their heads reading 'Congratulazioni' a tower of *struffoli*, a large dish of *tiramisu*, a bright white and fluffy Italian cream cake and champagne glasses sparkling with champagne and Aperol spritz laid out across the table. Glittering confetti decorated the white tablecloth.

Cheers erupted in the small space when the families saw Giulia and Louisa. Matilde made a dash for her mamma and Nanna eased out of her chair, her hand gripping the table for support. Louisa dashed over to her, helping her to her feet as her nanna cried, 'Cara mia, cara mia.' Once steady, Louisa met her nanna's glistening eyes. 'What did you think, Nanna?'

'You are magic, my granddaughter, magic. I would like to have

98

each dress in my size,' Nanna replied, touching Louisa's cheek. 'You have made me so proud,' she added. Louisa bent down and hugged her for the second time, not really wanting to let go.

'I cut the cream cake,' Zia Rosa announced. Louisa squeezed her Nanna; she might just let go for cream cake.

'Come on Nanna. Cake is calling,' Louisa said, with a wink. 'And, thank you, thank you for everything,' Louisa whispered, dropping a kiss on her nanna's soft grey hair. She then aided her in sitting back down, before wandering around their small party, receiving everyone's congratulations and helping Giulia serve cakes.

She stopped and squatted down to Matilde's level when she saw the little girl sat cross legged on the floor at the end of the table, a handful of *stuffoli* in a bowl resting on her lap. They discussed which cake was the best for a few minutes which made Louisa chuckle as Matilde had it all figured out. 'You have to have all the cakes to know which one is best.' Her baby-blue child eyes were wide with wonder and most likely sugar. 'That makes sense,' Louisa replied, to which Matilde popped up, shouting out to her mamma, 'Louisa said it is a good idea to have all the cake!'

'She likes you, I think.' Louisa jumped up at Luca's silvery voice. He was leaning against the alcove's wooden arch, a maroon apron over his crisp white collared shirt. His arms were folded as he drank her in, his shirt taught against his biceps. He gave her a side smile that sent any inhibitions she could possibly have about extreme PDA in a café full of people, into orbit.

She marched up to him, he stepped forward to meet her, and she flung her arms around his neck, breathing in his vanilla scent. Her body relaxed against his, a warmth settling in her stomach when his hands rested on the curve of her lower back.

'Thank you for this,' Louisa mumbled against his neck. Luca brought a hand up to brush back the wavy strands of hair that had escaped Louisa's ponytail during the whirlwind of outfit assembly from earlier that day. '*Amore*, the clothes you make were meant for the runway. You did amazing, no? This, you deserve it. We are proud,' Luca said, his voice soft as he gestured around the room at their families. She rested her head on his chest and looked around the room. Her chest rose with pride and satisfaction at what she had accomplished today. It had been a dream come true and, despite missing her sisters, she had done it.

Chapter 12

Nutella Cupcakes

Ingredients:

Sugar
Eggs
Butter
Vanilla
Pernigotti cocoa powder
All-purpose flour
Baking powder
Salt
Hazelnuts
Homemade chocolate spread (Nanna's recipe)
Icing sugar

What to do:

Beat sugar and butter together until fluffy.
Add eggs one at a time and vanilla and combine.
Combine baking powder, flour, cocoa powder and salt in a bowl.
Add dry ingredients to wet ingredients and stir.
Scoop into cupcake cases and bake at 180 degrees for 25 minutes or until spaghetti comes out clean.
Beat icing sugar with chocolate spread until thick. (Doesn't need to be stiff – don't add too much icing so it's too sweet and sickly – mix to taste.)
Spread on top of cupcake once cooled and decorate with a single hazelnut.

Amanda uncurled a tiny piece of paper from her pocket, placed it down beside her and got to work. She didn't want to be bothered by doubts or to dwell on the hole in her heart that seemed to be growing, making it hard for her to breathe this morning. She just wanted to channel her grandpa and cook. That would surely stitch up the hole that his absence was causing, right? She immediately relaxed as she read the recipe before her. Both she and her nonni didn't care much for exact measurements, cooking was something they felt – it was in their blood, something that brought out so much love and passion in them. It had always been funny trying to write down the ingredients as Grandpa told them to her. Each recipe read more as a visual, as a mini film playing in her mind as she could see Grandpa in his element making it up as he went along. She simply repeated his actions, almost like he was standing right beside her.

Manchester had been eerily quiet when she had left Dan sleeping in her bed at 4 a.m. this morning and made her way to her café. Her supply chef, Lauren, was already outside waiting, which had eased the heavy thumping in Amanda's head about staff not turning up and everything going wrong. A little small talk and a tour of *Torta per Tutti* later and Amanda was comfortable in Lauren's presence but only a bit less anxious, handing over some of her nonni's beloved recipes and leaving Lauren to make them. And Amanda accused Sabrina of being a control freak?

Three hours passed in a pleasant calm of happy baking. Lauren had been working wonderfully beside Amanda, listening to the odd instruction and following the recipes Amanda had set out for her without any qualms. *Cornetti*, focaccia and all kinds of breads were cooking slowly in the convection ovens, lemon cupcakes, banana and cinzano muffins and two different types of biscotti had filled up the cake counter; a pace had been set and a rhythm had followed naturally.

Amanda brushed her flour-coated hands on her favourite 'I

can't keep calm, I'm Italian,' apron and rolled her eyes catching sight of the words that she once found amusing. *Not today*, she thought, *not today*. A loud knock at the door made her jump. She nervously cast her eye over her lemon-shaped clock and swallowed back her panic. Why was she panicking? She still had over an hour before she officially opened, and the food was coming along nicely.

She rushed out to the front of the café and could hear the shuffle of people outside all nattering over each other on her doorstep. She couldn't decide whether her family being here, so full of enthusiasm and pride, made her feel more or less nervous. She didn't want to let them down. She fussed with the lock and opened the door to allow everyone to come tumbling in. They immediately sprang into action. Sabrina made fast friends with Kate, who was busy booting up the coffee machine and pressing keys on the till to spur it into action. Kate had only just let herself in through the back door five minutes ago and already she was blazing through her morning's to-do list.

Before questions could tumble off Amanda's tongue or she could divvy out tasks, Kate spoke. 'I've got it out here boss. I went over the table layout last night. When the other guys get here, I will give them their designated areas. I will manage the till. I'll shout through if I need you and keep you updated on what's selling. It's entirely up to you if you make more or if you'd prefer the "once it's gone its gone" concept. That might be trial and error after today, to see what you like.'

There was more fiddling of the till as Kate checked over the change Amanda had stocked it with last night. Amanda had really grown to like Kate and in that moment, she wondered if it would be deemed unprofessional to hug her. Sabrina was now leaning on the counter, watching this exchange with a smile as bright as her yellow nail varnish.

'I'll be around all day today too, so if you need anything at all Kate, just let me know. I can mill about with the customers and get a feel for what they think of the place, sound good?' Sabrina quipped.

Amanda nodded/ 'You are both amazing, thank you. I appreciate it a thousand-fold,' she said, her hands coming together in prayer position, her eyes wandering over to the clock, her stomach performing another gymnastics manoeuvre.

Amanda headed back into the kitchen, but not before pausing to take in her mum dusting down tables, her dad sweeping the wooden floor and her dear friends, Levi, Dylan and James pottering about helping Kate with the coffee bar while Sabrina read out today's special baked goods for Dan to write on the special's board. Catching Dan's gravelly voice asking Sabrina, 'Got it, what's next?' sent a bolt of pure love to Amanda's heart. Dan was sporting his skinny black jeans, long-sleeved printed loose shirt and his hair tied up in a high bun, now that it was long enough. If the paparazzi's signal hadn't gone off the minute that this specimen stepped foot outside Amanda's house this morning, then Amanda would be extremely surprised. She sighed, knowing she needed to pull her eyes away from him and her incredible family and get back to the kitchen.

Lauren had replaced the *cornetti* in the oven with the sweet breakfast loaves that Amanda thought would be perfect accompanied with a dollop of butter and a strong espresso. The cooling crisp *cornetti* filled the kitchen with memories of sunny days in Nanna and Grandpa's kitchen learning how to roll up the pastry to make the delicate *cornetti* shapes. This was it – her café was filled with her family and food made with love. Amanda felt like she was in a daze as she picked up her phone and texted Louisa to wish her luck for the fashion show and let her know that she missed her and was thinking about her. Amanda placed her phone out of the way on the counter and was momentarily stumped for what to do next. For some reason her emotions were torn; one second she felt pure excitement and delight, the next fearful and lost.

104

'Boss, I don't mean to alarm you, but I can't get hold of the front-of-house staff. They haven't turned up and doors officially open in fifteen minutes. But the good news is there is already a line around the block.' At Kate's words, Lauren looked up, eyes wide, meeting Amanda's blank stare. Amanda gulped, wondering where the last forty-five minutes had gone.

'Erm, right, let's go,' Amanda said as Kate marched back through the double doors leaving Amanda glued to the spot still watching Lauren.

'Is everything okay, hon?' Lauren asked, taking a moment away from the prosciutto she had moved on to slicing.

'Erm, yes, I'm going,' Amanda said, not moving, her legs feeling like jelly all of a sudden. 'Okay, Lauren, have you got everything under control in here?' Amanda asked, walking around the kitchen island to check on the ingredients she had put out for the Nutella cupcakes she was supposed to be making. Amanda had been excited to add these to her menu for the kids; it was something Italian that people would recognize, as she didn't want her very authentic Italian menu to intimidate customers.

'Yes, all good. I'll bring out the breads shortly and get them in the window. It's going to smell beautiful out there. It's like heaven back here,' Lauren replied with a sweet smile.

'Amanda, where are you?' Amanda heard Sabrina shout. God, she was dawdling, getting distracted by the food, she needed to be out front. She needed to officially open *Torta per Tutti*. It was time; two months of construction, grafting, failed plumbing, disappearing decorators, ninja paparazzi, snooty men in suits, and a dream that she had harboured since first stepping into the kitchen with her grandpa as a child, was about to come true. Her lips started to tremble, her eyes became blurry. *Stop it, stop it,* Amanda said to herself as Lauren guided her to the kitchen doors where Dan took her hand. Amanda looked around the café; Mum, Dad, Levi, James, Dylan, Sabrina and Kate were all waiting for her by the bay window. *Stop it,* her brain said more forcefully to herself this time. The tears were making it hard to see where she was going, the hole in heart threatening to tear it in two. She couldn't do this now. *Please don't do this now*, she begged of herself. But it was no use, in this moment, even when surrounded by people that loved her, she felt so very alone. It was in this moment that she felt every bit of strength leave her body. All the joyous memories and happy adventures she had accumulated over the past few months were outmatched by the need to hold his hand, to hear his voice, to live this moment together with him.

'I can't do it,' Amanda whispered, freezing on the spot, her head hanging low. Sabrina grabbed her shoulders and her mum clasped her hands, as the others stepped back to give them space. Tilting up her chin, Sabrina stared her dead in the eyes and wiped at her tears. 'You absolutely can,' Sabrina started, shaking Amanda ever so gently, 'You can, and you will, because, because you've never failed him before,' Sabrina finished, her voice cracking at the end. Amanda inhaled a sharp breath in, Sabrina's words at war in her brain. The thought that her grandpa had always been so proud of Amanda's skills in the kitchen, and how she took after him, was enough to fill her with a fierce determination. While at the same time, she felt crippled at the realization that he wasn't here to pat her on the back and kiss her forehead when she succeeded. He was supposed to be with her now.

'Sweetheart, look at me,' her mum said, taking over from Sabrina. Sabrina stepped back into Levi's arms and Amanda lifted her head to look at her mum. 'Sweetie, he's with you always. I promised you, remember? He's not gone anywhere. He's right here and I know he is so proud of you.' Her mum pointed at Amanda's chest, over her heart, before pulling her into a hug. 'Now, it smells incredible in here and I don't think us lot will be able to eat everything you and Lauren have whipped up, no matter how delicious,' she added, making Amanda snort though her sniffles.

'Have you not met my boyfriend?' Amanda chuckled, as Dan shyly stepped forward. Her mum released her, and Amanda kissed her cheek and whispered, 'Thank you,' as Dan reached out and took her hand. Kate wasn't kidding when she had said that there were already people queuing up outside. The rumbling of chatter was getting louder.

Dan leant down and wiped away Amanda's tears with a tissue. He then kissed her softly on the lips leaving her a little breathless from his touch. 'Your restaurant is my favourite restaurant,' Dan said, quoting something Grandpa used to tell her whenever she made him lunch or dinner. Amanda's chest heaved. Grandpa would chuckle and tell her that he didn't need to go out when he had the best chef he knew cooking for him in his home. She hoped she'd done him proud. 'Thank you,' she whispered to Dan, grateful for the confidence boost and reminder of her grandpa's words and belief in her. She couldn't give up now. Deep down she knew all this was for him, more than for her, to continue his legacy and all that he had taught her. Amanda lifted her head up and nodded at her loved ones. She could do this. She had to do this; for her grandpa, for herself and for them.

Before Dan could step away, Amanda pulled him down so she could reach his ear. 'Dan, did Kate say I don't have any staff?'

There was no time for him to answer as Sabrina yanked open the door and took Amanda with her, so they were both standing on the *Benvenuti* mat, in front of a crowd of over what had to be over a hundred people lining the street. Amanda couldn't believe her eyes. Her heart seized with elation, her sadness turned to joy. That was until a light bulb exploded above her head and she sent Sabrina a mock-angry glare, with an eye roll for good measure, before she erupted with laughter. Sabrina didn't seem to share the same funny bone as her face looked riddled with anxiety. Having no time to comfort or question Sabrina's nervous expression now, Amanda took a deep breath in, ready to address the crowd.

107

'Welcome to *Torta per Tutti*,' Amanda shouted to a round of applause. Her heart was rattling in her chest with adrenaline and amusement. There were wolf whistles and howls which only encouraged Amanda to address the elephant in the café and what she could only assume was the reason behind the queue of people eager to venture into her café, though she would be blissfully happy and surprised if it were merely their love for Italian delicacies. She couldn't believe that she hadn't thought about this before. She loved San Francisco Beat as much, if not more, probably more, than the crowd before her. So, if she could share the limelight with anyone on this day, she felt lucky for it to be them.

'For those of you who would like pictures with San Francisco Beat, can I ask that you remain out front and I will see to it that your dreams come true, before I hope that you will pop inside and treat yourself to a coffee or a delicious cake.' To Amanda's surprise it was a fifty-fifty toss between people who swarmed into the café and people that stayed behind on the street. Not bad, she mused. Then she looked up to the heavens, wiped at the stray droplets of tears that had remained with her from before and whispered, '*Grazie* Grandpa,' before shuffling into the crowd and going in search of Dan.

She spotted him being ogled at by a group of ladies who had claimed the table near the kitchen doors, where Dan had just come from carrying a tray of sliced lemon and thyme focaccia. *Would Dan make it out of today alive?* she pondered, as she prepared to throw him to the excited crowd outside. Registering one of the world's hottest singers carrying a tray of focaccia, Amanda had momentarily forgotten that she was down her front of house staff. She did a quick detour from Dan, checking in with Lauren in the kitchen to see how the more recent bakes were shaping up, but she only managed a few words before Lauren ushered her out of the kitchen and back into the fray with shouts of, 'I'm fine, I'm fine. I've got your Mum on hand.' So she focused on Dan and her task of satisfying the rowdy crowd outside with the other delicacies the café had on offer; four delicious musicians.

'Hey, my love,' Dan said when Amanda approached him. She began helping him fill up the tray in the counter with the fresh focaccia.

'Would it be possible for you and the boys to go outside and take a few pictures with a couple of your fans out front?' she asked, knowing that Dan would always make time for his fans and loving him even more for it.

'No problem. Anything for my number one fan,' he said, passing her the empty tray and gently grazing her cheek with his thumb as he walked past her. The playful smirk on his face did not go unnoticed. Watching him gather up the boys, Amanda couldn't even be mad that people had turned up to see them. But she didn't have time to join in ogling Dan; as he walked through the crowd of people, Levi, James and Dylan in tow, the café was packed and Kate was doing her best to keep up with the coffee demands. Amanda jumped on the till, while mouthing a thank you at Sabrina who was busy herself, carrying plates to tables. Tears threatened again at her family being so quick to swoop in and help her.

'Hi, sorry,' Amanda said, clearing her throat. 'Welcome to *Torta per Tutti*. What can I get for you today?' The lady in front of her looked to be in her late thirties, her hair was scraped back in a sleek ponytail and her makeup natural and glowing. She had faint bags under her eyes which Amanda attributed to the small children that clung to either side of her legs.

'My father is Italian and talks about home every day. It's not easy to find true, authentic Italian food around here. I was so excited when I saw on your blog that you were opening a café. I make your recipes for my papa all the time. To actually be able to taste what you have made is an honour,' the lady said. Amanda's heart swelled and she felt tears trickle down her cheeks once more. Had she really needed to bother with makeup this morning?

'I'm so sorry to have made you sad. I'm holding up the line, my apologies,' the lady stammered. Amanda was doing it again, crying in the middle of the café – what had gotten into her today? She waved her hands frantically trying to suppress her emotions and express to the lady that it was no trouble. Finally, she found her voice.

'No, no, I'm sorry, your words, they just touched me that's all. My grandpa would have been so proud. Thank you so much for coming in today,' Amanda managed, reaching out and resting her hand over the lady's.

The lady then proceeded to order one of every cake in the window, which caused her adorable children's eyes to grow wide with anticipation. Amanda boxed everything up, feeling an over-whelming sense of pride. 'Those ones are on the house,' she whispered as she handed them to the lady. Amanda had a feeling that was exactly what her grandpa would have done.

Chapter 13

Pizza Fritta

Ingredients:

Pizza dough (see recipe for Grandpa's pizza)
Provolone
Tomato sauce (made fresh, Nanna's way)
Salt
Pepper
Whatever else you fancy stuffing it with (Grandpa sometimes adds ham, but I like it best when he makes it with spinach and ricotta)

What to do:

Follow Grandpa's lead with the pizza dough.
Heat up a pan with olive oil, making sure to cover the bottom of the pan with the oil and making it deep enough to cover the pizza fritta.
When the pizza dough is ready, roll out discs as though you are making a pizza.
Place a few slices of provolone inside with a few tablespoons of tomato sauce and a sprinkle of salt and pepper.
Add a second disc over the top and pinch the edges together.
When oil is piping hot, throw in the pizza fritta. Allow to golden on each side before removing from oil.

The streetlamp outside flickered to life as the sky slowly lost its light, the sun fading behind the treetops. The open bulbs dangling from the wooden beams on the ceiling lit up *Torta per Tutti*. Gold glitter bounced off the painted walls and Amanda's snapshots of Orzoro – the small village on the Amalfi coast with its brave boats bobbing in the water, its market stall owners huddled together to thaw off the December chill, and its fig trees in full bloom at the height of the summer season – were glowing; the bright lights highlighted the wrinkles on the stall owners' faces, the shadows in the water and the sheer size of the fig leaves, making you want to reach out and step into the photographs. It felt cosy and quaint; it felt like a home away from home, one that Sabrina had no doubt their grandpa was looking down on. She couldn't have felt prouder of her sister, even if her phone had buzzed at least twenty times in the last hour alone and she hadn't been able to get to it.

Only now was *Torta per Tutti* starting to quiet down enough for her to hear it or acknowledge it. It wasn't like Sabrina to sit back when people were working around her, but she hadn't counted on being rushed off her feet today, serving people cappuccinos and *pizza fritta*. She couldn't exactly blame her big sister; all had been going rather smoothly until her staff hadn't turned up and Sabrina and her parents had sprung into action. Even San Francisco Beat had lent a couple of hands, though it was more their faces serving up gorgeous photos than their hands dishing out *cannoli* that was keeping the customers happy.

Sabrina had to admit that working together with her family and the success of the café's first day made her heart hum a happy tune. Having spent the past four years out in LA and missing her fair share of family events, she had been more than thrilled to play a part in it. And a big part of it she had played without actually meaning to. Fans had lined the streets for a chance to meet their idols San Francisco Beat. It had been an impromptu meet and greet and one that she hoped would be beneficial in making people aware of *Torta per Tutti*, like an unofficial press release for her sister's café. And it didn't hurt to have people talking about the boys and sharing their happy pictures on social media. Sabrina much preferred that form of publicity over fake magazine articles and rumours. The boys were always happy to engage with their fans and not one of them had a bad thing to say about them, unlike the media always looking for a story to twist. When it was apparent that the boys would be fine without her, Sabrina had kept her distance and her head down in the café, not wanting to make a scene or be caught hovering around Levi. He hadn't brought up the plane journey and her decision to not sit next to him, so Sabrina counted herself off the hook. Behind closed doors, life had continued dreamily. Sabrina was taking each day as it came regarding how to navigate her relationship with Levi, and not make it obvious that she was avoiding physical contact when there was a chance they could be papped. Did that make her a terrible girlfriend? She hoped not. She had only the best intentions at heart.

The last stream of customers exited the café chatting merrily about the lemon cupcakes and mint and sambuca chocolate mousse as Sabrina gathered espresso cups and plates from the table by the window. Picking up the dainty ceramic cups Louisa had sent from Italy, her heart tugged. The day had gotten away with her; she needed to call Louisa back to see how her fashion show had gone this morning. As though her little sister had read her mind, Sabrina's phone starting ringing once more. She deposited the dirty dishes into the basin behind the counter and caught the call.

'Lou, Lou, I'm so sorry. I've been meaning to call. I can't believe how late it is, how are you? How did everything go?' Sabrina asked, wiping her hands over her tired eyes and instantly regretting it; wondering if she now resembled a panda.

'It's okay, I knew you guys would be busy,' Louisa said in a perky tone as she started regaling the day's events. 'Brina, it was magical. I was nervous at first, but seeing my designs on the runway, it gave me such a high. I'm still on a high, or that might just be the amount of cream cake I have consumed and possibly the shots of limoncello too. Luca has had me celebrating all afternoon.' Sabrina's shoulders relaxed at the excitement in Louisa's voice. She wished she could have been in two places at once and witnessed her little sister's dream coming true today too, but she was so pleased that Luca was making the day special for her.

'That's amazing Lou, I'm so happy to hear it. Please send me pictures, I would love to see.'

'Of course, I'll send them over tomorrow. I think Luca was getting snap happy with his camera, he has a ton,' Louisa chirped. Sabrina's chest rose with love for both her little sister and for Luca – that he had been there supporting Louisa and taking lots of pictures for her family meant the world to Sabrina. A hiccup came down the phone making Sabrina laugh. Just how many shots of limoncello had her sister indulged in?

Just then Amanda burst through the kitchen doors. 'Is that Lou?' she shouted, her face flushed, her messy bun lopsided and her apron covered in so much flour you could barely read the print.

Amanda inched closer behind the counter to join Sabrina, while the rest of the family and staff piled out of the kitchen and took to the chairs in the café. They all wore tired eyes, their eyelids fluttering to stay open, but smiles still decorated their lips. It wasn't even 8 p.m. yet, Sabrina mused; this café business was no joke. After a brief three-way phone call solidifying their sisterhood once more, Sabrina made her way over to Levi. Safe in the confines of the café, away from prying eyes, Sabrina collapsed onto the bench next to him.

'Are you alright there, boss?' Dylan's voice caused Sabrina's eyes to fly open and she sat up, brushing her sandy waves out of her eyes. She had been close to drifting off, having still not mastered the art of coping with jetlag like the boys had and Levi's chest being as comfortable as a pillow.

'Yes, sorry,' she mumbled, wiping her eyes and cursing herself under her breath again. *Mascara Sabrina, remember you're wearing mascara*. It wasn't like Sabrina had never worn makeup before. Her years in the music industry had taught her how to wing out her eyeliner and to always use a setting powder when under the spotlights, but she much preferred a more natural look. The pressure for women to look glamourous every minute of the day in her industry was not something she cared to partake in. She wasn't opposed to going all out for special events, but that was if she wanted to. This attitude had been tested many times over the years, but she had been strict with herself; she feared if she let them get to her and added a little more to her makeup routine each morning, each dab of concealer and extra pat of foundation would lead her down a dangerous path of losing herself. 'What a crazy day,' she added, resigning herself to looking like a panda as she pulled at her eyelashes trying to keep her eyes awake.

'This place is awesome,' James noted, looking around, which received smiles and nods from the crew. Amanda brought out a tray of espressos and the day's leftover biscotti and bread. Sabrina was pleased to note that there wasn't a whole lot of leftovers, but she couldn't wait to dive into the biscotti that had been teasing her all day.

'*Salute* to a successful opening day, baby girl,' Dan announced to everyone raising their espresso cups and or piece of bread. Sabrina chuckled at the Italian scene.

'Thank you all for helping me and saving the day,' Amanda nodded. Sabrina could see her sister battling the adrenaline coursing through her veins and the exhaustion from having woken at three in the morning. She admired that tomorrow she would do it all over again.

Taking a bite out of a chocolate chip biscotti, Sabrina reveled in its crunchy goodness as her phone pinged with an email. Her heart began to spasm as she read Keira's words in black and white. She handed the rest of her biscotti to Levi, suddenly not feeling so hungry.

*

Sabrina pulled back the thick blush duvet on the bed in Nanna and Grandpa's spare room. When getting ready to return to the UK, Sabrina had spoken with Nanna, who had asked if Sabrina would care to stay at the house and ensure its upkeep. Mum had been popping in since Christmas to see to the post and make sure that the place was clean, but Nanna had shared her wish that it would make her happy should her granddaughter wish to fill the house with the love that it was once brimming with. At first Sabrina had felt some trepidation, unsure as to whether she would be able to handle living in the place they had lost their grandpa. Yet the minute she had walked into the house she had felt comforted by the scent of her grandparents.

It was home, a place where she had run around with her sisters building forts in the back room, enjoying countless sleepovers as a kid, waking up to the smell of sweet bread with lashings of Nutella, and where her love of music had only ever been encouraged during many weekends crooning to the sounds of Frank Sinatra and Massimo Ranieri. Here she could step back in time, be reminded of the simpler days and clear her head. When the time was right, she would see about getting her own place, but for now she felt content.

It wasn't until Levi jumped into bed that she realized she had been staring at her pillow, lost in a daydream of days gone by, swimming among the words Keira had written in her email.

'What's up babe?' Levi asked, propping himself up on his elbow and using his other hand to gently tug at her hand and pull her into bed. There wasn't a shadow of a doubt in Sabrina's mind that she needed to tell Levi what was going on. But her words kept getting lost on the way to her vocal chords. She needed to be strong about this. Levi would understand and so woul[d] rest of the band. City Heights Records had given them an am[azing] deal and a great opportunity. The boys were eager to get into the studio again. Sabrina knew they had plenty of songs ready to be recorded. Dan went everywhere with a notebook and she'd watched him scribbling lyrics down on their plane journey to Manchester, so they would be happy to oblige the record label's wishes without protest, surely?

'Hey beautiful, is everything alright?' Levi queried again, a line appearing between his brows from worry. He squeezed her hand for gentle encouragement to share her thoughts.

Sabrina turned to face him, mirroring his stance, one elbow propped up on her own pillow. 'We need to focus now, get our heads in the game for this new album. Keira sent over an email today with some upcoming media concepts and messages from your publicist. I'm going to arrange to speak with them all tomorrow so we can get the ball rolling for appearances. I've got some ideas for promotional campaigns as we get into the studio and create a buzz for the new music,' Sabrina said, then paused, biting her lip.

'Head is in the game,' Levi said, with a confident nod. Levi would go along with whatever Sabrina needed of him without complaint. He showed up, killed it behind the drums and charmed the journalists. If Dan needed help with a song, Levi would give his two cents and he wasn't afraid to speak up and tell the other boys if something sucked. Occasionally he would throw a song at Dan that he had written himself and the two of them would put their heads together to bring it to life. For the most part, Levi simply loved being in the band and took it all in his stride, not one to lose focus even after a night partying, due to his loyalty and love for his bandmates. Sabrina leaned over and kissed him softly on the lips, taking a moment to appreciate who he was and how all these things added up to make him the man she loved, and to possibly soften the blow of what she was about to say next.

'Okay, good,' she started with a smile. 'I'm going to need you guys to stay away from the café while we record this album and get into the groove of things with City Heights Records,' she finished, pleased with herself for sounding assertive and business-like. It was the right decision. She was San Francisco Beat's manager and she was the one that needed to make the right decisions, even if they were difficult ones to make.

Levi's smiled faded and the line in between his brows deepened.

'Are you sure Bri? Amanda is there from dawn till dusk; Dan is going to want to see her. And I like it there, I like being around your family. I thought we could have band meetings there and boost Amanda's outreach if we can,' he said, his voice light as though he could make her change her mind and see that the café wasn't any trouble at all. But Sabrina wasn't going to budge on her decision. Today she had slipped up, not informing the label of the band's spontaneous meet and greet. She had had no security in place, which could have been dangerous for the boys and extremely detrimental to Amanda's business should anything crazy have happened to a fan. And pictures had been snapped of Amanda and Dan kissing. While Keira had given Sabrina her word that whom the band dated were the least of her concerns if they were all happy, the boys' new publicist wasn't happy with the shots. Dan was one of the most sought-after and drooled-over lead singers in the USA, if not the world. The record label had made it clear to Keira that he was to give the impression that he was single, and Keira had passed this information on to Sabrina.

It wasn't something Sabrina was pleased with, but if it meant keeping Amanda safe and out of media scrutiny and her band in City Heights Records' good books, then she would have to do it.

'I'm sure. Just trust me on this, okay?' Sabrina said, putting her hand through Levi's hair and cuddling up to him. The soft-ness of the duvet and her body sinking into the comfy bed hit her all at once. Having gotten that off her chest, tiredness had moved into her brain.

'If you're sure,' Levi said, kissing her softly on the nose and wrapping his arm around her waist before she turned over, becoming the little spoon to his big spoon, and gave herself up to the land of nod.

Chapter 14

Spaghetti with Butter

Ingredients:

Spaghetti (homemade when possible)
Good quality butter (Grandpa liked the one with olive oil)
Parsley
Basil
Garlic
*Olive oil (Italy's finest, no blends please, you can taste the difference —
spoilt, I know)*

What to do:

*Cook your spaghetti as instructed or until lovely and tender. (No al dente
in Grandpa's kitchen. Grandpa is so right. Do what he says.)*
Chop garlic and place in a pan with olive oil. Allow to turn golden.
Chop parsley and basil.
Once pasta is ready, add to your saucepan.
Add your parsley, basil and a healthy spoon of butter.
*Season with salt and pepper and turn spaghetti over in the pan until
covered.*
Serve with grated picante or parmesan.

The booming and regal church bell rang out across the square
and this time it didn't cause Louisa's heart to plummet to the
soles of her feet. It had been over three months since that bell

had signified a mark of respect and homage to her grandpa, at his funeral, yet the pain of that day often weighed heavy in her chest. Today however, it made her heart flutter with pride. As she shaded in the intricate almond hem of the flowing gown she was designing, she thought of her grandpa; of how he had guided her here to Italy and how life had picked up and swept her off her feet in such a beautiful euphoria of romance and all the cream cake she could eat, not to mention designs to be drawn up and dresses to be made.

Her decision to stay in Italy for the Young Designers Showcase had been the right one. Though she had missed being with her sisters to celebrate Amanda's big day, the showcase had been a dream. Louisa had felt nothing short of inspired and had not put down a pencil except to pick up a fork and devour whatever Luca put in front of her. As for Luca, concerns about him being a holiday romance over Christmas had started to ease the more time they spent together, which to be honest was an awful lot of time; there was barely any room left for concern. It had been replaced by awe, infatuation and adventure.

As she sat tapping the end of her pencil against her sketchbook, lost in a daydream, her phone vibrated and shuffled a few inches across the table. Seeing Luca's name illuminate the screen, her eyes darted towards the clock on the wall of her tiny back office. Ten minutes past twelve. Louisa's stomach growled its disapproval at her being ten minutes late for lunch. She scooped up her handbag and headed for the back door. Louisa knew that the moment the clock had struck twelve, Giulia would have shut up shop and gone out to lunch herself; she did this every day when the two of them didn't have plans. Today Louisa had been thoroughly absorbed in her thoughts and mustn't have heard Giulia's familiar shout of, '*Fermati, è ora di pranzo!*'

The warm orange sun caressed Louisa's cheeks when she stepped outside into the small alley behind the boutique. She quickly retrieved her Dolce and Gabbana sunglasses from her bag, which had been a gift from Giulia for doing her proud at the fashion show, so Louisa could look like a true Italian fashionista. She rounded the corner of the elegant shop front and instantly bounced off a tall, solid object and was sent wobbling into the nearby bush. Louisa rattled her fuzzy brain and couldn't remember them having built a wall recently. She tried to loosen her sunglasses that had become imbedded in the bridge of her nose, as the wall reached out and offered a hand to help her up.

'*Amore mio*,' the wall sung out in a smooth velvet-like tone, that held a hint of laughter in it.

'Luca!' Louisa gasped registering that she had in fact bumped into a walking Luca and not a newly built brick wall. She reached up and took his hand, allowing him to pull her gently to her feet and back to a steady stance.

'Luca, I'm so sorry,' she expressed, wrapping her arms around his neck. Luca's watch now read 12.15 p.m. and those fifteen minutes were precious in Italy when it meant getting a table for lunch. 'I didn't mean to keep you waiting. I was drawing.' *And daydreaming of you*, she thought but didn't say out loud.

'It is no problem, Louisa. You work hard, *ma* now it is time for fun, *si*?' His lips curved into a bright grin as he wiggled his eyebrows. Keeping hold of her hand he swiftly moved them into the throngs of people, leading the way to whatever lunch destination he had planned for today. In the few months that Louisa had been in Italy, Luca had been to visit her at work on her lunch break almost every day of the week. Each day he had surprised her by whisking her off to a new and delicious location. Her stomach growled in anticipation of today's menu.

Luca weaved them in and out of the hungry pedestrians with skill. Each were wandering the streets following the rich olive oil-infused aromas that seeped through the cracks of the café doors. Italy at lunchtime was heaving with people all ready to put their feet up and tuck into some of the finest delicacies the world had to offer. Getting a good spot in any restaurant or café was serious business; the quick marching and fierce expressions etched on passersby's faces said it all. In a matter of minutes, it would all become serene again as people sat with their families and friends and enjoyed the food before them.

Fortunately for Louisa and her belly, the man in charge of their direction worked in arguably one of the best cafés in Orzoro, so she didn't have to worry about getting hangry. In fact, Luca had yet to see her hangry. That would be the bonus of dating an Italian and an Italian chef at that.

Today Luca was moving swiftly and effectively through the crowds. They had walked – or rather, jogged in Louisa's case, to keep up with Luca's giant strides – further than they had before. The crowds began to disperse, and the alley ways grew narrower. Louisa searched the stone walls, plant pots and worn painted door arches in search of a restaurant sign or name, but there were none in sight. As they moved further along the cobbles, the alley lead to an open clearing, almost like a town square, and opposite where they stood, she could see fairy lights wound around a worn brown framed window and a white awning that read 'Tony's'.

The place was only small; maybe ten tables. Once inside, Louisa's stomach did a somersault as the aroma of baked mussels filled her nostrils; that familiar scent of olive oil mixed with garlic, parsley and breadcrumbs. 'You are amazing,' she gushed. 'I have seen so many of Italy's hidden gems because of you. There is more beauty here than even I could have imagined. Thank you for bringing me here,' she finished as they took their seats at a tiny table overlooking the kitchen.

Luca reached across the table and took her hands in his. 'You are the more beautiful of hidden gems,' he said, dropping a kiss to her palm as a petite waitress with a sweet face came to take their order. Scanning the menu, Louisa's eyes bulged and her thoughts drifted to childhood as the descriptions of the dishes jumped out at her; mussels topped with fine breadcrumbs, parsley and garlic; spaghetti in a rich red wine tomato sauce – she felt lucky that growing up these were dishes she enjoyed weekly thanks to the chefs in her family.

Though Amanda took the lead when they were younger and stayed glued to their zias' sides, always wanting to be in charge of the wooden spoon and pushing Sabrina and Louisa out of the way on many occasions, Louisa had enjoyed the time together in the kitchen with them when they visited Italy – in addition to squeezing in besides Amanda every now and then to aid Nanna and Grandpa when cooking at home. Over the years she hadn't been exercising her kitchen skills as much due to having the most amazing chefs around her and much preferring Amanda's pasta to her own. It would be nice to make some more time while she was here to practice with her zias and her nanna once more. She could maybe even surprise Amanda with another recipe, as the *torta caprese* had gone down a treat. She smiled, thinking of how much Italy had inspired her, not only with her designs, but with a fresh zest for life in all areas, including love and cooking.

It wasn't long before the waitress came back, interrupting their discussion of the countries that they would love to visit one day, with a bowl of butter and garlic spaghetti piled high with a flower of baked mussels for Louisa and a mouthwatering lasagna layered with basil and mozzarella for Luca. Not able to wait a second for a sprinkle of parmesan offered by the lady, Louisa picked up her fork and began twirling the silky pasta around it. It was but an inch from her mouth when her phone rang. Immediately dropping her fork and sending Luca an apologetic closed-mouth smile, she dug into her bag to retrieve it. She hated to be rude at the table; phones were generally out of sight around an Italian dinner table and Louisa loved nothing more than switching off and enjoying Luca's company. However, living away from home meant her phone was never too far away in case her family needed her. Seeing that it was Amanda, Louisa answered it right away.

'Lou, hey, how's my Italian fashionista doing?' Amanda's voice came down the line, cheery with a hint of flustered that made Louisa reach out, squeeze Luca's hand and gesture 'one minute' with her index finger as she bowed away from the table to step outside. Luca, ever so understanding of how close she was with her sisters, waved her away with, 'It is no problem'.

'All is good here, what's up?' Louisa asked as she stepped into the April sunlight and began pacing the narrow, cobbled pavement that was lined with potted lavender and rosemary.

'It's good to hear your voice, I'm glad all is well,' Amanda said. Louisa was very aware that she was skirting around her emotions in typical Amanda fashion.

'Amanda,' Louisa said sternly, urging her sister to tell her what was so important she had to abandon a plate of mussels and buttery swirls of spaghetti.

'It's been two weeks Lou, two weeks. Sabrina has banned the boys from spending any time at the café. I know everyone's busy, but I've barely seen Dan and I don't know, it just seems a little drastic, don't you think?' Amanda sighed into the phone.

Louisa was momentarily stunned, watching a tiny lizard weave in and out of the ridges and cracks in the low stone wall and into a quaint flower bed. Such a rule seemed so out of character for Sabrina. It was Amanda's first few weeks running a café – she would need all the family support she could get. Taking the boys away from her, especially Dan, seemed harsh. She had to agree with her big sister's flustered state on this one. Sabrina wasn't being fair. But then again, Louisa had never overseen a rock band before; she didn't know the drills or the demands of a record label.

'Maybe it's just for a week or so while they get acquainted with their new label. Try not to worry and surely Dan can come by after hours or when they get a break in recording?' Louisa inquired, trying to be realistic and calm Amanda down. Maybe she could get Amanda to understand that Sabrina simply wanted the boys to focus on the music and not be distracted by Italian cakes. These all seemed like valid points. When recording sessions were over, Louisa couldn't see them venturing to the café as a big deal.

'No, it's like Brina doesn't want them to be associated with the place. She doesn't want them near it,' Amanda replied, sounding downtrodden. 'Anyway, sorry to moan. I shouldn't be complaining.'

'I'm always here to listen,' Louisa started, feeling happy to be needed given that phone calls with her sisters had been few and far between recently. 'And I don't think it's that, Amanda. Bri loves the café and is so proud of you. Speaking of which, how have your first two weeks been?' Louisa asked, hoping to turn the conversation around and end it on a happier note. She gently ran her hand over a sprig of lavender and brought it up to her nose, inhaling the sweet perfume it left on her palm as she waited her sister's response.

'Honestly, it's been a fairytale. Some nights I don't want to leave. Does that make me crazy? I could just stare at the tables and booths and coffee bar all night, it's all so beautiful and actually real you know? Maybe that's what's with my mood, I probably just need a good night sleep. And Dan is probably too focused on the songs in his head, he hasn't even noticed the time away from each other.' Amanda laughed. Louisa recognized the faint embarrassment in her sister's laughter. Amanda was not one to get emotional and fuss over a man, her time with Jason had made her a little hard around the edges and she tended to shut off her emotions, though Dan had been the exception to many of her rules.

Louisa chuckled. 'Dan not noticing your absence or lack of time together would be like an Italian not noticing there's no wine on the dinner table. Try and get some rest tonight. I absolutely can't wait to see *Torta per Tutti* soon. Oh, and try not to worry about Bri, I'm sure it's just new work jitters and she's trying to do a good job,' Louisa finished as her stomach grumbled.

'Thanks Lou. Right I best get back to baking. Please give Nanna and everyone my love and *tanti baci*. Love you.'

'Of course, love you too.' Louisa paused slightly before moving her phone away from her ear when Amanda disconnected. She watched the tourists and native Napolitanas roaming the streets of Amalfi. Some people had their phones glued to their ears, a calzone wrapped up in a to-go style paper as they munched on the way back to their office, their lunch hour drawing to an end, while others enjoyed a more leisurely lunch break, lazily chatting to colleagues while dipping *cantuccini* into their thumb-sized espressos.

Louisa wandered back inside. Reaching their table, she bent down and wrapped her arms around Luca, kissing his cheek in thanks for being so patient. He had not yet finished his dish, having waited for her. She smiled sweetly and received a dashing smile in return, his blue eyes sparkling in the sunlight that blazed through the glass pane. She wished to sit and stare into his happy crystal eyes for a much longer time that she now had left of her lunch. They tucked into their now cooler, yet still utterly delicious meals, and resumed their talk of travel and the adventures they would one day take.

Two hours later and Louisa found herself daydreaming of Luca as she worked on an outfit for an up-and-coming fashion blogger hoping to be the next Chiara Ferragni. She let out a buoyant sigh. She felt deliriously jovial, though that could also be because of the sheer amount of butter she had feasted on during lunch. Whichever it might be, she felt grateful for the happy distraction from thinking about the showcase results and the worry that her sisters were currently in a disagreement.

A tinkle of the bell in the front of the shop indicated a customer had just left. Louisa drew her eyes to the doorway of the office as Giulia walked in holding three garment bags. Today Giulia looked positively radiant in a little black dress with a chunky grey knit cardigan that Amanda would have been jealous of. Her face wore a pink hue from her light blush and her lips were plump with a slick of gloss. There wasn't a moment where Louisa didn't feel inspired by her. Today Louisa had paired her trusty white Converse, perfect for keeping up with Luca's strides, with black tights, a pink suede knee-length skirt and black fitted polo neck. All had received Giulia's appraisal when she had arrived at work this morning and it only motivated Louisa more.

'*Cara mia*, this lady wishes to have some alterations to her dresses. I want you to do it,' Giulia said, laying the dresses down across the small bench adjacent to Louisa's worktop. Louisa admired Giulia's straight to the point way. She didn't pull any punches with Louisa. Just like at the fashion show when she didn't stand for Louisa's self-doubt, here in the shop she challenged Louisa. If Giulia didn't like a design she would say so, for she didn't want to make it if 'Louisa was a crazy woman' and couldn't see its potential. Often all it would take was a look and a sigh from Giulia as she waved her hand over a sketch, for Louisa to glance over it and see what it was missing. Giulia truly was like her fairy godmother, turning rags into the most magnificent pieces.

Right now, she was challenging Louisa in taking on a task that Louisa wasn't quite comfortable with yet. She knew her way around a sewing machine, having grown up playing around with her nanna's and her mum's, but she had to admit to being a touch lazy at times, loving the drawing process much more; the maths aspect of sewing could tend to throw her and make her lose interest. Working alongside Giulia for the Young Designers Fashion Showcase had been an eye opener and she had had to pick up some slack and help Giulia to complete the dresses in time, when she had customers to see to.

Her confidence and knowledge behind a sewing machine was slowly but surely starting to improve, one stitch at a time. She placed her pencil down and went to look at the items the lady had left for alterations. Giulia was careful in taking the first one out of its bag and the minute she held up the hanger and undid the zip, they were both engulfed in a puff of tulle.

'Argh, I can't breathe,' Louisa chuckled. 'My goodness, it's incredible,' she added, gently trying to pat down the tulle so she could see Giulia's reaction. Louisa loved tulle and the way it created full skirts, swishing capes and extravagant trains that made you feel exquisite on a special occasion. Giulia on the other hand, preferred the sleek, A-line, figure-hugging sophisticated looks, but wasn't opposed to dramatic collars or flares. This piece was all Louisa, that was for sure. Another thing that Louisa was sure of was that this was going to be a pain in the butt to alter for someone who wasn't a genie on a sewing machine like Giulia. But something in Giulia's wide-eyed and pursed lips of an expression told Louisa that this was a challenge to keep her on her toes.

Untangling themselves from the plumes of ombre chiffon and tulle and battling the dress back into its garment bag proved to be a workout. Giulia hung the bag on the rack next to Louisa's worktop and nodded, 'You got it, right?' Louisa couldn't help the laugh that barreled out of her and was pleased to see that Giulia was laughing too.

'The lady, she needs them back in *due settimane*,' Giulia said through her laughter. Louisa stopped laughing abruptly. Two weeks was no time at all. Before she could persuade Giulia that she would require her help with this, Giulia winked and exited the office. Well, it was nice to know that Giulia had faith in her.

Chapter 15

Sfogliatelle

Ingredients:

For the pastry:

2 cups all-purpose flour
1 cup semolina flour
1/8 tsp salt
1 cup unsalted butter
½ cup water

For the filling:

1 cup of whole milk
¼ cup semolina
1 cup ricotta
¼ cup sugar
Zest of two lemons
1 egg
Cinnamon
Vanilla

What to do:

Make again and WRITE STEPS DOWN. Don't forget this time. Not everyone has a visual in their minds of Grandpa making them.
WRITE IT DOWN.
Should I share on blog?

The sounds of Andrea Bocelli emitted from the red CD player in the corner of the kitchen. Amanda was swaying along, her head down, long, wavy brown hair perched on top of her head in a messy bun, and the lemon rind that dipped in and out of the waves of custard as she stirred the mixture were keeping her thoughts light and distracted.

'Amanda,' came a shout. 'Amanda!' The shout came again, as Amanda realized she was now singing very loudly along to Andrea Bocelli and her voice didn't sound anywhere near as good as his. She looked up to see who was shouting her name, blinking, her eyes adjusting to the bright kitchen lights. She cast a look at Lauren, but she had her head hunched over the pasta machine and to Amanda's pleasant surprise seemed to be humming along to Andrea Bocelli too. This only cemented the fact that even though she had originally just been a supply sous-chef, Amanda had been right to offer her the position after how smoothly she had fitted in to life at the café. Lauren had been eager to learn more of Amanda's grandpa's recipes – another positive sign, Amanda had thought. Lauren was busy today trying her hand at *sfogliatelle*. Amanda watched as Lauren placed the dough through the machine until a cough interrupted her evaluating glance.

'Boss?' It was Kate.

'Sorry, is everything okay Kate?' Amanda asked, registering Kate by the doors and still whisking her mixture over the stove.

'We're not even open yet and three different media outlets have rung at least twice each,' Kate sighed. Amanda studied Kate's tired face. Today her cropped brown hair held two clips either side of her ears to keep the strands from falling in her face. She wore slim black trousers with a neat pair of black pumps and a short-sleeved white T-shirt. They had become fast friends over the past few weeks.

Kate had proven to be incredibly efficient keeping the café running smoothly out front and she turned up early every day to see if Amanda needed help making anything. The kitchen had been running like clockwork with Lauren's skills and the addition of Liam lending a hand every so often. More than once, Amanda had toyed with offering him a job, feeling like there was a chance that he might say farewell to his electrical endeavours and take it; he was here so much anyway. Amanda had been happy to teach Kate a few recipes in the early hours each day and it was at the point now that Amanda could trust Kate with whipping up the chocolate filling for the *cannoli* and the limoncello frosting for the lemon cupcakes. An extra pair of hands couldn't go amiss and in her grandpa's books, 'It was better to know than not to know'. After having her staff not turn up on opening day, Amanda thought it best that her team were familiar with each part of the café and knowing how to bake. And knowing how to bake Italian – well, forget the cherry on the top of the cake, that was the sambuca thrown in the cake for good measure.

'We're just going to have to ignore them. We must still answer the phone but as soon as they make themselves known I give you permission to hang up,' Amanda said, removing the custard from the stove top and placing it on a mat to cool. She was happy to see Kate chuckle. Kate had had experience working in cafés before, but Amanda was aware of how exhausting opening week had been, especially if you considered the unique addition of having world famous rock stars attending opening day, leading to every member of staff having been rushed off their feet with a welcomed, but all the same unexpected, workload. Amanda was grateful for the interest in the café; it was a dream having it brimming with customers, and she was also eternally grateful for her incredible team.

'Putting the phone down on celebrities and social media giants! Aren't we rebels, sticking it to Hollywood?' Kate laughed.

Amanda pondered this for a moment. She guessed it was true. She had never craved the glitz and glamour of the celebrity world. She wasn't about to lie and say she had never thought about what it would be like to be known as a highly sought-out chef the world over, but when Sabrina had gotten into the music business that bubble had burst. She was on the receiving end of her sister's late-night Skype calls when she'd got home at three in the morning after having spent the night being berated by Lydia or holed up in a toilet as paparazzi tried to barge their way in and get a picture of the latest pop star who'd had far too much fun for their own good. Not to mention reading articles about Dan that clearly portrayed what the media thought of him and dreamed him up to be, instead of writing about who he truly was. She was still getting used to that, especially now that they were dating. Dan being a rock star as well as her best friend was easier to digest when she focused on just that and avoided media outlets altogether. It was easier said than done at times, when paparazzi appeared on her doorstep, but she would then simply remind herself that they didn't know the Dan she knew and it would ease the nerves that tried to stir trouble in her brain. If she thought she had a thick skin before, it was nothing compared to what she had had to develop over the last few weeks since opening *Torta per Tutti*.

She wasn't happy that Sabrina was keeping the band away from the café. Yes, Amanda wanted to achieve success with the café without the suggestion that she was riding the coat tails of San Francisco Beat, which was how the magazines had so eloquently put it this past week. Kate had informed her of this news, and yes, she understood the boys were busy recording but she missed having them around and it only cemented her disdain for celebrity culture that Sabrina was enforcing such a rule because she couldn't have her rock stars being seen hanging around a very un-rock-star-like establishment; not that Amanda thought for a second that would concern any of their fans, so what was Sabrina's problem?

Her team here at *Torta per Tutti* would stick to their guns and prove to Sabrina they could handle the media. The boys could come back and everything would be just fine, as fine and as smooth as the creamy, glistening pan of custard she had to remember not to stick her finger in to taste. Old habits die hard, but there was no licking the spoon in this kitchen, not when you had health inspectors on the prowl. What happened in one's kitchen at home, stayed in one's kitchen at home, she mused. It had been easy enough to remember that when surrounded by Michelin-star chefs, in hot and steamy kitchens around the world, in the most professional of settings, but here at *Torta per Tutti* Amanda felt much more relaxed. She loved it. Her kitchen was bright and cheerful and felt like home; she firmly believed this made the food taste even richer, for when there is love and passion in the food, there is no beating it.

'Rebels, we shall be.' Amanda pulled her attention from the mesmerizing liquid to gather the next ingredients she needed and to go through her plan with Kate and Lauren. 'I have no problem with fans asking questions, but we can't be giving out details on the boys without Sabrina's permission. I'm okay with pictures being taken of this place, but if anyone asks questions, just try and keep it professional. We can't hide from it, there's bound to be more phone calls, but can I ask that we just keep our heads down and see to it that personal information stays within these walls as best it can? I have no doubt that once the reporters realize we won't take the bait on whether Dan is a "boxers or briefs" kind of guy, or what shower gel Levi washes with, they will get bored and move on,' Amanda noted, while adding flour to her bowl to prepare the pastry for her custard tarts.

'Ooh, so which is it?' Kate asked with a playful smirk. Amanda cocked her head at Kate knowing exactly what was coming next. 'Is Dan boxers or briefs?' Amanda snorted and blew a scoop of flour in Kate's direction, causing the girls to laugh along with her.

'I'm being serious,' Amanda said with a smirk. 'We keep our heads down and show Sabrina we can handle ourselves; she can put a stop to her silly rule, then you can see for yourself.' Amanda winked at Kate, who blushed a rosy shade of red.

'I'll open up. Francesca should be here any minute, she just had to drop her kids off at nursery,' Kate announced, changing the subject but leaving the kitchen with a definite extra pep in her step. It wasn't only Amanda that was missing the boys.

Amanda chuckled, tipping out the dough she had expertly formed while talking with everyone and beginning to knead it. Francesca, the lady that had tugged at Amanda's heart strings on opening day, had been coming in regularly with her children in tow and always brightened Amanda's day. Francesca recalled her childhoods spent up in the mountains of Calabria with her papa; of how they didn't have a lot but spending time with him hunting for food or braving the hikes down the mountainside to visit the markets were some of her fondest memories.

Amanda had learnt that Francesca had moved to England when her husband got a job here nearly a year ago. She moved her dad over with her when he got sick and though he was grateful that his time in England made him well, he missed his home in Italy terribly. Amanda loved talking to Francesca and sending cake boxes home to her papa. Earlier this week when Francesca made her usual visit, Amanda received a nudge from her grandpa up above and threw out the question she had been eager to ask her; 'Would you like to work here?' Francesca always seemed to enjoy her time at *Torta per Tutti* and Amanda sensed that she needed a friend and a place to belong, having not been in England very long and her kids occupying most of her time. Now they were at nursery, Amanda thought it would be a perfect fit. Francesca had jumped off her stool and embraced Amanda with squeals of glee, answering her question with a profound 'Yes!' – just thinking about it made Amanda smile. For *Torta per Tutti* to have that effect on people; for it to be a loving, warm and homey environment for others and not merely just a café – that idea was everything to Amanda.

*

It had been another successful and exhausting day at *Torta per Tutti*. Francesca had left around 4 p.m. to pick up her kids. Amanda had sent Lauren and Kate home a little after six as the last customers left, while she and Liam remained behind, tidying up the last bits and pieces in her beautiful kitchen. Liam had called by around five and jumped in with helping Kate with a few of the last orders of the day. Content that Kate and Lauren were heading home together in the evening sunlight, he had insisted on staying to close up with Amanda, knowing she often didn't leave until late. Leaving Liam to empty the dishwasher, she walked into the front of the café to find Dan was waiting for her. All six-foot-one of him was leaning forward on the coffee bar; his forearms resting on the top, fingers intertwined, his usual relaxed and effortlessly cool stance. His shoulder-length dark waves framed his face. When he saw her, he ran a hand through his hair, rustling up the floppy waves that gave him a 'just got out of bed' dreamy look, and stood up straight to greet her. He really was unreal. She made for him straight away.

'You smell good enough to eat,' Dan whispered in her ear, causing Amanda's whole body to tingle as his warm breath tickled her neck.

'As do you.' She managed a quick reply before Dan's lips were on hers. Time seemed to stop when he kissed her. She melted into him with no care nor concern for the world around her. She felt as light as a feather, happy to be whisked away by the breeze. He slowed the kiss, gently nibbling her lip before stepping back, his dark eyes filled with desire. 'You are a bad influence on me,' she said, lovingly shoving Dan, who she had no doubt read her mind as he caught her shove and bent down, peppering kisses over her cheeks and nose. Suddenly Dan froze and this time Amanda was fully aware of what had caused his sudden shift in demeanour.

'Looks like you don't need me tonight,' Liam said, with a light chuckle and a sheepish grin. Amanda smiled, genuinely appreciating Liam's kindness and good humour. She turned away from Dan to thank him with a chuckle of her own, trying to ease the tension that she felt radiating off Dan.

'No, but thank you for being here Liam. I'll see you tomorrow – the espresso and pastry will be waiting,' she said with a smile, not wanting Dan's presence to intimidate Liam. She very much enjoyed his company and she didn't think Kate would be best pleased if Dan drove him away because he'd got the wrong idea.

'Nice to see you again, mate,' he said to Dan.

'Good to see you too man,' Dan replied with a salute as Amanda gave Liam a quick hug and saw him out of the door. Amanda didn't waste time. She was aware of Dan's tired features and was all too familiar herself when it came to lack of trust in a relationship. She had Jason to thank for that, but she would not be having Dan thinking that of her.

'Come on you, out, out,' she cried, gesturing him towards the door, where she stood ready to lock up.

The sky over Manchester was a sheet of black with the occasional plume of grey swirls drifting by. The streetlamps cast an orange glow across Dan's prominent cheekbones, making the dimples in his cheeks pop when he pouted. Amanda didn't think there could be a face she was happy to see more at the end of a working day. She adored her job, if she could even call it that anymore, but that face was enough to make her hang up her oven mitts and curl up under the duvet with him for eternity; maybe, possibly, though she would be hard pressed to go without a morning *cornetto*. She'd have to get up and bake, then jump back under the duvet with him.

'I love you, you know,' Amanda said to Dan as they walked hand in hand.

'I told you to let me know if you needed anything?' Dan said, his raspy voice troubled, his eyes a swirl of something Amanda feared was deeper than just a hint of jealousy.

'And I will. But you do realize you are breaking all kinds of rules right now by coming to the café?' Amanda said with a laugh and a nudge of her elbow to Dan's side. What Sabrina didn't know couldn't hurt her, right? Getting to walk home with Dan, Amanda felt carefree and a little rebellious. She wanted Dan to relax, to enjoy every minute they had together and be sure of the love she had for him. He had no reason to be jealous.

'That I do.' Dan gave a gruff chuckle that wasn't quite believable to Amanda's ears.

'Dan, what's going on?' she asked, stopping to give him her full attention, her feet stinging for want of sitting down. Tiredness was catching up on her, but she couldn't give in until she knew Dan was okay; that they were okay. She didn't care for Dan's subdued silence, not when they promised to always tell each other everything.

'What did you need Liam for this evening?' Dan asked, his gorgeous brown eyes boring into hers. Amanda squeezed his hand.

'He sometimes walks me and the girls home when it gets dark, that's all. You don't have anything to worry about.' Amanda felt a slight urgency creep into her voice with her last words. She and Dan had been the best of friends for so long, they never argued or second-guessed each other. This felt odd.

'Just call me next time,' he replied, his voice a little off kilter to its usual confident bravado. Amanda turned away, suddenly feeling aware of her surroundings and not wanting to have this conversation out in the open.

'Dan, I can't call you. You have an album to record and a manager to appease. What have you got against Liam?' Amanda said, not liking the agitation that appeared in her voice yet feeling saddened by Dan's lack of trust in her. It was getting late and thoughts of her alarm clock going off in a few short hours were clouding her ability to sympathize with Dan right at this moment. Dan knew all about her past relationship with Jason, how he had cheated on her and lied to her on countless occasions. She would never do that to a person and Amanda felt Dan should know her better than that.

'Not a thing, baby girl,' was all Dan could offer, with a smile and a shrug Amanda knew was forced.

'So, how's everything at the studio? Is something else bothering you?' Amanda questioned, in an attempt to maybe get this evening back on track to how it had been only twenty minutes ago when she had walked out of the kitchen to see Dan's handsome face waiting for her. Talking about his music always cheered him up. They reached her front door and she rummaged for her keys awaiting his response.

'It's good, my love,' Dan replied, stroking his tense jaw as she twisted the key in the lock.

'I can't wait to hear the new stuff,' Amanda noted, shrugging herself out of her cable knit cardigan the minute she stepped into the house and tucking her bag away under the coat rack. She wanted nothing more than to leap into bed and cuddle up next to Dan but the air between them felt strained; he wasn't willingly revealing any more information. It wasn't like Dan to keep things from her; they had both tried that before, hiding their feelings from each other and it only led to a rift in their friendship. If there was something more to this than just a blip of jealousy over Liam being there for her when Dan couldn't, then he needed to speak up. Now there was a lot more on the line. If their relationship didn't work out what would that mean for their friendship?

'Hon, as strikingly handsome as you look when you pout, we're not going to bed arguing with each other,' Amanda said, catching Dan placing his loafers neatly by the door and closing the gap between them to fold her arms around his waist as he stood at the foot of the stairs.

'Who says we are arguing?' he asked, his features relaxing as his confident smirk made its debut for the evening, giving Amanda's heart a reassuring jolt. Even if Amanda wanted to address the flicker of sadness she saw in Dan's eyes, she didn't think it possible tonight as her eyelids drooped and the feel of Dan's familiar muscles at her fingertips lent themselves to her dozy state. 'Bedtime,' Dan said and Amanda had no energy to argue that she had wanted to stay up and talk to him and listen to him strum away at his guitar well into the night, having not had the pleasure of doing just that in what felt like forever.

Chapter 16

Tiramisu

Ingredients:

2 cups of espresso
4 egg yolks
3 tbsp Marsala wine (a little/lot extra for drizzling)
Two 7oz packets of lady fingers
3/4 cup of sugar
16oz mascarpone
Cocoa powder (The good Italian one)

What to do:

Make coffee and set aside.
Beat egg yolks and sugar until combined then add mascarpone and mix
until creamy.
Add 3 tbsp of Marsala and mix until combined. (I'm pretty sure Nanna
adds way more Marsala than this.)
Add a thin layer of mascarpone cream to the bottom of
the dish.
Dip lady fingers into prepared coffee and begin to layer into dish.
Follow with a layer of mascarpone mix and drizzle (drown) with
Marsala.
Repeat steps until there is a nice layer of mascarpone cream
on top.
Dust with cocoa powder and refrigerate.

The room was small and dark. The furniture, a simple coffee table and two settees, were worn and distressed, the brown leather bearing creases and cracks. With the sound boards, speakers and numerous computer screens there wasn't much room left for the luxury that the boys had been used to under Lydia's agency. San Francisco Beat fit snuggly into the sound booth, Levi having just enough room so his elbows didn't hit the walls each time he swung back to crash the symbols on his squashed drum kit. Sabrina liked it and, by the sound emitting from the speakers, so did the boys. Their sound was rich and enthusiastic. Sabrina felt the energy in every strum of the bass and crash of the drums. Watching Dan through the window, eyes closed, gripping the mic like his life depended on it, his voice sounded naked and bare, as though in such close confines it was forced to reveal itself. That or he was harbouring some pain that he was taking out on the music; he had been awfully quiet lately and not Dan quiet, but troubled quiet. Guilt stirred in the pit of Sabrina's stomach.

'I've heard about these guys, of course. I know they're huge in America and the whole world is starting to take note, but I admit I was never a fan of Jones Records and had them pegged to do perfumes and reality shows in the next year. I'm pleasantly surprised that the songwriting and sound is all them. I wondered about ghostwriters and their instrumental abilities, but you know your stuff lady, you've kept them real. I commend you,' the producer, Jack, said as he twisted a few knobs and played with a few dials on the soundboard, before turning to look at Sabrina. 'They're a great bunch of guys, I can see that already and they have an insane amount of talent. Thank you for bringing me on board,' he added, the creases around his grey eyes showing the sincerity in the smile at his lips.

'Thanks Jack, but I can't take all the credit. I'm thrilled Keira knew about your place. I love it and think it fits them perfectly,' Sabrina said, smiling back and blushing slightly at Jack's compliment. She sat in the black swivel chair next to him with her clipboard in hand, always ready to make notes, as they listened to the songs. She watched Jack fiddle with the computers, occasionally signaling something to the boys with his hands, to which the boys would nod to and then do their thing. It felt good to be back in this environment with the boys. They had been at it just shy of two weeks already and Sabrina felt confident that this album would be better than their first, and she loved their first one.

'How's it going, Sabrina?' came Keira's voice as she made her way back into the cozy quarters after having stepped out to take a phone call. Keira had arrived in the UK yesterday and Sabrina was thoroughly enjoying having her around and working together. Keira held her own clipboard which made Sabrina smile at their similar efficiency. Getting to work so closely had affirmed Sabrina's decision that City Heights Records had been right for them. Over the past twelve hours she and Keira had hit it off. With Keira's organization skills, her enthusiastic approach and with the respect she showed for the band's music and ideas, the boys had taken to her nicely too. Keira had been the one to recommend Jack's recording studio, informing Sabrina that it was one of Manchester's hidden gems and a treat for all true artists. The likes of The Smiths and The 1975 had recorded here, which had scored further points for Keira with San Francisco Beat, especially Dan, since he and Amanda idolized Jack Kerouac who The 1975 had been inspired by. Keira was taking the boys seriously which pleased Sabrina greatly. She had high hopes for the working relationship between all parties.

Jack pressed a button and motioned for a break through the glass, and the boys filed out all sticky and sweaty. Levi dived next to Sabrina on the couch and rested his head on her lap, the movement causing Sabrina to jerk up, very nearly spilling her coffee over her baby-blue flower print dress. She instantly cringed at her sudden and cruel reaction. What had gotten into her? Jack and Keira, that was what. She hadn't wanted Jack to see her and Levi getting cosy and she didn't want word to get back to the label about her and Levi's relationship. It was simply better to play it down. Though Keira had voiced her opinion that Sabrina and Levi made a cute couple, Sabrina didn't want to put Keira in a tricky position around other professionals. Sabrina couldn't make them both look bad. She was doing the right thing.

Levi's face however, made her feel far from right. This episode was far worse than the plane. His jaw was tense, and he was looking at the ground. It was the looking at the ground that made Sabrina feel dreadful. She'd hurt him and it didn't feel good. Gone was his dazzling smile and mischievous sparkle.

To add insult to injury, Keira chose this moment to go over emails and an important message from the publicist. Sabrina couldn't even pretend she had seen a spider or needed a wee when she had sprung from her seat, Levi would put two and two together with what Keira divulged next.

'If I remember correctly from my previous meeting with Sabrina we had, along with your publicist, discussed keeping your distance from Sabrina's sister's café after the spectacle that it became in the media recently. Dan, can I ask that you check in with us and inform us of your whereabouts, especially late at night? There are eyes everywhere. Last night's innocent stroll is this morning's gossip fodder. While I understand you all have lives outside of these four walls, the label and our publicist are not so forgiving.' Keira's voice was stern, but she broke her professional tone of conduct with her last words, making them softer – to make them sound less like a blow, no doubt. Sabrina had to give her credit, she really understood the band and was doing her best to work out a balance. Whereas the boys might appreciate this professionalism from Keira, Sabrina felt she would not be so lucky to receive the same treatment, if the penetrative glares she could feel from Dan, James and Dylan were anything to go by.

Levi was still staring at the floor, a hand rubbing at the back of his neck.

'What is it exactly that our dear publicist will not be so forgiving of?' Levi asked, addressing Keira with half a smirk and looking past Sabrina. She closed her eyes, bracing herself for what was going to come next. She should have told Levi that first day in City Heights Records' office when Keira had first warned her.

Keira glanced at her as if to say, 'You haven't told them?' which only made Sabrina feel worse. She shuffled from foot to foot.

'If we can just keep PDA to a minimum. I'm sure you know the drill – fans like to think it possible that they could date you. It helps with your image,' Keira explained, with a slight rosy flush spreading over her cheeks.

Levi's dark brown eyes illuminated with understanding as the dots of Sabrina's odd behavior over the last couple of weeks connected. 'Sure thing, boss,' Levi said, with a nod and small shake of his head before he wiped his perspiring brow and took a stand. 'Good meeting boys, shall we get back to it?' he added, walking past Sabrina coolly and straight into the sound booth, claiming his seat behind his drum kit. Even when he was mad at her she still loved him fiercely.

'You said you had some ideas to discuss with me?' Keira piped up, dragging Sabrina's attention away from her sulking boyfriend; she almost felt sorry for the drum kit for the beating it was now currently enduring with from Levi's frustrated strikes. Returning to her seat on the couch, Sabrina pulled out her notebook and the pieces of paper she had been working on for upcoming show promotions. Thinking about the boys getting out on stage again and performing for their die-hard fans, distracted her from the possibility that Levi wouldn't ever talk to her again. That, and she was certain that she would win him over with her plans. Getting stuck into business with Keira made her pulse steady and she regained her confidence in her abilities and what she thought best for San Francisco Beat.

'I'm thinking of a small gig here in Manchester – an intimate setting, one where the fans can get close; make it feel more personal and special before the album is released and the arenas come into play,' Sabrina told Keira enthusiastically. 'I fired off some emails earlier to our booking agent letting him know the plan and I'll look at speaking with PR to see if they can facilitate some interviews in the build-up and maybe discuss a few personal issues and get on the same page,' Sabrina finished, glancing away from her work and to the drum kit once more.

She felt grateful for the deal that City Heights Records had offered. The momentum from the boys' first album was still going strong, but there was an energy in the band going into album two that gave Sabrina a sense that this album was going to be something special; she was not about to spoil it with silly arguments over keeping their personal lives just that – personal.

Keira immediately tapped her fingers across the iPad on her lap. 'I think that sounds fab. If you can get back to me with what you arrange ASAP, I can help ensure everyone is working together and keep on top of them,' Keira said, her hands now moving at an incredibly speedy rate as she flicked her screen from one email to the next. 'I'm back to LA tomorrow, so I'd like to go over their schedule and your plan – estimate for the delivery date for this album and so forth.' Keira waved her hand in the air, not taking her eyes off her screen. She was a boss babe to be reckoned with. Not one to be outdone in that department, Sabrina pulled up her spreadsheets, contact list and rough proposal of the direction she had in mind for the band and set about getting in touch with all those she would need on board to make the plan a reality.

Four hours later and Sabrina finally looked up from her screen. Keira had left two hours ago, and the boys had been in and out of the booth for short breaks, mostly consisting of gathering around Jack to listen back to a song to decide on final cuts or retakes. Conversation was kept to a minimum while they all focused on work. She rubbed at her computer-strained eyes and held her stomach as it rumbled for her attention. While the boys were playing 'Midnight Angel' for the sixth time, she snuck out of the studio, informing Jack she would be back shortly.

It didn't take Sabrina long to cross town; the studio was, with a quick march, fifteen minutes away from *Torta Per Tutti* if she cut through the lush green of Piccadilly Gardens towards the more vibrant and off-the-beaten-path edge of the Northern Quarter. Amanda would be getting ready to close for the day. She hoped there would be a few leftovers that she could salvage for her and the boys. The smell of Kimbo coffee filled her nostrils first, followed by a sweet mixture of warm vanilla and citrus. When Sabrina turned the corner onto Amanda's road she felt as though she was seeing her big sister's café for the first time. The white and gold sign reading *Torta per Tutti* with blue and yellow accents around the windows, the likes of what you'd see on the finest Positano ceramics, teamed with the freshly potted sweet violets underlining the bay window – it was like a piece of Italy had been placed on the corner of Thomas street and Oldham street.

A few women fluttered out, excitedly talking about the fresh *cornetti* they had just devoured, and Sabrina's heart soared. She could just do with one of those *cornetti* right about now for an evening pick-me-up. Moving swiftly past the women and catching the door, Sabrina was engulfed with the full aromatic mouthwatering aroma that *Torta per Tutti* elicited. Goose bumps prickled on her arms.

'What can I do for you this evening, fine stranger?' Amanda's voice interrupted Sabrina's daydreams of sitting on the fountain outside of *Pasticceria Pansa* with her sisters as they sipped espressos and ate their weight in *cartucci*. She flicked her eyes open, having automatically closed them to appreciate her full sense of smell. Amanda was waving a cloth in her direction, one hand on her hip with a slight smirk on her face to go with her sarcastic warmth.

'Hey, how's it going? I feel like I'm in Amalfi,' Sabrina said

147

enthusiastically, the beauty of the café injecting her with a dose of giddiness. 'I love it so much.'

'Not enough to visit though, hey,' Amanda said with a note of disappointment. Sabrina drew her attention away from the cake counter where she had been eyeing up the remaining slices of *ricotta torta* and olive breads that Francesca and Kate were organizing into boxes. She sent them a smile and a wave and was given bright smiles in return. Her sister, it seemed, wasn't feeling as friendly. Amanda concentrated on wiping down tables, almost ignoring Sabrina.

'I'm sorry Amanda,' Sabrina sighed. Was everyone mad at her today? 'I know I've not been in much but we're in full-on recording mode and I've been swamped with marketing plans and strategies and getting to know everyone on the new team. Please don't be upset with me,' she whispered, not wanting to cause a scene in the middle of the café, though now it was empty, bar Kate and Francesca cleaning the coffee bar and counter.

'If that's your excuse does that mean the ban has been lifted and the boys can once again eat at my café?' Amanda stopped wiping the table and took a seat in the blue armchair by the bay window. Sabrina followed her but couldn't quite sit down in the yellow one opposite; she felt too antsy, she wasn't one for confrontation and especially not one for causing the hurt she could see upon her sister's face.

'Amanda, please understand what my job entails. I don't wish to hurt you, or Dan, or Levi, but image is everything and the publicist is insistent on the band keeping their girlfriends under the radar,' Sabrina explained, as she fiddled with the watch on her wrist.

'Ahh, that is until, of course, they're spotted with a hot celebrity darling or maybe someone more in their league and then they will be signing them up for every red carpet event and encouraging the paparazzi to take all the candid shots they desire. I'm sure if James were to dine here with a Victoria's Secret model it would make for quite the cute image of "rock star dining with model at quaint Italian café", Amanda said, running a hand through her hair, which she pulled loose of her messy bun, relieving her of the weight atop her head. Sabrina watched her. She wasn't shouting, which Sabrina took as a good sign, but the bags under her eyes indicated that was due to exhaustion and not for a lack of being angry with her. There was no hiding the dismay in her deep hazel eyes at what Sabrina had enforced.

Sabrina sighed, and her belly rumbled. She didn't know what more to say on this topic. In her mind she was doing right by her band and giving her sister the breathing room to run the café without hordes of screaming fans outside. 'I thought you'd all understand. It's the music business, it's the media; we have to cooperate and give them what they want,' she told Amanda, feeling disgruntled.

'What do you want Bri?' Amanda asked, raising her hands limply at her sides. 'I get it. I do. I'm not going to pretend that the paparazzi don't scare me, but what's worse is not seeing my boyfriend. I may not be the girlfriend the media or the record label want Dan to have, but I am the girlfriend he has, and I'd like to continue being that girlfriend. You being on their side and not thinking I'm good enough for Dan, it bloody hurts Bri. You of all people." Amanda paused. Sabrina felt the anger in her sisters' tone with those last words, her heart stung at how hurt Amanda looked and sounded. "It will be hard enough as it is when he's away on tour, but not being able to see him when he's around, well, it sucks. This relationship thing, it's all new to us and I'm not going to lie and say it's been a perfect transition because, well, it hasn't, and honestly, this whole ban thing hasn't helped. Dan has been super weird lately and I can't put my finger on it. It would be lovely to talk to him without getting berated the next day because pictures of us together are online,' Amanda finished, sitting towards the edge of the armchair, getting her cloth ready for more action.

'I'm sorry about that.' Sabrina started. Amanda shrugged. 'You're not out of his league and I didn't mean to have a go at you the other night on the phone. The publicist can get a bit pushy, that's all. And I just want to make the band successful, for them to do well and live their dream.' Sabrina plonked herself down in the yellow armchair opposite Amanda. Had she really made Amanda feel like she was second best to celebrities? Like she wasn't good enough for Dan? Sabrina felt hot all of a sudden. How could she argue her case now? How could she deny how she had made her sister feel? She always tried to encourage Amanda to share her emotions; now that she was doing so, she couldn't dismiss them. What was more important?

'All I'm saying Bri, is that you were all about the music; you've always been like that and you did a damn good job at keeping those boys grounded and fighting for them and taking the heat back at Jones Records whenever someone tried to steer them in a direction you didn't like. Don't forget that. Music is one thing. Image is another. You can correct me if I'm wrong and give me the inside scoop on the music business if I've got this all upside down, but I don't believe that my loving Dan interferes with his ability to make music,' Amanda said confidently. Sabrina let out a breath, her nerves relaxing slightly that she was getting to talk this out with her sister instead of being given the silent treatment – though she realized she deserved it. She had been neglecting them both recently and clearly putting success before family; since recording started she couldn't remember the last time she had spoken to Louisa on the phone.

'Quite the opposite, in fact. He sounds incredible on this album. It's different to the last one and I have no doubt you've inspired the lyrics,' Sabrina noted, playing with the hem of her skater dress and letting out a light laugh. 'I guess I'm scared,' she sighed, Amanda having become a bit like a therapist in the last ten minutes. 'This record deal is amazing. The control they've given the boys with the writing and their sound has been unprecedented.

I don't want to screw it up. But you're right, they're grown men with families and girlfriends, who make amazing music. That's their image, not some box that the label is trying to fit them in to suit media trends and fantasies. I can't believe I've been falling for it again and pushing Levi away,' she added, palming her forehead. 'He was so disappointed with me this afternoon. I didn't stick up for them this time. If it wasn't for the fact that I now go home with Levi every night, I'm repeating the same mistake as before, allowing the label to cause a rift between us, running away from our relationship.'

Amanda laughed and stood up. 'I can only imagine his pretty face pouting. It's okay to be scared, Sabrina. But you must give yourself more credit. The boys have girlfriends, so what? That has nothing to do with the music they produce or the art they create. They can't pretend to be people they are not, in hopes of shifting a few more records. The world will continue to fall in love with them for who they are and that's honest to goodness ridiculous musicians who, okay, yes, all have take-me-to-bed eyes, but that's beside the point. You're not repeating the same mistake. You're aware of what's happening this time so now you fix it and focus on running towards Levi and not away from him. Now, come on, I could hear your stomach growling before you even walked through the door, let's get you some food.' Amanda walked towards the kitchen and Sabrina jumped up to follow.

'You mean you started that whole conversation even when you knew I was hungry?' Sabrina asked, with a gentle shove to Amanda's shoulder as they both burst through the swinging double doors.

'We haven't had a good chat in ages. Which reminds me, you need to message Lou. She's been asking about you. I think you were better at staying in touch when you lived four thousand miles away,' Amanda said, with a teasing tut.

'Alright, I'm sorry. You've put me in my place. I've been a

terrible sister this past month and I'm sorry. Now please tell me you're not going to withhold that delicious looking *tiramisu* from me?' Sabrina asked, putting down her bag by the door and edging her way over to a bowl that was resting on the kitchen island.

'Only if you tell me that you're going to see to all this "banned from the café" nonsense and put Levi out of his misery?' Amanda said, taking two forks out of a kitchen draw and taking them over to Sabrina.

'I promise,' Sabrina affirmed, snatching the fork from Amanda's grip and tucking in.

Chapter 17

Nanna's Sugared Almonds

Ingredients:

Whole raw almonds
Icing sugar (I think Nanna said 1 cup for every 2 cups of almonds)
An egg white
Vanilla (maybe a tsp)
Cream of tartar (just a tsp too)

What to do:

Almonds need to be blanched and allowed to dry and then peeled.
(Don't rush Amanda, make sure they are fully dry.)
Once dry they need to go in the oven at 180 degrees for
5 minutes.
In a small bowl beat together egg white, icing sugar,
vanilla and cream of tartar.
Dip the dried almonds into mixture and then set aside to cool.

Louisa's eyes fluttered open with the first signs of light that crept up over the horizon. She liked to sleep with the curtains drawn back in Italy; the morning view made for a spectacular and rather magical wake-up call. It was a surefire way to have her jumping out of bed, and was a sharp contrast to her usual slow starts and lacklustre attempts to get out of bed to the brick and mortar views back home in Manchester. The birds were singing loudly atop trees near and far and the turquoise sea glinted as the early specks of the morning sunrise danced across it. Louisa had to blink a few times, still unable to believe that this was her life; a life that she had gone after when taking a giant leap out of her comfort zone and choosing to stay in Italy.

Shuffling out of the bed, careful not to disturb Luca during his one lie-in this week, Louisa pulled on a light cardigan and stuffed her feet into her slippers before creaking open the balcony doors and stepping outside. There was a gentle nip in the six o'clock air, the tweeting of the birds louder now she was on the other side of the glass. Louisa leaned over the railing, watching the fishing boats bob along the water. No other sounds could be heard expect for the water lapping against the boats, the birds chirping and the occasional tuk-tuk wheezing up the steep mountains of Orzoro.

Light, fluffy clouds teased the clear baby-blue sky. Louisa felt as though she could reach up and nibble on the cotton candy plumes that floated not too far above her head. She closed her eyes and tilted her head to the morning view, feeling no rush to be anywhere but in the moment. Adding to the comfort blanket that Italy provided her, were Luca's arms as he weaved them under her elbows, his hands resting on top of hers. So much for his lie-in, Louisa thought, while at the same time leaning back into him, appreciating his lack of pajamas as she felt smooth, tanned skin and the curvature of his muscles through her flimsy cardigan and camisole ensemble. Turning from one stunning view to another, Louisa spun around on her tip-toes to wish Luca a *buongiorno* and was greeted with a feathery kiss. They remained on the balcony enjoying the peace and quiet until the grand church bell signalled Palm Sunday was about to get under way in *Italia*.

Louisa could hear the steam whistling from the espresso machines as she and Luca rode past the quaint cafés. The spring sun had opened the potted plants that hung from the balconies and lined the streets and doorways, adding vibrant pops of purple and pink flowers everywhere you looked. The cracks in the turquoise and yellow walls on the passing flats were more prominent as the heat dried the paint. Nothing looked brand new or pristine, yet everything was charming and inviting. Even with its worn and modest exterior, each place stood proud in its own beauty and history, calling her and welcoming her with open arms. She got lost in the smells of the almond blossoms and the colours, and the constant thought that lurked in the back of her mind, no matter how many times she told herself to stop thinking about it; would she be getting a call today to be informed she was the winner of the Young Designers Fashion Showcase?

Suddenly a car horn shrieked obnoxiously, scaring Louisa out of her daydream as she studied each tile and brick they passed and envisioned herself winning the prestigious showcase, while absentmindedly forgetting the narrow roads and the need for cars to get past. In most cases the cars treated her and her bike as one of their own and allowed her to blend in with the stream of traffic; however, one wiggle or swerve into their space and they weren't afraid to use their horn. You'd do well to not get in between an Italian and their need for speed on the road.

'*Amore, stai attenta*,' Luca shouted from somewhere behind her. Louisa daren't look back for fear of wobbling, losing her balance and crashing into a parked car.

They passed a couple more streets before a twinkly bell in the distance from Luca signalled for her to pull over. She carefully dismounted her beloved cream bike with a white wicker basket, which she had treated herself to with her first paycheck from Giulia, and retrieved the lock from her backpack. Luca pulled up beside her and upon getting off his bike, kissed her on the cheek before tying up his own bike – deep grey in colour, a little rusty round the edges, with a black wire basket.

'Sorry,' Louisa apologized to Luca, staring up at him from under her mascara-covered lashes. He brushed a hand against her cheek. '*Va bene*, you give me a fright. Where does your mind wander?' She reached up and took his hand, finding his concern for her sweet and endearing.

'Right now, my mind is wandering to wherever that delicious smell is coming from,' Louisa said, casting her eyes around the small street, willing her brain to focus on something other than the showcase results. *I will not talk about the showcase, I will not talk about the showcase*; she repeated this mantra over and over again in her head. It was Palm Sunday which meant that most Italians congregated around the churches while the odd nonno and nonna, zia or zio remained at home preparing the lunchtime feast. This was the case with her nanna and zias. With the weather heating up and the three hundred plus steps to get to the church, her nanna and zias wouldn't be making it to mass today. It was Luca and Louisa's job to get the olive branches and confetti – sugar coated almonds shaped into flowers – blessed this morning.

Louisa was excited to be in Italy for this special holiday. Easter was a huge deal and she hadn't experienced Holy Week – the week leading up to Easter – since she was a child. She wanted to celebrate every second of it. 'Do you think I have a good chance of winning?' The words slipped out before she could stop them, as she danced along the street holding Luca's hand and waving her cheese, rosanna and chocolate loaded olive branch in the other. Easter time in Orzoro conjured up such childlike joy, the feelings of utter excitement and wonder made her flutter alongside the rumbling nerves of finding out the results for the showcase. She couldn't help herself or push it quite far enough in the back of her mind to relax and not think about it today, no matter how hard she tried.

'Si, *ma* of course.' Luca indulged her question. His handsome face bore a five o'clock shadow and it looked good on him, making his blue eyes pop and giving him that dishy Italian look. 'You are talented, Louisa. You can do anything,' he added with a stellar smile as they walked hand in hand up to the church.

Louisa had stayed over at Luca's place, which she did occasionally when he had a day off from the *pasticerria*. He had a beautiful little apartment, a ten-minute walk from her zia's house, that made her feel like she was living in a dream. The kitchen was a small square; pots and pans dangling over an island, a white porcelain sink with turquoise tiles and a nook in the corner that overlooked a neat rose garden and vegetable patch. Luca kept his place tidy; his living room was home to a simple coffee table and cream couch that lent itself to the rustic vibe, and potted herbs decorated each room. It was cosy, had a modern flare and was very Luca; a mix of old-fashioned meets new, stylish and fresh.

When she stayed, they often curled up in the nook watching the sunset as they chatted away, each with a glass of wine in hand. Louisa savoured these moments with him, where she could slow down and unwind for a minute and appreciate the beauty around her. She felt a long way from her frazzled days in London as a receptionist when she didn't have the foggiest clue where she was heading.

Now she was in control and making sure to open her eyes to the journey she was taking. Luca still spoke of his dreams to travel; though he loved Italy, he wanted to explore other cultures, but like Louisa, he worried about letting his family down. He loved working at his family's *pasticceria* and had done so since he was a young boy. Taking a break from it or leaving it behind was a decision he found difficult. Last night, over their wine and homemade lasagna, he had told Louisa how she had inspired him, how she was a good sister but also learning to do things for herself too. He hoped maybe he could take a holiday soon, just a short one so his family would not struggle, but so he could take a step in finding the right balance in doing all the things he desired. Her heart had expanded at the thought of the adventures they could take together.

'*Grazie amore*,' she cooed at Luca, her eyes glowing with love as she adored his side profile, his jawline strong and defined. Luca caught her staring and gently pulled her into him. Draping an arm over her shoulders he dropped a kiss on her light brown hair, which she had tied back in a cute ponytail.

They walked hand in hand and chatted excitedly about travel, Amanda's café and how they couldn't wait to hear San Francisco Beat's new album, all while Louisa tried not to poke anyone in the eye with the small tree she was holding and its swinging balls of cheese.

Walking with the flow of the crowd up to the church, Louisa's phone rang out from the depths of her maroon tailored coat. 'Argh,' she called out as she fumbled with her olive branches, getting them tied up in her hair. Her heart rate went from a gentle pace to Formula-1 speed as one of the branches slipped through her fingers, cheese hitting the ground by her feet as she searched manically for her phone. Luca ushered her towards the low wall, so she did not get trampled by fellow pedestrians, put his branches, laden with mini salami and chocolate eggs, and confetti down, and started to untangle the olive branches from her hair.

Hunched over, with Luca's hands in her hair and one arm still holding onto a bunch of olive branches, she finally clasped her hand around her phone and yanked it from her pocket with a gasp of anxious breath. Swiping it to answer without even looking she put on her poshest voice.

'Hello, Louisa speaking.'

'Hey Lou.' The silvery voice sounded familiar. Louisa dared a glance at her screen, moving it away from her ear as Luca freed the last olive branch from her hair.

'Jesus Christ, Levi … I am so sorry,' Louisa yelled, staggering back against the wall then registering the disapproving glares from the churchgoers. She winced, quickly looking at Luca, hoping she hadn't offended him. To her relief, he was chuckling. She apologized a few more times, bowing her head as she did so, her hand on her chest, calming her heart rate. 'Sorry, Levi. I thought you were someone from the showcase. I'm waiting for a call,' she stammered. 'Is everything okay?'

'No worries, Lou Lou. I won't keep you long, but I wanted to ask you a favour,' Levi said, his voice quiet with a hint of desperation that concerned Louisa.

'Sure. What do you need?' she replied, brows drawn together with nervous anticipation.

'I had something special planned for Bri, but if I'm honest, since joining this new label things have been off.' His voice was low and shaky. Louisa could see him threading a hand through his hair, something she'd witnessed Levi do on occasion over the years, usually when he was out of his laidback comfort zone. 'I'm not sure I should go ahead with it. She can't even stand next to me when we're out in public these days.'

Louisa scrunched up her nose and chewed on her bottom lip. It didn't seem like a very Sabrina thing to do; Sabrina adored Levi, Louisa knew that much. She had a feeling this was all to do with her banning the boys from the café like Amanda had told her, though Louisa had only thought that to be a first week jitters kind of default rule. She hadn't believed Sabrina would still be enforcing it nearly a month later.

Louisa played with her ponytail, giving her bobble a wiggle to loosen the tightness she felt at the back of her neck, trying to avoid a headache that would no doubt creep up on her should she not help resolve this. 'Have you tried talking to her Levi? Has Amanda spoken up?' Louisa crouched, hovering over the low wall, resting her thighs against it.

'I've tried, but it made things worse. She got upset that I didn't trust her direction and spoke to me like we were in some sort of business meeting. It was all about the image of the band and how it would help our profile. I support her one hundred per cent Lou, I think she's amazing. I appreciate her knowledge and don't want to undermine her professionalism, but it was like some sort of spiel straight from the publicist's email. I don't believe for a second it's what she believes in. I know she visited with Amanda yesterday, but they haven't seen much of each other lately and last night she was, what's that word you use? Frazzled? She kept muttering something about figuring it all out, that she had something to do. I hate seeing her so worked up.'

'Hmm,' Louisa pondered, swishing her ponytail left to right and clicking her Converse together for a sign of inspiration for how to fix this. 'It's balance, Levi. She wants to do right by the company and prioritize you guys as a band first, which in all fairness is her job. It might be a big ask, but if you can figure out a way to make her see that record sales won't drop and fans don't care if you're dating and show the label that you're a solid team both in work and out, then I think you might stand a chance. So, in other words, Levi, this album needs to be undeniably kickass, in every way,' Louisa said, with a laugh to soften the laundry list of tasks she had just given him.

'Now, that I believe I can do,' Levi replied, with a laugh of his own and a dash of his usual charm back in his tone. 'She's so sweet Lou. She's had her head buried in papers since last night, pushing me away, telling me she needs to fix it. I don't want her to think she has to do it on her own. I'm worried I got too angry with her and now she thinks I don't care.'

'I'm sure she knows you care Levi. Try not to worry. When she wants to figure something out, sometimes you just have to let her. And Amanda?' Louisa asked, standing up and stretching her legs. She squeezed Luca's bicep to signal she wouldn't be long. She didn't want to rush Levi –it had been a while since she had spoken with the boys and she wanted to make sure he was okay before bidding him goodbye.

'I haven't seen much of her, I'm ashamed to admit, it's been pretty difficult with this whole ban in place. I spoke to her on the phone last night and apart from sounding exhausted everything sounds awesome at the café; you'll love the place when you see it, Lou. Her and Bri haven't been talking much. You girls know how to work hard; they've both been crazy busy, but Amanda seemed in a better mood after they spoke yesterday. She told me the same as you, just to let Bri figure this one out. Speaking of being busy, I have another favour to ask. Don't feel pressure, but do you think you could make it home for Easter? I know you're super busy with work there but if you could make it, that would be amazing. We're doing a small gig over Easter weekend and I think you're right, I have to show Bri that we can have the best of both worlds and I think my plan might solve that.' Louisa couldn't remember if she'd ever heard Levi talk so fast before. And he was not done. 'Flights are covered, I can send you all the details if you think you can make it. I have flights for Luca, Nanna and your zias too, if you say yes.'

Louisa stopped pacing and stood gob-smacked against the low wall. She didn't know what to say. Levi had organized flights for her whole family and Luca too. He wanted them all to be in Manchester for Easter. Her eyes grew wide. What was going on? Oh no, what was she right about? What had she just encouraged him to do?

'Erm. Levi. That sounds pretty fantastic. Erm, I'd have to speak with Luca and Nanna and everyone. Easter is a pretty big deal over here and it might depend on if I win this showcase and I have a bunch of dresses to alter. But yeah, I can see what I can do,' she said, shrugging at Luca, whose sparkling blue eyes were looking at her intrigued.

'Great. If you can let me know as soon as you can. I mean no rush, but the sooner the better,' Levi said, his tone spritelier and more Levi-like than at the beginning of their conversation.

'I will do. And Levi, is everything alright?' Louisa asked, pushing a strand of hair that the breeze had blown in her eye out of her face.

'Yes, everything is fine. Sorry to burden you. You're right, I need to give Bri space and be more understanding, she's only been trying to do her job. Oh, and Lou?'

'Yes?' Louisa stopped leaning and stood up straight again, waiting for Levi's next words.

'Can you not tell Sabrina or Amanda? It's no big deal, but yeah, erm, don't tell them you're coming, if you can come. I hope you can come.'

'Oh, yes, of course. Don't tell Amanda and Sabrina. Okay, got it,' Louisa said as Luca looked at her quizzical expression and mouthed, 'What?' To which she replied with a shrug.

'Okay, thanks. Talk soon then. Give that Italian stud our love,' Levi said, back to his playful self, before hanging up.

Louisa dropped her phone in her pocket as she briefed Luca on what Levi had asked of them. His face lit up at the idea of going to Manchester, but he did his best to act nonchalant as Louisa went through all the pros and cons of taking a trip at such short notice. She would soon be finding out about the showcase and to prepare for a magazine spread would take time. Then again, if she went home, she could celebrate her win with her family. Not to mention the workload she had at the shop with the stack of dresses she had to alter. She shook her head, aware she was rambling to Luca and she didn't even know if she had won the showcase yet. This trip would mean she could finally see *Torta per Tutti* in person and see all Amanda's hard work and it would be lovely to surprise her family. And, best of all, Luca could live out one of his dreams and travel with her, which was very kind of Levi to do. And Levi – Levi was planning something special that it didn't sound like she could miss.

Louisa took a deep breath, reeling in all her positives and negatives. She unloaded Luca of her olive branches, really one olive branch would have probably been sufficient but Nanna and her zias had given her practically half the tree.

'It sounds nice; we celebrate together, *ma* if you think not, you have work, we don't go, if you think we go, maybe we go,' Luca said, a smile on his lips and a twinkle in his eye. He was ever the sweetheart and a voice of reason in her undecisive mind. Louisa's heart skipped as she took him in. Getting to take Luca to her home would be rather special. Whatever it was Levi was planning had sounded important. Did she really have to miss another family event? It was part of the reality of her decision to stay in Italy, she knew she shouldn't be mad about it – but all the family hadn't been together since New Year over three months ago, and Louisa had never been away from home this long either, so it would certainly be wonderful, if she could make it happen. Levi's words took precedent in her mind, sending a few drops of adrenaline pumping through her veins; her sisters had been fighting, her family needed her and maybe she could make her sisters focus on all the incredible opportunities and dreams they were living out, what with Amanda and the café, Sabrina and the new record deal and her with the fashion showcase and a steady workload. Amazing things were happening; there was no need for bickering.

Louisa had more of a pep in her step by the time they stepped into the square, where they were met with a magnificent site. Everywhere she turned there were olive branches baring colourful chocolate eggs, bright red rosanna sweets, mini *carciocavallo* and salami, as well as bouquets of confetti, so elegant, so pretty, decorated with pot flowers, feathers, baby pinks, yellow daisies, and baby blue birds. The priest in his gold, white, and red robes made his way out of the church and the crowd immediately began to follow his footsteps down the path to a large clearing overlooking the sea, where he would say a prayer and bless the palms and confetti. Louisa had a new wave of energy built on a mixture of happy adrenaline at the thought of going home, nerves over all she had to do at the shop, her need to help her family and the beautiful blessings the priest was showering them with. There were a few disconcerted looks in her direction after the priest rained water down on them and Louisa jumped, sending two cheeses pinging off her branches and rolling across the ground, when she realized it was her phone disturbing the peace.

She sent another apologetic look Luca's way to find his blues eyes crinkled with humour. She smiled hesitantly, pulling out her phone while bending down to collect the cheese. As she did so, Luca shook his head and ushered her away to concentrate on her call while he collected the scattered produce. She blew him a kiss, took a deep breath and answered her phone.

'Louisa speaking,' she said as she tucked herself away behind the corner shop. Her stomach gurgled with nervous anticipation and she paced past the window's Easter display. Italian Easter eggs were truly something else.

'*Ciao* Louisa. I ring to say thank you for presenting your designs at our showcase. For a fresh designer we see you show potential. *Ma*, your work is very new and needs some refining. We wish it to represent you. To truly show your flair, your style. We hope that you will return to us next year for another chance at our magazine editorial, when you have more experience.' Louisa's throat felt constricted and tears instantly puddled in her eyes. She held up a hand to shield herself from the sun and cover her tears in case Luca was looking. Moments ago, she had felt untouchable – helping Levi, the idea that she would see her family again soon – but now she felt like the air had been let out of her lungs. She had failed. She hadn't won.

'Thank you. *Grazie*. I appreciate your time and I would love to come back next year. Thank you,' Louisa choked out as confidently as she could muster. She was grateful and she had appreciated the opportunity. But she had failed. She had missed Amanda's grand opening and had nothing to show for it.

'*Grazie signora. Ciao*,' the lady quipped before disconnecting. As quick as a flash Louisa's heart had gone from happy to devastated. She swiped the tears from her eyes as she watched the water spout from the hand of the Virgin Mary and run into the basin at the bottom of a small fountain hiding in the wall. She homed in on the calm sound of the running water before it made a small splashing noise as it hit the pool. She thought of the fountain at her zia's house – the one with the brightly-coloured crystals that her mum had decorated it with when she was a child, and she willed herself some strength. What was she going to tell her sisters? What was she going to say to her mum and dad? She had been given this great opportunity from Giulia and she had let her down. Oh, how was she going to tell Giulia? She curled a loose strand of hair around her fingers and bit her lip. She had to turn around now, stand up straight and face Luca and the bustling crowd.

'*Amore*, everything is okay?' Luca called out as she neared him and the congregation, all of whom were now chatting and making their way back to the church in procession, olive branches aloft. She couldn't keep him waiting, weighed down with olive branches and cheese. 'Eh, *mamma mia*, what can I do?' Louisa muttered one of her grandpa's favourite sayings to herself. 'We did try, right Grandpa?' She patted down her wet face and pulled her ponytail a little tighter like she was encouraging herself to pull herself together, before she was close enough to Luca to tell him her news.

'I didn't get it.' Her voice betrayed her and came out in a wobble. This time it was Luca's turn to drop the contents piled high on his forearms, to wrap her in a warm hug. She wrapped her arms around his waist and rested her head against his firm frame. A few minutes passed before Luca placed a hand on the back of her head and spoke. '*Amore*, I am proud of you. You do not have to win to be a success. You did it.' Louisa sniffled. His positivity spoke volumes to her. If Luca believed in her after only knowing her a short time, surely she could believe in herself? He knew of her weaknesses and when she was selling herself short, and also when she made excuses out of fear, yet none of that mattered; just like Giulia he didn't allow her to bring light to her excuses or remain down for long, he simply believed in her. Now, she just had to work her butt off for next year.

She stepped back, instantly feeling colder away from the heat of Luca's body. 'Thank you. I just wanted so badly to do it for everyone,' Louisa said, her voice still wavering.

'I know, *ma* you do it for you and we all are proud,' Luca replied, brushing a hand over her cheek as she squinted up at him in the sunlight. She tip-toed up to him to kiss his cheek. *So, no magazine editorial*, she told herself in her head, *but you helped Levi today and your sisters are still successful, life is still good*. Her stomach was in knots. Louisa breathed in Luca's vanilla scent, trying to loosen the uncomfortable tightness the knots were causing. It was simply a minor setback. Now she had experienced the runway, she knew where her purpose lay. She would do it again.

'Let's not tell anyone how many times this cheese has touched the dirty floor,' she whispered into Luca's ear making him laugh. That laugh was certainly climbing the ranks of things that made her heart happy. It was closing in on her Grandpa's pizza. 'Thank you, Luca,' she added, before planting her heels back on the ground and bending down to retrieve their goodies off the floor and round up the runaway cheeses.

'*Va bene*,' Luca said as he joined her. He was doing a better job of juggling the olive branches and palms in his hands than she was of not smacking herself in the face with salami while coordinating holding loose cheeses and confetti. '*Amore*,' he chuckled as he helped her to get a better grip of her things while sneakily taking the cheese from her and adding it to his pile. Once upright and stable, they headed back through the markets and crowds towards their bikes. Somehow the Italian people shouting, children in smart waistcoats and gorgeous dresses giggling and chasing each other around the square, the purr of vespas buzzing along the cobbles and in and out of market stalls dropping off more fresh produce and the tantalizing smells of *pizza fritta* floating along the breeze, eased Louisa's disappointment in herself and the heartbreak over not winning. She still had *la dolce vita* and a thought occurred to her that made her squeal with glee.

With not having any immediate appointments on her calendar

besides the beautiful dresses she needed to finish before Easter, her thoughts drifted back to her phone call with Levi. She wondered if Giulia would mind her taking a small trip and if she could finish the dresses in time.

'Luca, what would you say to taking a little trip to England?' she asked, a genuine smile creeping onto her face. She might not get to raise her glass to celebrate her own success, but Louisa had a feeling there would be plenty to toast.

Chapter 18

Pastiera

Ingredients:

For the pastry:

Eggs (1 or 2 – depends on how many pastiera you are making)
Flour
Butter
Sugar
Vanilla
For the filling:
Ricotta (tubs or cups?)
Barley
Candied peel
Eggs
Vanilla
Sambuca (and lots of it)

What to do:

Wing it! Follow your heart and do what Grandpa did. (Very informative Amanda. Need to note down recipe properly if you use for blog.)

Scattered across the kitchen island lay multiple trays of pastry that would soon become *pastiera*, one of Amanda's favourite recipes to make with her grandpa and an Italian Easter tradition.

A tradition that Amanda and Grandpa had done together since Amanda was teeny tiny and he would let her pour in the amount of sambuca she felt necessary. Grandpa would always get a kick out of the bottle being too heavy for Amanda to hold, meaning sambuca would stream out of it before he stepped in to save the day. She could still hear Grandpa chuckling and shouting, 'That should do it!' She never told him the bottle wasn't heavy, she just loved the smell of the sambuca and Nanna had secretly told her, 'The more the merrier'.

Amanda smiled at the memory as it wrapped a hug around her heart. It was their first Easter without him, her first Easter in *Torta per Tutti* and she wanted to make him proud. After her initial breakdown moments before opening her café over a month ago, Amanda had managed to keep her tears at bay. The more she baked for her customers, the more mouths she fed and the more hours she spent in her kitchen, the closer she felt to Grandpa. And with the *pastiera* laid out before her, she felt especially close to him today and wanted to get them just right.

When the egg whites formed perfect peaks, she would add them to her ricotta, barley, candied peel, sambuca and egg yolk mix, scoop thick ladles full into each one of her pastry shells, before latticing strips of pastry over the top. They would then go in the oven until golden brown and cinnamon danced in the airwaves.

'How are the eggs looking Lauren?' Amanda asked over the noise of her handheld whisk. Though her stand mixer was better suited for the rush of the café Amanda wanted to take her time with the *pastiera* and make it exactly how she made it with Grandpa.

'They're beautiful. How many more are you needing?' Amanda glanced over to Lauren's station where an array of multi-coloured eggs rested on a table cloth to dry, her eyes doing a quick count.

'You can go ahead and dye a couple more and we should be good. Thank you,' she said, excitement in her tone.

'Can do,' Lauren replied merrily. The Easter menu had been a hit with the customers so far. Luca and his family at Alfonso's had all been stars and worked closely with Amanda to aid her in importing the best produce Italy had to offer for her café, and she was still stocked up with the surprise parcel of salamis and cheeses Louisa had sent to her on opening day, but now the counter and windows were piled high with Colomba and Baci and Kinder Easter eggs. The café looked positively Italian and Amanda couldn't have felt prouder.

Torta per Tutti was settling into a nice groove where Amanda knew the regulars, the coffee lovers, the cake connoisseurs and the Italiophiles, who she could always count on to Instagram and spread the word about her place being the only place in Manchester to serve the freshest, most exquisite, authentic Italian food. She appreciated their love greatly, especially considering that the main media had chosen to focus on calling the place out for its attention-grabbing media scheme of riding *San Francisco Beat's* coat tails and using them to draw people in. Amanda had had her fair share of noses turned down at her from the other local restaurateurs and acclaimed restaurant reviewers. She had heard the rumours that had been circling; most of them to do with Liam coming in and out of the café, (would magazines ever tire of creating drama between couples? They now had a poll on pitting rockstars against electricians.) pictures of Dan with any woman he remotely got within a metre of, and of course Dan arguing with women in the street. (There had indeed been eyes everywhere when Dan had visited the café that night and the media had twisted their discussion in the street to make it look worse than it had been.) She'd had to laugh. Amanda couldn't lie and pretend it didn't hurt. It did but speaking with Sabrina yesterday and getting her thoughts off her chest had felt good. She'd seen that the media had been getting to Levi and Sabrina's relationship and that Sabrina had been letting it control her decisions with the boys, causing it to have a negative effect on not only her own relationship with Dan but Levi and Sabrina's too. Amanda had finally come clean and expressed her concerns to Sabrina that the media would always say and do what it wanted and people would always think of them what they would, but they could not let it control how they lived their lives. She just hoped that Sabrina would put her foot down with this and speak with City Heights Records so that Dan could come visit her at work and see all the Easter goodness she had put together. She wasn't exactly angry with Sabrina anymore, but she hoped that it wouldn't take her sister long to get things sorted. Easter was one of her favourite times of year; she wanted Dan around so that whatever was bothering him with Liam would be put to rest and they could enjoy some family time.

Glossy white peaks formed before her, whisking her back to reality. This was her café, her pride and joy, she would not let the paparazzi or rumours knock her spirits and take her focus away from it. While she might not be certain of her and Dan's relationship status or why he had become distant lately, she was ridiculously certain of every baked good that made its way onto her customers' plates.

Spring time always brought with it a surge of inspiration, due to this being her favourite time of year for Italian baking, and she couldn't wait to share the *pastiera* and *casatiello* with her customers; especially the customers who had been dropping hints for weeks about the out-of-this-world Italian Easter desserts that they hadn't had in years since they visited Italy.

Just looking at the *pastiera* made Amanda's heart soar. After combining the egg whites with her barley mix, scooping the mixture into the pastry shells and latticing the tops, Amanda pulled the olive and rosemary focaccia from the oven, replacing them with the *pastiera*. It would take well into the evening, and both convection ovens, to cook them all, but she had enough goods in the counter to see to it that the late afternoon customers would be fed.

171

Content that Lauren was more than capable of dying eggs without her and that the kitchen was relatively tidy, bar her small mess at her station from whipping up the *pastiera*, Amanda sliced up the focaccia and headed out into the café. Behind the counter and coffee bar, Kate and Francesca were cheerily serving customers and there was a warm buzz in the air.

'I was thinking about putting up your recipe for *casatiello* on your blog this Friday, so your readers can prepare it for Easter,' Francesca piped up, after the two women she was serving walked away with a plate of *struffoli* and a Nutella cupcake.

'Sounds good – it gives them chance to get their ingredients but is simple enough that they can make it Easter morning too. Perfect Francesca, thank you,' Amanda said with a grateful grin. Francesca, it turned out, was a dab hand at technology and an avid blog reader, Amanda's being one of her favourites. With Amanda having very little time to spend on her blog these days Francesca had taken over and transformed the café's Instagram, snapping gorgeous shots of her food and the rustic Italian vibe of *Torta per Tutti*. She had posted a recipe earlier this week on the blog and had talked with Amanda about sharing them twice a week. She had also replied to comments on the 'before and after' café post Amanda had done, that had gained a lot of views. Francesca was creating the vision Amanda had had for herself regarding her community and keeping people connected, and Amanda adored her for it.

Francesca always made sure to run things by Amanda first, to triple check which recipes Amanda was happy to share, but Amanda trusted her judgement. She was grateful to take a backseat if it meant she could focus on the baking and avoid the headlines for a little while and not have to be the butt of social media jokes between her sisters and Nikki, who got on with Sabrina and Louisa like a house on fire when it came to taking the mick out of Amanda. Those four-way Skype calls had always been a blast for Amanda. Of course, avoiding online headlines was one thing, but journalists and reviewers were everywhere.

'Sweetheart, why do you suddenly look as pale as a sheet?' Francesca asked, concern etched on her pretty face.

Amanda watched the man's movement's carefully as he surveyed the fully decorated and clean café. Had she made a mistake last time when she kicked him out? Was he actually in cahoots with Jeff or was this man really a bigwig health inspector or secret reviewer ready to take her down? She gulped. Fake news over Dan's latest fling or Liam being her boyfriend she could handle; health inspectors and restaurant reviewers live and in person she only hoped she could cope with. She sent up a prayer to her grandpa to have her back on this one as her palms grew sweaty.

'Apparently, that man there,' she pointed in Tom's direction, 'is a health inspector or maybe a reviewer, though a real one of either, I'm not quite sure. I thought it was just Jeff trying to scare me a few weeks ago and so I was a bit abrupt and maybe just a teeny bit sarcastic to him.' Kate choked on a laugh. 'You, sarcastic? Never,' she said through gritted teeth as she smiled at the customer she was serving before turning to Amanda and Francesca. Francesca gently shoved her saying, 'Shh.' Amanda smiled and shrugged; her sisters would be high-fiving Kate for that one. Tom was now inspecting an empty table, moving the napkin holder and examining the menu. Amanda groaned, not knowing what to do. She had to get back into the kitchen to warn Lauren and tidy up without drawing attention to herself.

'Hon, you go. I'll distract him,' Francesca said, gently pushing Amanda's arm towards the kitchen door. Amanda nodded and opened the door as gently as she could manage while Tom was distracted by the picture of the Amalfi Coast Amanda had taken from her zia's balcony in Orzoro. The picture was mesmerizing. It had been evening, the water glistened under the moon's pearl glow, the only light coming from kitchen windows and the odd streetlight. It was like a smattering of fireflies glowing across the mountains.

'Kate, would you like to take this man's order?' Amanda heard Francesca say, as she busied herself with clearing away the odd pots and bowls she had left in the sink and filling in Lauren who was frosting the last batch of lemon cupcakes for the afternoon. The *pastieria* in the oven were keeping the kitchen nice and toasty and smelling rich with vanilla cinnamon and the lemon added a touch of freshness to the mix. Amanda inhaled deeply to calm her nerves.

There seemed to be some commotion followed by a clatter out in the café. Amanda heard a screech of a chair and, 'No, no ladies. I am not here to indulge. I'm here purely for business.' Tom was apparently protesting Francesca and Kate's Operation Distract. Just then a light bulb pinged above Amanda's head and she thanked Grandpa up above for sending her Francesca. She nodded at Grandpa, who she knew was somewhere in the kitchen alongside her (she always felt his presence) and followed Francesca's lead.

Amanda held her head high and walked through the double doors into the café. There she was greeted by Kate who had a smile plastered across her face and was stood towering over Tom, who they had managed to get sat down at a table. Kate was going through every cake on offer, explaining to Tom which part of Italy they originated from and which were Amanda's grandpa's favourites. Francesca sat beside Tom at the table they had enforced he sat at and was nodding along to the menu, occasionally inputting how authentic the pastries were and how her own Italian grandpa craved them each day, telling him that they gave him a taste of the home he missed.

Amanda's heart flared with love for the two women before her. She pinched her cheeks to give them some colour, so she didn't look too drained from the 4 a.m. starts and carried the tray she had prepared over to them.

'Tom, how lovely to see you again.' She did her utmost not to sound sarcastic, but it was a struggle – her body felt tense and her toes were curled up in her pumps. She caught Kate smirk and painfully controlled an eyeroll.

'I would love if you got to experience *Torta per Tutti* properly this time. Here you have a *sfogliatella*, that Kate here was just telling you about. It's my nanna's favourite and was made fresh in the extremely early hours of this morning. Actually, everything before you, the *cannolo* and olive bread, have all been baked fresh this morning. I have a pastry chef, Lauren, working alongside me, who is incredible. Please dig in and I will fetch you a coffee.' Amanda didn't wait for a reply; she had faith that he wouldn't be able to resist the plate she had placed in front of him, not least because Kate and Francesca were staring at him expectantly.

By the time she made her way back with a tiny cup of espresso (she used the good ceramic cups, the ones Louisa had sent as a surprise gift in her opening day parcel), Tom had bitten into everything on the plate. 'Here you go, the finest Kimbo coffee all the way from Italia.' Amanda said, loosening up a little as the aroma hit her nostrils. Amanda could have sworn Tom's lips curved up at her as he took the tiny cup.

He wasn't exactly mean-looking and he didn't resemble a weasel like Jeff, but smiling definitely helped his greased back hair, sharp jawline and beady eyes look less menacing. He took a sip of coffee and Amanda stepped back, not wanting to over-crowd him. She gently tapped Kate on the shoulder and nodded at Francesca for them to move away, in hopes that Tom would finish what he had started to eat. She would let the food speak for itself, just like Grandpa would have advised her.

At that moment, a straggle of women came in, gasping as their eyes took in the photographs on the wall. Kate stepped up to the register to welcome them and Francesca said hello's and began chatting to them about what they should try. *Don't think of Tom as an intimidating reviewer or inspector, treat him like you would anyone else who walks through that door*, Amanda told herself as she watched the ladies, excitement in her bones as they spoke highly of the décor and of the mouthwatering smells.

Her toes uncurled, her stomach untangled, and her heart slowed back to its steady pace. Tom was human just like the rest of them.

For the rest of the afternoon Amanda wanted to fill the café with nothing but love and positive thoughts. She would be sure to make them feel like family, as Grandpa would have done, and give them the full Italian experience. She would walk around and offer everyone a piece of the freshly baked Italian focaccia and make sure their coffees were topped up. She would let her guard down just for an hour or two about business and worrying over what Tom might say in some prestigious magazine or online publication. All she could do in this moment was be herself and if Tom didn't like it, then that would be okay because she did. Words, she noted to herself, that she could do well with telling Sabrina too.

Amanda picked up the tray of focaccia and a few biscotti and wandered around the café, stopping by each table and offering every person a slice. She engaged with the customers, finding out what they were enjoying from her menu, and learning about holidays they had been on to Italy and how they found out about her. She made mental notes of any tweaks to the menu or requests her customers had; her spirits were lifted with joy that this was what *Torta per Tutti* was all about.

As Amanda came upon Tom's table, she watched him take his napkin off his knee and gently wipe his mouth before placing it on the table next to his empty plate. There was no mistaking the smile on his face. She took a soft step to the side of his table, so as not to frighten him, and offered the plate of focaccia.

'I couldn't possibly,' he said with a shake of his head and a wave of his hand. The smile had been replaced by a thin line upon seeing her. Amanda forced hers to stay in place. 'I'm terribly

176

full,' he added. Amanda wasn't sure if it was a good full, a content full, or the food was marvelous kind of full, and no matter her confident pep talk from mere moments ago, she daren't ask.

'That's no problem at all. I will wrap a piece up for you to take home. I can't possibly let you leave without trying some,' she said, a surge of joy coursing through her knowing that Grandpa would do the same thing. She meandered around the counter, wrapped up two thick slices of focaccia and placed the parcel on Tom's table, smiling genuinely. His face remained stoic.

'Thank you so much for coming Tom, I truly hoped you enjoyed the food,' she said, without an ounce of sarcasm. She did hope he forgave her for their last encounter and that the food today had made up for it. He nodded. Amanda did the same. Tom's lips didn't budge from the thin line and he made no attempt to engage in conversation. Amanda couldn't help the sadness that settled in her stomach at the thought of him not having enjoyed her food or the atmosphere. She marveled at how in a room full of laughter, chatter and empty plates, that she would hold this one man's opinion above the rest; at how negative reviews always seemed to override the positive. But, no, she couldn't do that, where was that thick skin of hers? And what had Dan told her back in January after they had purchased the café and the nerves had set in?

'Baby, you are not to let what happened at Rusk, with Jeff, or rumours, or the idea of any negative review seep into that wonderful mind of yours. You created your recipes and built the idea for *Torta per Tutti* from that beautiful mind. Do not allow negativity into your space – just look at all it is capable of when it is filled with love. The right customers will gravitate to you, they will find you. You cannot change based on a bad review or because of the need to please everyone. If you let it change who you are and how you do things, you are giving up your authenticity. The world needs what you have to offer.'

Dan had been right, of course. Reviews would always be there, good or bad, but what mattered the most was staying true to herself and delivering the best food possible to those who walked through the door. Amanda knew that deep down she had it in her to fill *Torta per Tutti* with warmth, heart and irresistible food and in turn see it succeed for the long haul. She couldn't dwell on her fears of Jeff sabotaging her again or the San Francisco Beat media fiasco that called her café a phony – the people that understood what *Torta per Tutti* was all about would find her and make it their home.

Thinking of Dan, her chest tightened. She missed him and hoped that things would get back to normal soon. The café was brimming with people and the counter nearly empty. She excused herself from Tom with a smile and went to check on her *pastiera*. Before she walked through the double doors, she couldn't help glance back at Tom with curiosity; anxious to see if he picked up the wrapped focaccia. He did. Amanda hummed a satisfied hum as she pushed open the kitchen door.

The smell of *pastiera* caused a wave of delight to wash over her. She picked her phone out of the bowl she had reserved for knick-knacks – to keep her kitchen tidy and the worktops free of electronics, pens and bits of paper – and exhaled the tension that had been building between her and Dan and his more recent reservations when speaking to her. With the whirlwind that was flour, eggs and butter from the moment she woke up in the morning, maybe she hadn't been the best at putting Dan's mind at ease when it came to his jealousy over her relationship with Liam. Amanda hadn't meant to frighten him, but Dan questioning her loyalty to him was something she hadn't been prepared for and it seemed to have come out of nowhere. Dan oozed confidence with the ladies, which wasn't something Amanda had gauged from the media, but through the man she had gotten to know over the years and been witness to when with him and the boys in San Francisco. It came from the late-night phone calls discussing dates and girlfriends and his manner always being so chilled and laidback when recalling such events with her. Whatever skeletons had gotten to him now, maybe she needed to do her part in helping to diminish them like he so often did for her insecurities.

'I love you. Hope you're having a rad session today. XX' she texted with a smile.

'The *casatiello* is prepped for tomorrow and I've put the eggs in the fridge to keep until we need them. The Easter menu is looking fab,' Lauren said, snapping Amanda's eyes away from her phone.

'You're a star, thank you Lauren. You can head out now if you'd like. I'll see to the *pastiera* and cleaning up the last of my mess.' Amanda chuckled, glancing at her work station that was still dusted with flour and scraps of paper she had been noting down recipe changes on, next to her book of her nanna and grandpa's recipes that was bulging with similar torn pieces of paper. So much for keeping paper to the bowl on the counter, she thought. 'And help yourself to a coffee and anything you'd like before you go.'

Lauren discarded her apron, washed her hands and thanked Amanda before exiting the kitchen just as Amanda's phone beeped.

Amanda spun around and grabbed it from the bowl. If her sisters had been in the kitchen with her now, they would have wondered if aliens had altered her brain seeing her spin so giddily. It was true that Dan had the ability to make her walls crumble and give butterflies the right to permanent residency in her stomach and possibly her brain.

'Hey. Is Dan with you? If he's sat eating sambuca biscotti before work, I will be very disappointed … only if he doesn't bring us all some. It's been a long day. PS. Working on lifting the ban so please tell him to have patience with me and keep on the downlow. XXXX'

The butterflies in Amanda's stomach went into a mad, fluttering frenzy as Amanda read Sabrina's text. If Dan wasn't at the studio, where could he be? Had she been too late in putting his worries to rest? Had she not taken his insecurities seriously when he had done nothing but dote on her and support her when dealing with her own in the past? Had she been so focused at the café, harping on about all Liam's help, unaware that Dan was battling with problems in his head? Were her and Dan better off as just friends? After all, had she just proven to be a terrible girlfriend? If these thoughts weren't occupying her mind she might have just laughed at that fact Sabrina just said, 'Keep on the downlow'.

The kitchen door swung open, making Amanda jump. 'I'm going to lock up out here, boss. You need any help back here?' Kate asked.

Amanda cleared her throat as the oven chimed, momentarily making her forget her worries. *Pastiera* she could focus on. *Pastiera* wasn't complicated. *Pastiera* she was good at. 'No, I'm all good back here. Thanks Kate,' she said, grabbing her lemon-printed oven gloves and getting lost in the fragrant aroma of barley and cinnamon, as she began taking the golden-brown pans of deliciousness out of the oven. She had no doubt Dan would turn up at the studio soon. It was not like him to be late. And Amanda was sure he would have a good reason.

Chapter 19

Nanna's Baci Cookies

Ingredients:

½ cup slithered hazelnuts
1 cup of roughly chopped Perugina milk chocolate
1 cup of sugar
2 cups of flour
1 cup of melted butter
1 egg
Pinch of salt
1 tsp baking powder
Drop of vanilla

What to do:

Mix together the sugar and butter in a mixing bowl.
Then add the remaining ingredients and combine.
Roll small chunks of the dough into balls and place on baking tray.
Flatten with palm slightly and bake at 160 degrees for
10–15 mins, until golden.

'What are the two of them doing? They are late again, and this makes Dan late for the third time this week,' Sabrina said, exasperated, as she stood in the sound booth with Dylan and James, away from Keira and Jack. 'What's going on with Dan? He is never late and now Levi too. Well, okay, so that's a tad more believable, but ten to fifteen minutes, not an hour.' Dylan and James were not soothing her frustration by looking from each other to her and shrugging.

'They'll be here soon, no worries boss,' James said, attempting to reach out and stroke her forearm, but Sabrina was pacing too quickly for him to connect, so he simply wobbled precariously against the stool he was leaning on. Sabrina was baffled by their collected demeanours – Dylan's even more so than James. James and Levi were as thick as thieves, the two most likely to be getting up to trouble. Dylan was more on Dan's wavelength and did not care for tardiness. Why was he cutting him so much slack? This should be bothering him, why wasn't it bothering him? Sabrina stared at Dylan with narrowed eyes, trying to study his face for hints and intimidate him. He simply stared back, a smirk playing at the side of his mouth, his fierce, bright hazel eyes not wandering from hers and very aware of what she was doing.

Sabrina huffed when Dylan didn't offer up any information on their whereabouts.

'Did we say six tonight, boss? Maybe we scheduled for seven-thirty?' James queried, his hand propped up under his jawline, his dark eyes squinting playfully. But she was not in the mood for games, not tonight, not when she had a Skype meeting scheduled in an hour with Keira and their publicist to talk about San Francisco Beat's image, which was causing her anxiety to already be through the roof.

'Do some work, you two,' Sabrina started, shaking her head at James and withholding a smile that proved slightly challenging when you had two ridiculously good-looking rock stars in front of you who were trying to turn on the charm with just their facial expressions. Sexy smirks be damned. 'Maybe warm up your vocal chords and practice a few beats on the drums, in case I have to fire your best buddies.'

'Anything for you, boss,' James called after her, unphased by her order, as she marched out of the record booth and plastered on a smile for Jack.

'Sorry Jack, they're just caught up and should be here any minute. No need to worry,' Sabrina said airily, trying to convince herself.

'It's all good love. We've no rush,' Jack replied, while performing hand gestures through the glass to Dylan who picked up his bass and followed Jack's instructions.

Sabrina sat down to rifle through some of her notes for later and to check over responses for the upcoming gig she had initiated with the label. All involved had given her the go-ahead which meant she had been working around the clock with the labels, booking agents and events promoters to make it possible. But it was difficult to concentrate, and she felt uneasy with Dan and Levi's absence. After speaking with Amanda the other day, her relationship with Levi had begun to improve but she knew it would be better once she got this meeting out of the way so she could be less jittery. She had apologized for her behavior, and normalcy had crept back into their relationship with simple ease. She hadn't realized how tiring it had been building a wall whenever her natural instincts wanted to hug him or kiss his cheek. Of course, she was still a professional but those subtle gestures of togetherness – a graze of hands, a hand on the knee when sitting next to each other during a long day – reminded her of how much she and Levi were a team and why they worked so well together. It felt great to feel like her work and life balance was steadying out, or it would feel great if she didn't now want to strangle Levi for being late.

Stepping into the darkness of the corridor to get some air, away from the cramped recording studio, Sabrina heard voices coming from the tiny reception area. There was a weak ray of streetlamp light coming from the crack in the front door and though she knew other musicians sometimes stopped by, there was no one about; the receptionist had already left for the evening. The voices made her freeze.

'Who knew keeping a secret like this would be so difficult? How are you holding up with Amanda?' Levi's voice was soft and anxious. Sabrina's heart was pounding in her chest. What was Dan keeping from Amanda? She would kill him if he hurt her.

'Dude, can we not talk about it? It's all good. I will make it up to her.' There was no mistaking Dan's raspy voice. However, it contained a slightly troubled infliction, that contrasted with the smile he was giving Levi that Sabrina could just make out in the shadows.

'But how are things between you guys, dude? You've not been yourself lately. I know she's the one and you know she's the one. You're not like your dad and she's not either man. If you're bugging out, you gotta talk to me,' Levi said, a softness to his voice that was reserved for Dan and that Sabrina had only been privy to over the years if something was going on with Dan's family and Levi was concerned. It tugged at her heart strings how close these boys were – they weren't just best friends, they were brothers. But now her worrying brain sped up a mile a minute agonizing over what was bothering Dan, in addition to her mind repeating the words 'the one' and homing in on Levi mentioning a secret. Didn't people usually talk about 'the one' when referring to marriage? Was Dan going to propose to Amanda? Sabrina let out a small gasp of excitement, before clamping her hands over her mouth and squinting her eyes as if it would make her hear better in the dim lit corridor.

'God, I know.' Dan's gruff voice sent a spasm straight to Sabrina's heart, an air of vulnerability in it that didn't often accompany Dan. 'I'll figure it out man.' Sabrina could make out Dan stroking a hand over his chiseled jaw that this week bore a little stubble; seemingly representing Dan's more disheveled and unusually out of control vibe.

'Yeah? I need to meet this guy, Liam, who's got my boy shook up. Must be a real heartthrob,' Levi noted with a teasing inflection. It may have been dark, but Sabrina could see the cheeky glint in his eye and the cocky smile that Levi was no doubt wearing. Dan let out a laugh. 'And thanks man. I owe you,' Levi said, patting Dan on the shoulder, before Sabrina heard footsteps; they were heading her way.

'You don't owe me anything. You can just tell Dylan and James they're on their own when ...' Dan stopped abruptly when he noticed Sabrina fumbling with her phone trying to pretend she had only just entered the corridor and was too busy dealing with business to have even noticed them. Dan's eyes gave her a knowing look. Levi's on the other hand looked like they were about to pop out of his head. He at least looked sorry that they were late and that they might have possibly just been overheard. Dan remained as cool as a cucumber. Sabrina shook her head, waving her phone in the air. 'Busy, busy,' she muttered with a sigh, then remembered that she was supposed to be mad at them both for being late. If she was to keep up her charade that she hadn't heard a peep, she needed to snap back into manager mode and do her thing. Yet, Dan's eyes were still on her, which had the annoying effect of somehow calming the mixture of confusion, excitement, worry and anger, that had been bubbling up inside her for the past hour due to their tardiness and then now upon hearing their conversation. She didn't want to be calm, she uncharacteristically wanted to yell at them both for being way past unprofessionally late, or squeal with glee and beg them to impart whatever secret they were keeping from Amanda. She wanted in on proposal plans.

'I apologize for our delay. I had a family matter to address and got held up speaking with my mom. I hope you don't mind that I needed Levi to see to some things for me,' Dan said, his tone relaxed and matter of fact.

Sabrina's hands were on her hips, as she tapped her foot. She looked away from Levi who was nervously scratching the back of his neck and eyed Dan suspiciously. His dark eyes didn't blink; he held her gaze. Of course she cared about the wellbeing of

Dan's mum – Amanda raved about her – so she momentarily let her guard down, feeling slightly deflated that Dan had not just offered up information on his secret.

'Is everything okay? How is your mum?' she asked, hands still on her hips, her head tilted with yet another thing to add to her list of worries.

'She's wonderful, thank you,' Dan said, reaching out and placing a hand on Sabrina's forearm, his brown eyes boring into hers with warmth. 'Now, I'm sure that my boss is going to fire me should I not get my ass in that record studio this instance, so if you will excuse me.' He removed his hand from her forearm with a gentle squeeze and stepped past her. Sabrina's eyes followed him.

'Me too, and I'm rather fond of our boss, I'd hate for that to happen,' Levi said, making to follow Dan. Sabrina caught his arm, while still watching Dan. 'Not so fast,' she said. She watched Dan hesitate, not taking his next step. He seemed to contemplate something for a second before pushing open the studio door and continuing in.

Sabrina spun around, trying to ignore the flex in Levi's forearm as she gripped him tighter. *Don't you dare get distracted by his muscles* she told herself sternly. When she met his brown eyes, they were wide, his eyebrows drawn in, awaiting her words.

'Is Dan's mum really okay?' Sabrina asked, eyeing the door that Dan had just walked through, making shapes with her lips as she figured out how to question Levi without giving away that she had heard their conversation.

'Yes, she's fine babe. I'm sorry, we got caught up talking to her, that's all,' Levi replied, placing his hands on her shoulders and drawing her attention back to him.

'Is Dan okay? I know I haven't helped matters with the rules that I set recently. I promised Amanda no more ban and I will see to that today, but is Dan happy? Is he mad at me?' Sabrina said, aware that she was becoming more flustered as each word escaped her lips. Levi rubbed her shoulders.

'Bri, he's good. I promise. Nothing I can't help him with and yes, I think allowing him some freedom to be Dan and not some sought-after sex god twenty-four seven would be nice. He misses his girl and wants to pick her up from work without everyone and their brother giving him their views.' Sabrina cringed at how bad her judgement had been on banning the boys from the café.

'I'm sorry about that,' she started, placing her hands on Levi's hips and stepping closer to him. 'Amanda mentioned something about Liam the other day. She said there was tension in the air and Dan has never been jealous before; she was struggling with how to handle it and upset that Dan doesn't trust her now.'

Levi hesitated and dropped a kiss in her hair. 'I haven't got all the answers for that one right now baby. I do know that Dan never had anything to be jealous of before; he's never loved anyone more.'

With Levi's words, Sabrina squeezed him tight around the waist, understanding Dan's feelings. Ever since the day she and Levi had kissed on the balcony of San Francisco Beat's debut album launch party, a little over two years ago, she had loved him. She had loved him even when she had pushed him away. She had loved him even when he was dating other women and she was dating other guys trying to forget about him. She loved him when she watched him play the drums. She loved him when he wrapped his arms around her at night so he could fall asleep holding her. She loved him when he made her coffee just the way she liked it and the way he winked at her when she bossed him about or ran through the band schedule with him. She loved how he didn't take life too seriously and how that megawatt smile of his, the one that was very rarely void of mischief, always made her heart beat faster.

'Ahh, okay. But they're going to be good, right? He's not keeping secrets from her?' Sabrina spoke, her head tilted against Levi's chest. She knew she risked him learning she had overheard his conversation with Dan if she said too much, but she hoped she had said it in a way that sounded nonchalant. Everyone could tell that Dan hadn't been acting himself recently.

'I think they will be fine,' Levi replied, wrapping his strong arms around her neck so she could nuzzle on his biceps.

'How can you be so sure?' she asked quietly.

'Because Dan and I have been friends for over twenty-five years. There's nothing I wouldn't do for him and I'm not ashamed to admit that I love him. He's stuck with me and I'm stuck with him, for forever at this point. Amanda loves him something fierce and I know that Dan doesn't take that love lightly. He adores her, he respects her and loves her something terrible. You don't walk away from that kind of love, even when it gets tough, and he will do anything to make sense of his demons and not allow them to ruin what they have.' There was something about the way Levi took a step backwards to look at her, his brown eyes big, his hands on her shoulders, his knees bent slightly so he was at her eye level, that made her worries melt away. The fact was she did trust him; she trusted the man in front of her. There was a truth in his eyes that rendered Sabrina speechless. No words were forming in her brain, she simply stared at Levi with glassy eyes.

'Come here, I have a secret to tell you,' Levi added, pulling her into him. She shuffled her feet making him work for it, which he was game for, practically lifting her off the floor back to his embrace. 'I love you,' he whispered in her ear, his warm breath tickling her neck causing goose bumps to rise on her skin.

'I love you too,' she whispered automatically, putting her head against her favourite pillow – Levi's chest – her eyes closed, melting into him. 'But that's not a secret,' she added, with her own playful smirk.

'But it made you forgive my tardiness,' he whispered into her ear, then gently kissed her neck before she pushed him away, held open the door and gestured for him to get inside.

*

The orange and yellow flames danced around in her nanna and grandpa's fireplace, flashes of blue catching Sabrina's eyes, as she kicked off her slippers and flopped onto the couch. It was nearing 2.30 a.m., they had just wrapped up tonight's incredible studio session and everyone was spent. But the problem with the late-night sessions was that even though everyone was tired, it was often hard to fall straight to sleep due to adrenaline. Sabrina could still hear Dan's raspy vocals in her head. His husky tones and deep melodic sounds mixed with the words for what they had decided this evening would be their first single. The lyrics of 'All of You' were now ingrained in her mind. It was one of her favourites and she had no doubt it would be one of Amanda's too when she heard it.

A whistle and a hiss came down the chimney, the soft spring wind present in the early hours, but the fire soon warmed the room. Her meeting earlier had started off as well as expected, with the publicist not being all too willing to go along with Sabrina's ideas or seeing it from her point of view. But Sabrina had put her foot down. With her family's best interests at the forefront, Sabrina had laid it all on the line. The boys would remain true to themselves, they weren't going to parade around and draw attention to their personal lives, but they would not shy away from living them. Their music was honest; they weren't about to build their success on the false pretense that they'd jump into bed with anyone who fancied them. They had families and girlfriends, and this was something they valued and believed their fans would value too. Sabrina had also touched on the new songs and the lyrics that had been coming through in Dan's writing. He was going through a new stage in his life with Amanda; it poured into his words making for the most vulnerable and heart-felt songs and Sabrina anticipated this truly connecting with their fans and audience. She had finished her argument by saying this was the only way to move forward and that the label could work with them or against them, it was up to them. A weight had lifted off Sabrina's shoulders when she was reluctantly given the go-ahead to proceed as she wished.

Now, she nestled into the couch, picking her phone up from the armrest and contemplating messaging Louisa. Amanda had been right again the other day; work had been getting on top of her – she had been getting caught up in the mad game of it all and disregarding her family. Granted, they knew how much getting the boys signed by City Heights Records was a huge achievement that brought with it an awful lot of work, stress and strain, but it was no excuse. Her sisters were working just as hard too, though they probably had the sense to be sleeping now. Amanda was getting an early night ready for tomorrow's Easter rush and Louisa had mentioned through text that she was preparing for a busy day at Giulia's boutique working on a few dresses that had been giving her some trouble. Hopefully with the shop closed for the Easter holidays, Louisa would have fewer distractions and be able to get them finished. Sabrina was happy to know that, despite her little sister's heartbreak over not winning the showcase and the dresses being quite the challenge, she sounded in good spirits.

A yawn made Sabrina stretch and return her phone to the armrest, not wanting to disturb anyone for the night. Tomorrow was Saturday, the day of the show Sabrina had been busy working on with the booking agents and events team. It was the day before Easter and Sabrina had thought this a great day to bring people together; people who may or may not celebrate the holidays could spend some time with the boys and have a place to belong. It was an intimate gig, only released on San Francisco Beat's club members website. Sabrina hoped it would be a lovely way for their die-hard fans to get a little more up close and feel appreciated. On Sunday, she and the boys would then be taking a break from the studio to enjoy the Easter celebrations. Sabrina couldn't even pretend not to be jealous that Louisa was getting to spend it in Italy. It was one of the girls' favourite holidays to celebrate there. They had so many fond memories from childhood; she had texted Louisa earlier telling her to eat a Baci chocolate egg for her and to take lots of pictures. Thinking of Easter, Sabrina would have to pop in and see Amanda tomorrow at *Torta per Tutti*, after all the kerfuffle, which had mostly been her own doing due to succumbing to pressure. She hadn't spent much time in the café since opening day, or catching up with Amanda. Tomorrow she would make an effort to call by before it was action stations with preparing for the boys' gig and that way, she could tell Amanda that the ban had been lifted. Sabrina hoped that things would settle down with Amanda and Dan. She felt terrible for the tension she had forced upon them and played a part in, though she felt something else was bothering Dan. Suddenly her stomach did a flip. Maybe this would be the week Dan popped the question? Maybe he'd just been ridiculously nervous for the past few months building up to it. Now that she had lifted the ban, it could happen any time. She patted herself on the back, just a little.

'Hey baby.' Levi's smooth tone brought her thoughts back to the present.

'Hey,' she replied, gratefully taking the mug of decaf coffee he handed her. She really wanted to ask about Dan's possible proposal but didn't want to give the game away and spoil the surprise. But surely Levi trusted her not to spill the beans? Sabrina looked at him over her mug, contemplating his gorgeous features. She squinted her eyes almost as though she was telepathically trying to tell him she knew what he knew so he could talk to her about it. 'So, weddings are fun, huh?' she chirped as casually as she could manage, wriggling her toes towards the fire to warm them up, an air to her voice that she thought sounded unsuspecting enough.

Levi choked, spluttering on his coffee. 'Hot,' he noted, waving his hand in front of his mouth then carefully setting his mug on the coffee table as he sat down.

'Are you okay? I wasn't talking about us, don't get your knickers in a twist,' she chuckled, rubbing his back. 'Do you think that's why Dan has been so anxious lately, being late for sessions and getting jealous over Amanda? It's all just not very like him.' Sabrina shrugged, placing her coffee mug next to Levi's so she could turn to face him. She put her legs across his as she did so, making herself comfy.

Levi had turned a wonderful shade of pale. She felt bad for having scared him. Though she had loved him from the moment she met him, they had only been dating a few months and she didn't want to pressure him with the idea of marriage even if she had briefly let thoughts of marriage and babies with him occasionally float around in her mind.

'Sweetheart, you're right that Dan hasn't quite been himself recently, but let's not get ahead of ourselves. He wouldn't propose to Amanda while he's got troubles fogging his mind. You know our boy is more sensible than that,' Levi said matter-of-factly, rubbing the back of his neck, his cheeks now turning a rosy shade of red.

'I guess that makes sense,' Sabrina noted, prodding his thigh playfully with her big toe, before scrunching up her nose with concern. 'What's troubling him? Anything I can help with?' she added, feeling worried now that if Dan wasn't about to propose, then what had him and Levi been discussing when they said 'secret'?

'I love that about you, you know? I love that you always want to fix everything and help everyone,' Levi started, an elbow propped up on the back of the couch, his hand playing with her wavy hair. Sabrina scoffed.

'Cause problems more like. It's my fault Dan has been struggling, isn't it? Me enforcing a silly rule that he had to stay away from his girlfriend. How horrible am I? But he has no reason to worry about Amanda and be jealous over Liam, they're just friends,' Sabrina told Levi, as she fiddled with the drawstring on her lemon print shorts. Levi sighed.

'Bri, you've seen the media attention Dan gets right? But you know none of the women he's been caught with are ever anything serious. With Amanda it's entirely different. He worships the ground she walks on and it's a huge transition. She makes him feel all these things he's tried to keep bottled up. Not being there for her over the past month, someone else stepping into help, well, it threw him for a loop. He wants to be there for her, give her all she needs,' Levi explained, stroking Sabrina's cheek with his thumb, easing the guilt that was rising from the pit of her stomach. 'But it's all good. And don't beat yourself up. It's not your fault. You're our manager – we get it and I should have been more patient and understanding. And yeah, being away from the café didn't exactly help but it's Dan's mind he's got to address. He knows it's unrealistic him being around her 24/7. He's just got to get his head around it.'

Sabrina caught Levi's stroking hand in hers and kissed it, before resting it on her lap. 'I understand,' she said softly. 'I hope he knows Amanda would never do anything to hurt him and that she loves him a crazy amount.'

'He does, baby.' Levi paused, as if unsure whether to continue. 'You've met Dan's mom?' Levi asked, Sabrina nodded, realizing it was more of a statement that a question; he had been there when she met her. She was a lovely lady and it was easy to see where Dan got his looks and penchant for being both a charmer and a sweetheart from. Though Emma was a lot more boisterous than her son.

'She didn't have it easy throughout her married life; her husband sucked. Dan vowed never to be like his dad. He was a cheat and Dan was the one his mom turned to for support. He was her shoulder to cry on, but he was a kid when it all started. His mom is his world; he would never dream of putting a girl through the suffering his mom went through, but it plagues him. He's never gotten serious with anyone before fearing the worst – fearing that he'd become like his dad. I guess now it's come

193

out in an ugly way, Dan doubting Amanda too and fearing someone else can give her things he can't.' Sabrina gulped down the lump in her throat. Levi wiped the trickle of tears that had sprung involuntarily from her eyes.

'I didn't know that,' she whispered, her voice small, her cheeks burning up from the flames. 'But Levi, does Amanda know this? Maybe it would help. She's been so busy at work that she's been getting frustrated that he doesn't trust her when she's putting her own past behind her to focus on him. Surely he needs to talk to her and work on doing the same?'

Levi shrugged and brushed back his messy locks.

'He doesn't like to talk about it. His mom is doing great now, but I spent nights at his house when she was struggling to cope, witnessing the arguments when she took her husband back only to find out he'd done it again with someone new or never stopped seeing the women when he said he had. His poor mom fought depression and Dan felt helpless when she loathed herself and lost her confidence. But hey, that's all in the past now. I just want you to know Dan's a good guy. And like I told you, a love like theirs isn't going anywhere. Amanda trusts him, I can see it and deep down he trusts her too. They will figure it out together. That's what love is,' Levi finished, touching a knuckle to Sabrina's chin and flashing her his dashing smile that sent tingles down her spine. Sabrina was trying to comprehend all that he had just told her about Dan and his mum. Her heart broke for what they had been through, but it also made her feel content that Amanda's heart was in the right hands. Amanda and Dan had both known hurt, they would look after each other. She stretched her legs above Levi's thighs and raised her arms above her head. Her yellow pajama tank top rose above her toned stomach. No sooner had she brought her arms back to her sides did Levi have his hands on her waist pulling her on to his lap.

'How about after tomorrow's gig, we take our minds off work

and enjoy us?' Levi said, raising his right brow and planting a kiss on her nose.

'Hmmm,' Sabrina pondered. 'How about us and chocolate cookies?' she said, brushing a finger over his lips.

'Ooh. You got it,' he replied, his voice rough with lust for her. His hands shot up to her face to pull her to him so he could kiss her. The kiss made Sabrina's doubts ebb away. She felt like she had been on a rollercoaster these past few months. Though her heart ached for Dan and Amanda, she had faith in their love and she also had faith in her band and that the fans that would stick around no matter if the boys were loved up and off the market. But Levi was right – she felt it would do her a world of good to take her mind off anything that didn't revolve around cuddling Levi, kissing Levi and eating chocolate cookies come Sunday.

Chapter 20

Grandpa's Cheese

Ingredients:

Milk
That weird name of a product Grandpa used to talk about,
but I can never remember — it begins with 'R', I'm sure
(ask Nanna)
Salt

What to do:

See also, ask Nanna.
Find Grandpa's cheese making tubs.

'Pfft, pfft.' Louisa was simultaneously blowing and wafting tulle away from her mouth, trying not to choke on tiny specs of glitter sprinkling from it. She was buried underneath the dress that Giulia had been adamant Louisa work on the alterations for herself. Even on the mannequin, the dress looked like something out of a fairytale. Louisa had tapered in the waist from underneath the mass of plumes, added another layer of an extremely delicate lace over the skirt to add more detail and dimension and she just had the neckline to alter before she would be able to leave the boutique for the night.

It was already way past home time, but after the news about the showcase just days ago she had ashamedly allowed herself to stew in an uninspired funk. So now, while the rest of Italy sipped their evening wines and tucked in to bread and burrata, she was being suffocated by tulle trying to get this dress – which she truly adored and really wished was hers, but also kind of hated right now – finished before she left for the UK the next morning.

Giulia had left her three hours ago; she wasn't kidding when she said these dresses were all up to Louisa. She was one straight-to-the-point and stubborn Italian and though Louisa was grateful for her belief in her, she also felt a tiny bit sick at the thought of ruining such stunning masterpieces. She stepped back to take in her work so far and eye up the alterations of the neckline and nearly brought the whole mannequin with her.

'Oww,' she exclaimed to the walls, as her hair tugged, caught in the mesh of the fabric, pulling her back into the dress. '*Mamma mia*, Grandpa, I could do with some help,' she cried, making herself laugh. She didn't know if the laughter was because of nerves, tiredness or the fact that she could picture her grandpa laughing at her current state, but whichever it was, the giggles were needed. She managed to spin into the dress, her hands fiddling with the strand of hair, pulling it free, before she lost her balance. 'Uh, we've got to get this done, Grandpa. How would you do this neckline?' she asked the heavens with a chuckle, once she succeeded in taking a step back to give the dress a once over.

Squinting her eyes, Louisa tilted her head from left to right and pursed her pale pink glossy lips. 'I think if we took the neckline to a deep V and meet the waist band and add a sheer lace, almost like a bandeau, just over the chest, that would make the top just as elegant as the rest of it. There's too much fabric on top,' Louisa said out loud, waving a pen in the air as she took to her sketch pad to test out her theory. 'Thank you, Grandpa. If the lady doesn't like it, I'm blaming you.' She chuckled to herself once more.

With one knee kneeling on her stool and the other leg planted on the floor, she hunched over her worktop, picking up coloured pens, shading, drawing and rubbing out until she was satisfied. 'Yep, wow, I love it,' Louisa gasped. 'Right.' She busied herself grabbing fabric scissors, thread, needles, pins and a measuring tape, before gently, albeit with some difficulty, trying to lift the dress off the mannequin.

'*Amore*?' came a soft voice just as she was getting to the tricky bit of lifting the final piece of the dress up and off the mannequin. It got stuck and she was once again suffocating under a blanket of tulle. Was this to be her life? Not being good enough for the top designers and being left to drown in a sea of fabric? Okay, now even *she* thought that was a tad dramatic. It had been a little harder to let go of her devastation of not winning the showcase than she thought. Amanda had been gutted for her but sent her love and words of encouragement to keep going and Sabrina had actually texted a few days ago to apologize for being a bad sister while sending her support for Louisa to keep her chin up and not give up. Her mum and dad had gushed about how proud they were of her over the phone and how it was the designer's loss, not hers. And Nanna had pinched her cheeks and told her good things were coming. Somehow all their positivity made her feel more like a disappointment. But she didn't have too much time to dwell on it, due to this other worldly behemoth of a dress that was occupying all her time and energy. The other two dresses were complete but her trip to England for Easter was resting on the balance of finishing up this one.

She was pried away from her thoughts and saved from a humiliating death by Luca, who after scaring a hiccup out of her, rushed over and helped her lay the dress on her workspace.

'*Grazie*,' she said, smoothing down her hair and patting down her red pencil skirt to dust off the glitter it was now sprinkled with.

'*Buona sera*,' Luca said with a coy smile, humour in his eyes. He often gave her that look. Flashing his dazzling pearly teeth, his blue eyes piercing in to hers, his lips curved at the edges like she surprised him.

'Well, I'm glad my troubles amuse you, Luca. I'm happy to have been able to put on a show for you. At least one of us is smiling.' She was aware that as she spoke her lips too creased into a smile. Luca's smile was infectious. She couldn't exactly be frustrated right now – he had swooped in and helped her out – but she couldn't wait to start on the dress, and she was pretty sure Luca had brought cheese and wine if the wicker basket by the door was anything to go by.

'*Amore*, no,' Luca said with a chuckle, stepping towards her and kissing her on each cheek. 'I like to watch you work. If I can help, I help,' he added, moving back towards the door and presenting her with a wine glass. She eyed it suspiciously, then put it down a safe distance away from the dress.

'Luca. *Grazie ma* no wine for me this evening. Give me all the cheese but no wine. I must make sure this dress is perfect. I can't work on it while tipsy,' she said as she glanced at her design and nodded at each of the tools she had set aside, mentally ticking the boxes in her head to make sure she had everything she needed.

'*Ma* of course *amore*,' Luca nodded and sat down against the door frame. 'I am not here,' he said, holding up his hands and sending an innocent grin her way. He meant it too. He hadn't come to distract her. He had come to be with her and keep her company and to be there when she locked up in the dark. He was a sweetheart, he tugged at her heart strings. Though she couldn't help laughing out loud. It would be hard to pretend he wasn't there, with all six-foot-three of him crouched in the doorway, his tight navy jumper hugging him in all the right places. She watched him for a few moments as he rustled around in the basket and plated up some warm focaccia from Alfonso's and an array of meats and cheeses. Her stomach growled – she couldn't remember when she last ate. This dress was quite demanding.

Touched by Luca's kindness, she sat down next to him, kissed his lips softly, catching him off guard and helped herself to a slice of focaccia. '*Grazie mille*,' she whispered.

'You eat, then work. It is better like this,' he replied, taking a sip of his wine. She couldn't argue. The focaccia and nibble of parmesan settled her stomach's grumbles and just a small sip of wine fired her up ready to create a masterpiece. Because that's what she was going to do – create a masterpiece that would make the owner of this dress fall in love with it all over again. Love was what it was all about. You had to love what you were wearing. It made life fun.

'You cannot wear this dress, no?' Luca asked as she busied herself cutting into the neckline and pinning where she would need to sew a new hem in place.

'I wish,' she muttered through the pins in her mouth. 'Isn't it gorgeous?'

'I think it suits you, to make your pretty eyes pop,' Luca said, with a casual wave of his wine glass.

'Thank you. I hope they love it, whoever gets to wear it,' Louisa said with an enthusiastic smile as she took the dress to the sewing machine. Tonight, she couldn't fear the machine, she had to use it with confidence. 'So, are you excited about visiting Manchester?' Louisa asked.

'Of course,' Luca said enthusiastically. 'You make my dreams come true.'

'How were your mamma *e* papa when you told them about being away for Easter?' she asked, while placing the dress precariously under the needle of the sewing machine. She wanted to get the shoulders secure with the machine, but the rest would have to be stitched by hand. There was no way the girth of the dress would allow her to use the machine for it all.

Luca popped a piece of cheese in his mouth and chewed thoughtfully. He had such a careful way about him, as if how he made people feel mattered to him. He genuinely loved his family and cared for their happiness. Louisa knew she could always talk to her sisters about anything and everything, but when it came to her fear of hurting them or worry over being selfish, Luca understood her.

'They make some loud noises at first, *ma* I think it is because of you that they are happy for me to go. And I tell them I must take things to Amanda.' Luca let out a small laugh. 'Food is important, *ma* love is important to them also.' Louisa took her foot off the pedal; only the sound of Luca lips against his wine glass and the swish of the wine inside could be heard.

'That's very sweet of you and them,' she said, gently caressing the fabric, pausing to take in Luca's words before making her way back to her worktop. 'I think they worry about missing you and about you being safe. They can't protect you when you are far away and.' She too let out a chuckle in thinking of how she had been brought up with her nonni and the traits her mum had picked up, 'Italians have hearts of gold, but they are stubborn to boot.' Luca raised an eyebrow at that phrasing – it had come out in English as she didn't know how to translate it in Italian. 'They can be set in their ways. Believe they are right and know what is good for you. It takes some time for you to figure out what you think is good for yourself.' Her eyes washed over the room, her sketches, the material silky soft in her hands and then down to Luca. She was figuring it out, she thought, and it wasn't so scary now she had taken that first initial step; saying yes to uprooting her life and taking a chance on Italy.

It wasn't until she looked at him this time that she noticed a stack of boxes peeking out from by the door frame.

'Luca, what are those?' she asked, pointing at the edges of a tier of boxes. She abandoned the dress and walked over to the door where she found five boxes stacked, biggest to smallest, like a Christmas window display.

'We take them to Amanda,' he replied, sitting up straighter, excitement in his eyes.

'Luca, I already have a bag full of cheese and salami,' Louisa tried to protest.

'*Si, ma* she will need more. I pick a few things extra and Papa wanted to send wine to celebrate and meats you no find in England.' He was looking at the boxes when Louisa turned back to look at his face. This evening his designer stubble made him look neat yet rugged. It suited him. His dark brown hair had grown an inch or two and Louisa liked it. He was strikingly handsome. When he turned to meet her gaze, a bright smile spread across his beautiful features.

'*Mamma mia,*' Louisa shouted which made him laugh shyly. She squatted down next to him and began peppering his face with kisses. She only stopped when he gently caught her bobbing head and planted a passionate kiss on her lips. When he let go, she felt an overwhelming surge of happiness course through her veins.

'You are one in a million,' Louisa expressed. 'Grandpa would have loved you.' He truly would have, Louisa thought, casting another look at the boxes, and he would have done the exact same thing. Amanda was in for a treat.

*

'*Veloce, veloce!*' Shouts of 'quickly' burst from the mountain top, in between the sound of the rising cockerels. Orzoro was still covered in darkness, only the streetlamps, Nanna's bedroom light and her Zia's kitchen lights were on to aid in this morning's rush.

Louisa and Luca had been up since before the crack of dawn, having only slept two hours once the dress was done. Dressmaking was serious business and so was eating cheese and drinking wine until the sun came up. They had scrambled to get to her zia's house to pick up Nanna and her zia's. Louisa was running on empty, but she was determined not to miss their flights and to be home in time for San Francisco Beat's gig and whatever it was that Levi was planning that had required her not to tell her sisters of her arrival just yet. But with boxes galore in tow, the taxi had been a squeeze and they had spent a good portion of the early morning derailing the schedule as they tried to fit everything in the boot.

Now, Louisa stood staring at Zia Sofia who was trying to cram not one, but four *caciocavallo* cheeses into a carry-on bag. '*Mamma mia*' Louisa sighed. 'Zia, no, *non posso*, I can't.' Her zia simply stared at her, her bluey-grey eyes shining with sheer determination and a look that read, 'Italians don't joke when it comes to cheese. It's going in the bag.' Louisa gave up and tried rallying the rest of the troops instead.

Two taxis could be heard beeping at the bottom of the one-hundred-step staircase, while Luca and Louisa tried frantically to get four elderly ladies to put down the salami and focus on getting safely down the steps.

'Nanna, *vai, vai,*' Louisa said, signaling to Luca to start ushering Nanna out the house and down the stairs. 'I'll help the others, they're masters at this, you see to it that Nanna manages.' she finished, rushing past Luca and sitting on the suitcase that Zia Sofia was doing her best to close, the bulges of cheese making it very difficult. Zia Sofia offered her an innocent smile that under any other circumstance would have made Louisa want to cuddle her, but she was already sweating at the thought of going through customs. Cuddles were not on the agenda this morning, not when her brain was focused on smuggling a hundred pounds of dairy products through the airport.

Once Nanna was making her way to the waiting taxi, Louisa cajoled her zias to the front door and got their bags on to the balcony. Taking the key from Zia Rosa, she pulled the heavy steel door to a close and triple-checked that she had locked it correctly. Her zias, though elderly, were accustomed to the uneven steps and long walk down to the main road. They did it almost every day, often carrying heavy shopping bags with them too. Still, Louisa was impressed by how smoothly they walked and with no complaints. Halfway down the stairs, Luca ran back up to meet them and help them with the rest of the way. Small beads of sweat were forming on the crease of his brow which tugged at Louisa's heart strings; he truly was a gentleman.

When they reached the taxis, Louisa had to wipe the sweat from her top lip. The sun was only just starting to rise in the distance over the boot of Sicily, but it was already shaping up to be a scorching Italian spring day. Luca took her bag from her and indicated for her to take a seat. She hesitated, knowing that there were more bags to be brought down, but before she could argue that she needed to get the rest of the bags, Luca dashed up the stairs to retrieve them. Again, her heart struck another love chord.

Louisa braced herself for the journey ahead. She passed around bottles of water and took two travel sickness tablets before offering them to her nanna and zias. They waved the medicine away with hearty laughter. She nodded at them in admiration. Maybe one day she could conquer this road without being medicated.

Luca came bounding back, three mid-sized suitcases in tow. He placed them in the boot of the minivan with the help of the taxi driver, before coming over to check on them all.

'I drive with the small car,' he said, helping himself to the tablets resting on Louisa's knee. He took big gulps of water and winked at her, knowing all too well himself the road that lay ahead. When he was younger, he had told Louisa, his papa would make him drive the long route of one thousand turns to make cake deliveries. It had been his initiation into the family business, proving that he was a hard worker and would not let the family down. Even after this practice, Luca dreaded the road. His stomach had never quite got used to it.

'It will be okay,' Louisa said, stepping out of the taxi to give him a hug and a kiss on the cheek. With most of the boxes taking up the backseat of the small taxi, her zias had done well to order a minivan. There was now more space for everyone to fit comfortably. 'Keep your eyes on the road ahead *amore*, okay?' she finished, as she checked her watch and kissed Luca quickly before taking her seat and getting buckled in. She watched Luca run around to the front of the small taxi and climb in before signing the cross that she would make this treacherous car journey without fainting and that there would be no sniffer dogs at the airport.

Chapter 21

Nanna's Chocolate and Sambuca Biscotti

Ingredients:

6 tbsp butter
²/₃ cup sugar
½ tsp salt
2 ½ tsp vanilla
1 ½ tsp baking powder
2 large eggs
2 cups of all-purpose flour plus extra*
1 packet of chocolate chips
¼ cup of sambuca (this is a guideline, but more sambuca = more flour)

What to do:

Beat the butter, sugar, salt, vanilla and baking powder until creamy.
Add the chocolate chips and sambuca and mix.
Beat in eggs.
Add your flour until smooth and you are able to make a dough.
*With the addition of the sambuca, more flour will be needed so the
dough isn't too wet or sticky.
Place the dough onto a baking sheet and shape it into a log.
Bake for 25 mins at 180 degrees.
Reduce oven temperature and take out the biscotti. Allow it to cool for a minute
while oven is cooling and then slice into separate half-inch biscotti slices.
Bake at 170 degrees for another 30—35 mins.

There she stood outside *Torta per Tutti*, her face beaming, the sun shining gloriously in the clear blue summer sky. Raised high above her head she held a trophy. The trophy was shaped like a *cannolo*, bearing the inscription 'Best Italian café in Manchester'. Her nanna and grandpa stood by her side – in fact, the whole family were there spread out across the double pages of the proclaimed *Food* magazine. It was the perfect scene.

'Grandpa?' Amanda heard herself saying. 'Grandpa?' she repeated, this time more forcefully willing him to answer. Suddenly her eyes flew open. She promptly sat up in bed, a chill sweeping over her entire body. Taking in the light pink walls and vintage posters of San Francisco and Jack Kerouac book covers that adorned the wall, she took a sharp intake of breath, feeling a tight pain shoot through her chest.

'Bloody hell, Grandpa,' she said wiping her eyes and shaking her head. It had all been a dream. If the corny *cannolo* trophy hadn't given it away, her Grandpa certainly had. It took Amanda a moment to compose herself and to register the fact that Dan had shot up beside her.

'Hey baby girl, hey,' he said, reaching over and rubbing her back. Amanda breathed in a huge gulp of air. Dan gave her a minute, not rushing her to speak, allowing her to process her feelings, showing they mattered. Amanda surveyed the bedroom once more, her eyes resting on the postcard of Italy she had pinned to the wall. It was one her grandpa had sent from one of his trips back when the girls were younger. His words had jumped off the page right into her heart. She could only see the colour of the postcard faintly thanks to the light from the streetlamp outside, seeping in through a crack in the curtain. It was still dark out. She turned slightly and caught a glimpse of her alarm clock; 1.30 a.m. Another two hours and she would be getting up to begin her day at her café.

Dan was rubbing his hand in circles at the small of her back; his touch warmed that part of her body, making the rest of her icy in comparison. She quickly shoved her arms under the duvet and leant back into Dan's chest. She stayed there for a moment, not saying a word, tracing the tattoos on his forearms. Her favourite – a black and grey rose – she knew was there but couldn't quite see in the dark. The feel of Dan's skin on her fingertips soothed her.

'It's our first Easter without him,' she breathed softly, closing her eyes as Dan brushed his lips over her hairline. The familiar touch of his plump lips made her feel at home; made her feel strong in her most vulnerable moments.

'And look at what you've created. Honey, I think your grandpa would be impressed, you've gone above and beyond with all you have done at the café and you're only just getting started. The smiles you brought to all those people yesterday, how happy they were with their *pastiera* … he's proud of what you've done, keeping his spirit alive,' Dan finished, dropping a kiss on her bare shoulder. Sending home all her customers who visited *Torta per Tutti* yesterday with a *pastiera* and *colomba* had been a tradition her grandpa started at their house. No one would ever leave without a homemade *pastiera* courtesy of Amanda and Grandpa during the Easter holidays and it was a tradition Amanda had known she wanted to uphold in her café. She was looking forward to giving more out today and adored the thought of everyone slicing into them tomorrow.

Dan's words wrapped a hug around her heart. He was right. She missed her grandpa terribly, but the hole in her heart had been somewhat filled with barley and ricotta like every loving scoop of it she poured into her *pastiera* this past week. Easter at *Torta per Tutti* was truly spectacular and Amanda had felt her grandpa's presence with every *casatiella* she made and every Kinder egg she had sold this week. She had gone into work every day with an extra pep in her step.

'Thank you,' she whispered to Dan, tilting her head and turning to face him. The thin strap of her camisole slipped down as she did so, making Dan's eyes stray from hers and wander over her lips, to her shoulder. She could feel the heat coming of his body. When he brought the strap back up to her shoulder with his gentle touch, grazing her collar bone with his fingertips, a spark ignited in her stomach and Amanda felt a rush of heat to her cheeks. She ran a hand through his floppy brown hair and kissed him tenderly. When she pulled away, she watched the familiar way he kept his eyes closed savouring their kiss, his long lashes beautiful, his cupid's bow perfectly pouting. Amanda wanted to enjoy this moment, to enjoy his company with no one else in the room, but she couldn't shake the nagging insecurities in her mind. The media image, Dan doubting her trust, the late nights, Dan being out of sorts and the tension between them recently – it had all been adding up and they still hadn't really talked about it or got to the bottom of what was niggling at them.

'Dan, do you trust me?' Amanda asked, her words confident with a hint of a wobble. She would never put Dan through any of the things Jason had put her through. Dan was the person she wanted to be with and that would never change. It hurt her to think that he thought otherwise, enough to question her friendship with Liam. She wasn't going to sugarcoat this one. They had hidden feelings from each other before and she had thought all that was in the past. If something was wrong, he needed to respect her and tell her. If he thought they were better off as friends, he needed to speak up. Though her stomach knotted at the thought that he wasn't happy and how she would cope if that were the case.

Dan's eyes flew open; tiny golden specs flickered in his dark pupils with the trickle of light coming through the curtain. He shook his head, her hand still cupping his jaw. There was hurt inside his eyes.

'Of course, my love,' he uttered, his voice croaky with the early hour, stroking a hand over her hair.

'Then why have you been so distant lately? And I'm not talking about the whole stupid ban from the café thing. You're not telling me something, I can see it in your eyes. Since when do you get jealous and question my friendships or turn up late to studio sessions? And don't think I haven't noticed your hushed phone calls.' Dan leaned into her palm.

'I'm sorry. I promise there is nothing to worry about with us,' Dan said, while Amanda could see the flash of turmoil in his eyes like he didn't know how to open up. This wasn't like Dan.

She shifted so she was fully facing him now and in a sitting position, her legs crossed on the bed. 'Dan. That is where you are wrong. If something is bothering you, I am here for you. I can help you and we can figure it out together, you can't keep it bottled up because I will worry, and it will affect us in the long run if you don't let me in.'

Dan was still sitting up, his muscled torso evident in the morning sunrise. He truly was beautiful. Amanda loved him. They needed to get through this blip because he was her best friend, she couldn't be without him. Dan turned to prop himself up on his elbow.

'Trust me, baby girl,' he whispered into the darkness, making Amanda's chest deflate. She couldn't do this, she couldn't feel shut out from him. But was what he was asking such a bad thing? After all she was asking the same of him; to trust her? She trusted him, of course she did. Didn't she? Was she letting her own fears creep into her subconscious? Was she forcing Dan to speak up based on her own needs rather than putting Dan first and giving him the space he clearly wanted? Her mind seemed to answer for her as she got up and walked towards the door. Dan didn't speak and didn't get up after her.

It bugged her, Amanda couldn't deny it. She wished her grandpa was here to offer her advice. He and Nanna had been together for over sixty years and they were very much in love till the day he passed away. What had been their secret? Amanda racked her brain with memories of her grandpa, of his words of wisdom, as she made her way down the stairs and into the kitchen.

Before she knew what she was doing she had pulled out the eggs, flour, butter and sugar from the fridge and cupboards. Grandpa had never been a fan of her previous boyfriends, but he had loved Dan. Was her experience with Jason interfering with her ability to be patient and understanding with Dan's feelings or did she have a right to be frustrated that he wasn't letting her in? She placed the mixing bowl on to the counter with a thud. With Jason she had felt frightened, weak and pathetic. Was this how she made Dan feel? What had she done for Dan not to trust her? He had just moments ago told her that he did. So, why was she having such a hard time believing him? Something felt off. She chopped the butter with vigour and threw it into her bowl. They had only been dating nearly four months; was this a sign that they had been better off as friends?

Amanda rubbed the butter into the flour, not measuring anything, just trusting her instincts, like Grandpa taught her in the kitchen. 'They are right, no?' he would say when her instincts produced the most delicious pizza dough or homemade pasta. She laughed at the memory. She certainly had her grandpa's love of cooking and fiery passion. Louisa had most definitely got his ability to love without logic or fear. And Sabrina had picked up on his will and determination to see things through no matter how tough. It made her a good leader. Amanda added a splash or five of sambuca to her mixture along with eggs and a touch more flour to soak up the liquid, using her hands to combine her ingredients. Suddenly, strong arms wrapped around her waist. She closed her eyes, focusing on her hands, kneading the soft dough into a ball. Dan swayed from side to side, not saying a word, his cheek buried in her hair. Once she had her dough, Dan simply moved with her as she placed it onto a baking sheet and manipulated it into a log. She wiggled out of his grip to put the tray in the oven and washed her hands.

When she turned around, Dan was holding the tea towel while leaning against the fridge, just standing there ever so casually in

211

his boxer briefs. His eyes looked weary. It was the first Saturday in a long while that he had had the opportunity to stay in bed and rest, yet here he was, standing right by her side at two in the morning, looking like some sort of rugged, tattooed heavenly creature and it terrified her. Dan had never, not once in all the time she had known him, terrified her. She loved him so much. Her heart felt good about this. Her soul screamed that this new relationship was right; them being so intimate with each other was one thousand per cent right, so why was Dan being distant?

Dan handed her the tea towel and still no words passed his beautiful lips. Then he moved past her and set about retrieving the cafetière, coffee, and sugar, and filling up the kettle. He knew where everything was now. After the three weeks he had spent here in January, he knew her routine, her systems, where she kept everything. It was easy for him. He fit into her place like the missing piece to her puzzle. Dan wasn't an overthinker like her. To others he might come across as mysterious and sure, he had layers – he knew what he wanted the world to see, what he wanted to share and what he didn't – but with Amanda he lay it all bare. Well, except for now.

The kettle boiled. Amanda leant against the counter watching as Dan spooned the right amount of coffee into the cafetière, added the water, mixed it around with a spoon, placed the lid on and waited a few moments before pushing it down. He was a good student, remembering exactly what her nanna had told him. It wasn't exactly rocket science, but her nanna and grandpa knew a thing or two about Italian coffee and Dan liked his coffee and loved his food. He pulled two cups from the cupboard and took them to the table. Then went back for the cafetière. The kitchen light bounced off his olive skin, the veins in his biceps visible when his arms tensed.

This was the unfiltered, un-photoshopped, raw version that the media didn't get to see. It was intimate. It was special. A smile curved at her lips as Dan took a seat at her small kitchen table.

He placed half a teaspoon of sugar in her coffee and stirred. Then with all the grace of a god, he looked up at her, flicked his messy, yet stylish, locks back and offered her a slight smile. It wasn't cocky. It was simply sweet and reassuring. The timer beeped on the oven, reminding her that she was baking. Dan stood up. A faint chuckle left her lips. It wasn't often that Dan left her to it in the kitchen. In Italy he had loved watching her and her zias cooking together and was always ready to lend a hand. When they returned to England in January, it had been their first taste at living together and Amanda quickly found out that cooking would no longer be a solitary thing for her. And she wasn't complaining. As much as she loved pottering around the kitchen by herself, she loved having Dan pottering with her more. They would talk about anything and everything as they busied themselves with chopping and mixing. Dan would suggest ingredients and, in typical Grandpa fashion, Amanda would tell him why they would or wouldn't work. It was currently a tie between who was right regarding what worked and what didn't. The foodie in Dan had some good ideas. Amanda would tell him this. Sometimes.

Amanda saw to taking the *cantuccini* from the oven while Dan grabbed a chopping board. Amanda placed the log on to the board. After a few moments she carefully sliced it. Dan picked up the slices and spread the biscotti evenly on the baking sheet before Amanda put it back in the oven for twenty minutes. Then she wandered over to the table to sip her morning coffee. Dan walked behind her chair and put his hands on her shoulders. The feel of his calloused fingertips resting on her collarbone had goose bumps running wild all over her skin. He lowered a kiss on the top of her head. Was Amanda right to let her guard down, to smile and gloss over what had just happened some thirty minutes ago? Was it a sign that whatever problems they faced, patience was key, and they would get through it? Because this – right now in the kitchen – she wanted to keep this, and she wanted to keep it with Dan.

Amanda swiveled around on her chair into a kneeling position, better to reach Dan. She looked up, meeting his all-encompassing deep brown eyes. She was about to break the silence when Dan spoke.

'Honey, I haven't forgotten our conversation from earlier,' he said, his fingertips brushing over her lips; she hadn't either. But she was grateful for this moment when she let her soul guide her and not her wandering mind. 'We can talk more later. Okay? Just give me some time.' His rough and raspy voice sent a warmth through her body as her hands explored his. Patience, she could give Dan patience, couldn't she? She could and she would trust him because he needed her to. She just had to trust that whatever Dan was struggling to tell her was not that he thought they were better off as friends.

'Later. Yes,' Amanda mumbled through a kiss that was growing steamier by the minute. Suddenly the timer on the oven sent a loud continuous beep through the kitchen. Twenty minutes! Had they been making out for twenty minutes? She carefully pulled away from Dan, her lips tingling, her neck stiff from tilting to reach him and her knees creaking from having been knelt on the wooden chair lost in a kiss for twenty minutes.

'Shoot, the *cantuccini*.' Amanda pulled away from Dan and stepped towards the oven. He grabbed her wrist, pulling her back into him.

'Later,' he said, his big brown eyes wide, a flicker of innocence behind them now. He looked cute. Her rugged, muscly, tattooed boyfriend actually looked cute. Amanda let out a hearty laugh.

'No, not later. They'll burn,' she said. Dan threw her a charming side smile and a disarming wink, before seeing to a fresh cafetière of coffee.

Chapter 22

Grandpa's Cannoli

Ingredients:

For the shells:

Flour
Egg
Oil
*Marsala (be careful, not too much this time — drowning it does
not work for this recipe)*

For the filling:
Ricotta
Perugina dark chocolate
Amaretti biscuits
Vanilla

What to do:

Combine all shell ingredients into a bowl to form dough.
*Chill for a while. (Maybe a good hour? Grandpa could get impatient; it
didn't do the pastry any harm.)*
*This is the tricky bit. Copy what Grandpa did, rolling out dough and
forming small discs to wrap around Cannoli tubes.*
*Fry in sunflower oil or vegetable oil (heck, I'm sure Grandpa used olive oil
once, but don't do that, it takes away the sweetness) until lightly golden
brown. (Doesn't take long.)*

Leave to cool on plate, with kitchen roll to absorb excess oil.
Combine ricotta, melted chocolate, crushed amaretti and vanilla until
they form a nice smooth paste.
Fill pastry bag and fill shells.

It couldn't have been a more perfect spring day. There wasn't a cloud in the sky, leaving it a dazzling clear blue. Golden beams of sunshine were lighting up the daffodils and cherry blossoms in her nanna and grandpa's garden, and the air was warm. Sabrina had on her favourite baby pink and white polka dot skater dress with her hair in a high ponytail and was stood on the doorstep gripping onto Levi's muscly bicep.

'Baby, I told you. I've just got to nip out and do Dan a favour. I will not be late for tonight's gig, I promise. Stop pouting,' Levi said nibbling her bottom lip and groaning. He looked extra soft and cuddly this morning in his bright blue hoodie. Sabrina whimpered a little and gave him a flutter of her eyelashes to no avail. Then she stood on her tip-toes to further entice him with a kiss. 'I know what you're doing, but I've really got to go. I love you,' he said, kissing her nose and stepping out into the April sunshine. Those words from his lips rendered her speechless; all she could do was smile, wave and watch him walk away as she tried to float back down to earth.

When Levi was no longer in view, she did a quick sweep of the house; lights switched off, straighteners unplugged, paperwork and bits and pieces she would need later folded neatly in her bag, check, before throwing her trusty pink Chanel bag over her shoulder ready to head into town.

A short bus ride and a walk through Piccadilly Gardens later and the familiar smell of Kimbo coffee and sweet Italian breakfast pastries made Sabrina's taste buds come alive with anticipation. *Torta per Tutti* looked positively Italian with its bold and bright ceramic plant pots underlining the bay window out front, making Sabrina's shoulders rise with glee. A good, rich

Italian coffee and a large slice of *pastiera* with a side of *cannoli* was what she needed.

Upon seeing the sun bounce off the display of Easter eggs decorating the café window, Sabrina's mind drifted to Louisa and how she would be enjoying this Easter in Italy. Oh, how the girls had adored Easter in Italy when they were kids. The Easter eggs were something else. The shiny plastic silver and gold wrappers – sometimes multi-coloured, pink, purple or yellow, or printed with the likes of *The Avengers* or Disney princesses – the secret toys inside and the creamy decadent chocolate made her eyes twinkle like a child on Christmas morning, and her mouth water. They had the same effect now. Sabrina lit up seeing the display that Amanda had managed to import with Luca's help.

Thinking of Luca and Louisa, Sabrina quickly checked her phone before stepping inside the café and getting lost in the drool-inducing cake counter. She still hadn't heard from Louisa, which seemed odd considering her little sister always texted without fail on show days. Maybe Louisa was giving her a taste of her own medicine. She really had fluffed up a lot over the last few months. Now though, with the ban lifted on where the boys could and couldn't venture and their publicist not being quite so hard on her dictation of the boys being something they weren't, Sabrina hoped balance would be restored in her brain; work was work and home was home. She could now get back to not walking on eggshells whenever she was out in public with Levi and she could get back to being there for her sisters more now that she wasn't caught up in pushing her family away in order to appease other people.

Francesca greeted her with a smile as warm as the vanilla-scented air while Kate was seeing to other customers. Sabrina waved over at Kate, happy to see the café bustling with people all wearing cheerful expressions, their tables full of one of every-thing in the counter and coffees to wash the treats down with. Francesca saw to getting Sabrina a coffee so Sabrina snuck into the kitchen to say good morning to Amanda while it brewed.

'Hey Brina,' Amanda said, her head down and focused on carefully folding *cannoli*.

'Hey, how's it going? It smells divine in here,' Sabrina gushed, her eyes wandering over the production line of produce, mixtures and bakes ready for the oven. She wondered if there was a bowl she could lick. Patience often eluded her and Louisa when it came to waiting for Amanda's food to come out of the oven.

Amanda chuckled, drawing Sabrina to turn her attention away from the tray of Italian rocky road that looked majestic, like a unicorn had sprinkled it with every rainbow sprinkle ever made.

'The bowl for that is just by the sink,' Amanda noted, looking up from her *cannoli* making to wink at Sabrina. Lauren smiled and nodded in the direction of the bowl. Well, if they both insisted. Sabrina quietly devoured the remnants of sprinkles, amaretti, crushed biscotti and cherries that had been left behind while getting to witness her big sister in her element. Of course, over the years she had watched Amanda in the kitchen at their nonni's house, parents' house and her own house when cooking up feasts for everyone, but she had only ever heard tales about the fast-moving, straining and stressful life on the line as a chef. Both Lauren and Amanda worked smoothly and efficiently, fiddling with the intricacies that were *cannoli* and *sfogliatelle*. The oven beeped, meaning Amanda had to carefully stop what she was doing without ruining the delicate curl of the *cannoli*, to see to it that nothing burned. It was non-stop when your counter was nearly sold out at only ten in the morning. Sabrina felt grateful for this moment to sit back and appreciate her sister. And then Amanda spoke, spoiling the moment with her sarcasm.

'Are you going to stand there and stare at me all day? I thought you had rock stars to wrangle and a gig to put on,' Amanda said through a side smirk.

Once Sabrina was certain she could not scrape anymore Perugina chocolate from the sides of the bowl, she placed it in the sink and left it to soak in some hot water before addressing her sister by sticking her tongue out.

'I expect to see you all there later,' Sabrina said with a wave of her hand as she pushed open the kitchen door.

'I wouldn't miss it for the world,' Amanda shouted through the back swing as Francesca handed Sabrina a coffee. Sabrina gave her a hug and a thank you, collected a box of treats for the crew and boys for tonight's show and with a belly full of Italian chocolate headed for the venue to manage *San Francisco Beat* for the first time under City Heights Records.

*

An energy filled the room that only forty-five minutes of Tyler Wall and his guitar could conjure. Mum was wiping away tears, Dad was clapping enthusiastically while shaking his head muttering 'Fantastic. Absolutely brilliant,' and Amanda's throat was horse from singing her heart out down Sabrina's ear. Sabrina was still swaying to the last strum of Tyler's guitar that vibrated in the airwaves as he left the stage. It had been a long time since she had had the pleasure of seeing Tyler perform; he blew her away every time. She was pleased that he had been more than happy to open for San Francisco Beat when he was such a big star in his own right, but he had agreed with an enthusiastic yes and that he would love nothing more than to be graced with such an opportunity.

'God, that guy is good,' Amanda croaked. Sabrina could see her big sister following the movements of Jamie, the sound tech guy, as he replaced Tyler's stool and mic stand with Dan's mic. Amanda's eyes looked lost in a daydream as the room grew quiet, the lights lowered, and San Francisco Beat took the stage. Sabrina recognized her sister's 'lost to the world around her' look; it was the one that only Dan could procure from her. Amanda's upbeat attitude and happier demeanour had not been lost on Sabrina today. She hoped that her sister and Dan were doing okay now, and it wasn't just the promise of chocolate later that was giving her sister a dopey romantic expression.

'Things okay with you guys?' Sabrina nudged Amanda and whispered, as the boys settled into their spots.

Amanda leaned into her. 'I hope so,' she said, as Dan grabbed the microphone, his eyes instantly locking on to Amanda's. Sabrina watched as he brushed his tongue seductively over his lips, into that irresistible side smirk of his. His dark eyes sparkled in a way that made it clear there was only one person in this room his heart desired. Sabrina was pretty sure every woman in the crowd melted on the spot. 'He is unreal,' Sabrina laughed, unable to stop from shaking her head and shoving Amanda. Surely that fire in his eyes was a good sign that Sabrina hadn't done any irreversible damage to their relationship and that Dan would be able to overcome the fears his dad embedded in him?

'I know,' her sister replied, a smug but adoring look on her face. She didn't take her eyes off Dan. Dan had that magnetic front man thing down to a tee for sure. Even Sabrina struggled to peel her eyes away from his enigmatic allure. But she did and when they found Levi as he counted his band down to the first song, her heart soared. Tonight, she wasn't watching him play from the side of the stage as their manager, tonight she was front and centre simply watching her boyfriend destroy the drums. Tonight, she wanted to witness San Francisco Beat the same way everyone else in the room was, except with the bonus that she did still get to get up close and personal with them after. She chuckled to herself, relaxed her shoulders, closed her eyes and let the music wash over her. The record label could trust her, they truly were special; their music like no one else's. To the fans, all that mattered was what was happening on stage right now and it was pure art.

*

'Sabrina, can you come up here please?' Sabrina's eyes flew open to find Levi with a microphone reaching for her hand. Her cheeks flamed. 'What?' she gasped, her insides freezing. 'Can you join us on the stage baby?' he added to a round of 'awws' from the crowd. All eyes were on her. Weren't they just in the middle of 'Choose You'? How did Levi get to the front of the stage? Who gave Levi a mic? Sabrina's eyes darted to each member of San Francisco Beat. When they caught site of Dylan's, he seemed to register her panic. She watched as he walked over to Dan's mic.

'Two and a half months ago, we signed with this awesome new label and this, folks, is the woman behind the San Francisco Beat machine. We appreciate you guys sticking with us and hope you dig the new sound, but we couldn't have done it without this woman right here.' Dylan finished his speech and nodded at Sabrina encouragingly. That was kind of him, she thought. What a lovely thing to say. She smiled back as Levi caught her hand and guided her up on to the stage. With the bright lights on the stage casting the audience in a dark shadow she focused her attention on Levi. Levi with a microphone. Levi not behind his drum kit. What more did he have to say? Dylan's speech would do. It was very sweet of them to acknowledge her in this way, though she already knew that they appreciated her. She didn't crave the spotlight on her, she tried to communicate this to Levi with a stern glare and small smile. But his brown eyes were zoomed in on her lips, his Adam's apple trembling, his palms sweaty. Suddenly she didn't care that two hundred people were watching them, she wanted to hug him and rid the worry on his handsome face. Why was he worried? She wondered.

'Dylan's right. We couldn't have done this without you. Your belief in us, your patience with us and your guidance have given us more than we could have ever dreamed.' There were more 'awws' from the crowd as Levi spoke, but he didn't stop there. 'Sabrina?' Sabrina felt her legs turn to jelly as Levi's usually light and playful tone turned serious. 'Sabrina, I don't know how you always manage to smell like sunshine and flowers or how you remain calm and kind even to those people who don't deserve it. You always have a bright smile to offer me that matches your dresses and knocks me for six every time I lay my eyes on you. Your need for organization and sheer stubbornness to keep things neat and tidy and put everything back in its place has a way of driving me crazy while challenging me to be a better man. As odd as that may sound, it's the little things. The first time we kissed I knew I wanted more of that and more of you. I let you go back then, but I never want to make that mistake again.' Levi bent down to put the microphone on the floor, so now only she could hear him. Who was she kidding, you could hear a pin drop in this place right now. Levi didn't get up, he released the microphone and dropped down to one knee, rummaging in the pocket of his cargo shorts. Sabrina's hands flew to her mouth. Tears rushed to her eyes. She was most definitely sweating through her pink dress. Did they actually make deodorant for these kinds of situations? She didn't think so.

'Sabrina. This world likes us to abide by rules; to tell us what we should or shouldn't be doing, who we can and can't love, but forget all that – as far I am concerned you are my world and I adore you.' Levi paused, fiddling with a tiny box, not dropping his gaze from hers. 'Will you marry me?' Levi asked.

Sabrina's knees shook, she gasped into her hands and promptly flung herself onto him. Levi wobbled but caught her around her waist. 'Yes, yes, yes,' she whispered in his ear as she held onto his cheeks planting kisses all over his face. When he put her down, she kept hold of his sweet face. His brown eyes glistened with tears, he touched his lips to hers and kissed her tenderly.

'I think that's a yes, folks!' James' voice sang down the microphone, reminding Sabrina where they were. The crowd erupted with applause and woos, but she wasn't focused on them, just the man she loved with all her heart placing an engagement ring on her finger.

'I cannot believe you. You are mad,' Sabrina said, shaking her head and grinning. Levi's features relaxed into his mischievous smile. 'No matter what, you and I can take on the world, together,' Levi said, placing the stunning, simple pear-shaped single stone diamond ring on her finger. His words touched her very core. They had achieved so many of their dreams together since Amanda had sent San Francisco Beat her way over three years ago. They had stood by each other's sides navigating the crazy world of celebrity together and Levi had been her right-hand man whenever she needed him most; at her grandpa's funeral last year and in facing Lydia's constant put-downs. He made life fun. He was her partner in crime. They were a team. And now they were going to be husband and wife. She squealed and flung her arms around him once more. Levi scooped her up and walked her off to the side of the stage kissing her forehead and hair.

'We've got one more song. Will you wait here for me?' he asked, putting her down and holding her hands. She gazed at the ring on her finger and back at the man she loved.

'No, I'm going to go back down there to watch. I'll be like your number one groupie, front and centre,' she laughed, pushing him back on the stage and blowing him a kiss. He winked then did a little jog to his drum kit as James started up the last song with his guitar riff.

Sabrina skipped down the three steps and immediately got ambushed by Amanda and their mum and dad. 'Congratulations darling,' Dad said, kissing her forehead. 'Congratulations sweetheart,' Mum echoed, giving her a big hug. 'I think it's safe to say you are doing a stellar job and Levi likes your work,' Amanda gushed, excitement in her teasing tone. She winked, pulling her in for an embrace, which made Sabrina laugh and roll her eyes. Her body didn't quite know what to do with itself, she felt high from the nerves and happiness mixing together. The boys were halfway through 'Right Side of Love' – the crowd were singing along to every word with a new abundance of beautiful energy – but then it hit Sabrina.

'What about Louisa and Nanna? Do you think they are going to be sad they weren't here? I feel like we've left Lou out?' The questions tumbled out of Sabrina's mouth as she fiddled with the white-gold ring sparkling on her finger. Amanda looked to their mum and dad as the boys thanked the crowd for joining them for today's incredibly special and intimate gig. They wished everyone a good Easter and told them to stay tuned for the new record coming soon. Sabrina looked up. Amanda and their mum and dad paused to clap and cheer the boys off stage. The crowd began shuffling out of the room, glancing at Sabrina and offering her waves, smiles and thumbs up as they left. Sabrina smiled back, waving her gratitude and thanks. She felt an overwhelming sense of love for the community they had built together; for the people that didn't know her personally yet were happy for her.

'It will be okay, love,' Dad said, rubbing her shoulders. 'We can FaceTime once we get home.' She gave him a half hug in thanks, her brain swirling with pure joy and a dose of anxiety over Louisa's absence from this once in a lifetime event.

But once the room was empty bar her family, Sabrina's eyes caught sight of a group of people sitting in the stands at the back of the room. Tears flooded her face in an instance. Amanda followed her gaze to Louisa, Luca, Nanna, Zia Sofia, Zia Rosa and Zia Emilia, who were sat with both Levi and Dan's mums.

'Bloody hell,' Amanda expressed, rather loudly, catching Louisa's attention. Louisa mouthed, 'Surprise!' before jumping up and racing over to them. Sabrina wrapped her arms around her baby sister as Amanda did the same and the three sisters jumped up and down on the spot, hugging each other tight.

'Incredible band you're managing, Bri. Bit too much talking on stage if you ask me, but excellent music,' Louisa said with a teasing smirk as Sabrina let go of her. Amanda burst out laughing and nudged Louisa. 'Nice one,' Amanda said, before Louisa hugged her too.

'Congratulations Bri. That was ridiculously romantic and so beautiful. I'm so happy for you,' Louisa added. The girls' mum and dad watched their daughters' interaction, their eyes beaming with pride. Just by looking at her mum's wide grin and her dad's casual reaction to Louisa bouncing over, Sabrina knew they had been in on all this all along. Amanda, it seemed, didn't have the foggiest. Sabrina had a feeling she knew what secret Dan had been keeping all along.

'When did you get here? And did you know about this?' Amanda asked Louisa.

'Literally a few hours ago. And Levi didn't say anything other than asking if I could come home for Easter. And, well, with the opportunity falling through with the showcase and with the boutique closed for the holidays, it made sense and I had my suspicions,' Louisa said, as the family started to rise from their seats and head in their direction. Sabrina couldn't wait to squish her nanna. She left Amanda and Louisa to debate the boys' lack of trust in them keeping secrets, and raced over to Nanna.

'*Cara mia*,' Nanna said, reaching up to grab her cheeks and kiss her. 'This Easter is more special than any one before. *Che bella, che bella*. We celebrate.' Sabrina cuddled her nanna with tears in her eyes before her cheeks got pinched three more times by her zias and she showed off her ring to everyone. Levi's mum didn't hesitate to envelope her in a giant hug or hold back from saying, 'I told you so. I knew it was you all along.' Sabrina's heart soared; Joanne had always made Sabrina feel like part of her family. She happily engaged in conversation with Sabrina's zias like there was no language barrier at all. She squealed like a teenager when greeting the girls' mum and got on with everyone like a house on fire. Though Sabrina had never thought to worry about hers and Levi's families getting on, she felt somewhat relieved watching these exchanges.

It wasn't long before the boys made their way to the party

congregated near the stage. Levi made a beeline for Sabrina, picking her up and spinning her around, which received a round of applause from all the family. Sabrina let out a mixture of a squeal and a shriek, unable to hide the complete high she was feeling from this evening. The show had been extraordinary to say the least and not just because of San Francisco Beat's stunning performance. Though she wondered how she was going to explain this one to the publicist tomorrow.

Chapter 23

Nanna's Easter Antipasti

Ingredients:

Melon (always juicy, fresh melon)
Prosciutto
Boiled eggs
Mozzarella
Bread (homemade to crunchy and soft perfection)

What to do:

Slice your melon so they look like smiley faces. Layer around
your serving platter.
Place a bed of prosciutto in the middle with sliced and quartered
boiled eggs.
Add balls of mozzarella between the gaps so the prosciutto doesn't go
soggy. (Make it look pretty.)
Serve bread on the side.

After the exhilarating high from last night's San Francisco Beat gig and Levi's proposal, Amanda had allowed herself to switch off her alarm and indulge in a lie-in. It was Easter Sunday, her bed felt extra fluffy, the mattress extra soft and the hunk of a man next to her extra snuggly. She didn't think she would ever be able to pry herself out of this bed now, until her stomach grumbled informing her that it too was awake; food was calling her name.

'Always hungry,' Dan mumbled sleepily next to her, his face buried into his pillow propped up on his bulging biceps, his hair sticking out every which way.

'You got that right,' Amanda croaked, pushing his hair away from his eyes so she could see him better. 'Are you good this morning?' she asked, stroking his cheekbone. Dan opened his mesmerizing brown eyes that pierced into her hazel ones after a few blinks. Minutes passed as they gazed into each other's eyes; Amanda gently caressed Dan's face, the swirls in his pupils indicating to her that he was thinking. He shuffled, pulling one arm out from under the pillow and propping himself up on it, head against his hand.

'My dad was a liar and a cheat. I never told you before because when you came to San Francisco you were trying to find yourself and get away from a man that had been treating you the same. It killed me inside. I wanted to tell you, but I feared that you would think me like my dad. Over the years I've wanted to get it off my chest, but the media didn't help my case with the stories they liked to spin. I thought it was best just left in the past.' As Dan spoke, Amanda stopped her caressing and her hand stilled on his cheek. Dan's eyes did not desert hers. She didn't want to rush him or bombard him with questions. She wanted to be patient for him; she had to learn.

Dan took her hand and sat up against the bedframe bringing her with him, so she was sat on his knee, nose to nose.

'I didn't know how much it still haunted me until we got together. But again, I chickened out of telling you, too afraid that you would think I was the same and I didn't want you to relive nightmares of what you went through with Jason. In not telling you, I haven't been able to get it out of my mind. I've been torturing myself over becoming him, not being there for you, hurting you and not being able to give you all you need. It's not that I didn't trust you or Liam, baby girl, I didn't trust myself and I acted foolishly and through jealousy, with not knowing

228

what to do about it. I'm deeply sorry,' Dan finished, reaching out and twirling a wavy strand of hers around his fingertips.

Amanda was momentarily speechless, not quite sure how she could fully express the magnitude of the love she felt for him or the desire to protect him and get rid of his pain and so she closed the gap between them and kissed his lips softly and sweetly.

'Sweetheart, I will never judge you based on someone else's actions. You are what I need, all of you, that's it. Our flaws, our faults and everything in between. We can't predict the future, but I am here for you every day, to fight for you and for us. We have to be in the moment and give each other all the honestly, kindness, care, ups and downs, and love we've got. I admit, maybe at first there were niggles, little sprouts of old insecurities that popped up, but when I look into your eyes, when you kiss me, they disappear. I'm a different person now than I was back then. You said it yourself that in San Francisco I was finding myself and you gave me the time and patience to do that. I'm happy Dan. I'm happy in myself and I don't need you to be perfect to make me happy and I don't need you to give me anything but you, if you want to and are ready to give me that. You are not your dad, you are not Jason, you are you and I love you with every piece of me,' Amanda said, an urgency to her voice as she cupped his face and looked deep into his eyes, wanting him to understand. 'I am here for you whatever you need to get through this. I promise to be more understanding of your time for yourself and I'm so sorry that your mum had to go through that. But all I ask is that you try not to shut me out.' Amanda paused while Dan brought her hand to his lips and kissed her fingertips, not breaking their eye contact. She smiled a small smile, allowing Dan's confession to sink in.

'I'm sorry for getting frustrated with you.' she said, pressing her free hand to his chest. 'I'm sorry for not understanding and not knowing all of this.'

'Honey, I appreciate you saying sorry, but you have no reason to apologize to me. You didn't know any of this because I didn't offer this information. The honesty we share empowers me; I was silly to shy away from it now, especially after four years of knowing your heart. But it is a lesson for me and one that I am sorry caused you doubt.' Dan's gruff voice touched her core. This was how it was supposed to be. They were good like this when they let each other in. They listened to one another; even when they each had their own troubles they listened to each other's fears and never made each other feel like either of their emotions didn't matter.

'It is a lesson for us both, I believe,' Amanda agreed, tracing her fingers over the black and grey praying hand tattoo just above his right pec.

'Thank you, my love,' Dan whispered in his gravelly tone, sending tingles up Amanda's spine. 'I'm all in for this, as long as you want me?' His eyes flickered with a hint of inner turmoil; the confident Dan trying to beg off the negative thoughts and need to ask such a question.

'I'm all in, Dan,' Amanda said softly, resting her forehead against his. Dan's eyes closed, a peaceful moment passing between them that further bonded their souls, deepening their connection, now no secrets were being harboured. 'You're stuck with me Mister, for better and for worse. You shall be my guinea pig for life,' she added, kissing his cheek and jumping off the bed, Dan groaning and grabbing at her San Francisco Beat T-shirt as she did so.

'Where are you going? I'd like you stuck right here,' he said, pointing at the bed while brushing a hand through his messy locks. Amanda faltered for a minute, Dan's come-to-bed eyes and kissable lips making her question whether the Easter feast she had to prepare was really that important.

Her belly grumbled once more. Food. She gave Dan a teasing smirk and blew him a kiss before bounding out of the bedroom.

Food was most definitely important. As was cooking for her family. The gorgeous man sprawled out across her bed; well, she knew he'd forgive her once he got a taste of today's menu.

*

'Oh my god!' Louisa shouted the minute she stepped foot out of Amanda's car in the small parking lot opposite *Torta per Tutti*. 'This is not your café! I don't believe it. You did this?' Louisa practically screeched as she ran around the bay window, her eyes darting over the awning, the paint and trying to peak through the closed blinds. Amanda couldn't help chuckling at her sister's enthusiasm and the attention it was drawing from passersby.

Amanda didn't even have it in her to crack a sarcastic comment about bringing her sister to someone else's cafe. A clever line had got choked up in her throat with the fact that she had in fact bloody done it and yes, this was her café. Quickly swatting away her tears she unlocked the door while Louisa jumped up and down behind her, eager to see inside. Over the threshold Louisa gasped, 'It's stunning, it's absolutely stunning. *Brava* sis. Wow,' before she ran off to admire the place.

Bustling behind Amanda signalled her family's arrival; Dan getting closer with Nanna on his arm and his mum following closely with her mum and dad.

Suddenly Amanda felt ridiculous; her cheeks flamed. She blinked a few times to get rid of the fuzziness in her head, but it dawned on her that this was the first time Nanna was seeing *Torta per Tutti*, the first time her zias would be welcomed into her home, the first time Dan's mum would get to see the crazy vision her and Dan had been rambling on about for years. For weeks she had worried about what the press were saying about her café. She had been agonizing over what restaurant reviewers would say about her food, but that was nothing compared to the bubbles that gurgled in her stomach now. These were the people that mattered; what her nanna thought meant everything to her. Would her nanna think that Amanda had done good by her grandpa too?

'*Mamma mia, cara mia*,' Nanna said, reaching Amanda's side. 'It's marvelous.' Tears sprinkled down Nanna's face and before Amanda knew it, her face was wet too. Amanda cursed her eyeliner for her not being able to wipe away her tears.

'Your grandpa would be so proud, *cara*. So proud,' Nanna said, squeezing Amanda's arms before pulling her forcefully down to her level with all the strength only an Italian nonna possessed, to hug her and kiss her cheeks. '*Grazie* Nanna,' Amanda said, wrapping her arms around her nanna's neck and hugging her tight. Amanda's cheeks were then pinched and kissed until raw as Zia Emilia, Zia Rosa and Zia Sofia congratulated her. '*Brava, bambola, brava*,' Zia Sofia whispered, tears sparkling in her own eyes.

When Amanda was content that she had shown her Nanna and Zias every nook and cranny of the café, she inched towards the kitchen, eager to start cooking today's menu. First, she would get the coffee brewing, pull out a few leftover pastries for breakfast and set them up out front as her family milled about. Sabrina and the rest of the boys would be around later, and she had offered her Easter dinner invitation to Tyler, Francesca, Kate and Liam too and would love it if they were able to make it. Her heart was full that she was able to host this Easter in her very own café and the chatter she could hear while cooking gave her food that extra dash of love.

*

All her favourite people in the entire world were in her café, safe, happy and together around the table. *Screw the eyeliner and mascara*, Amanda thought as she tried to quell the tears that trickled down her cheeks due to laughter from the current conversation she was having and the sheer overwhelming love in her heart from the scene around her.

'You mean to say that you kept it all from Amanda?' Emma mock-admonished her son from across the table for being so sneaky. Dan shrugged casually, that confident side smile of his causing a dimple to appear in his cheek. He wasn't fair. 'He didn't tell me anything, not a sausage,' Amanda said, swatting at Dan's leg that was next to hers, but he caught her hand in his and brought it to his chest. Through his loose buttoned silky shirt and beneath his tattooed pecs, she could feel his heart beating. Why did this man always cause desire to flood through her at the most inappropriate of times? Maybe she should have let him see to her desires this morning instead of succumbing to breakfast. He smirked at her knowingly.

'We can keep secrets, you know. We wouldn't have told her,' Louisa said indignantly, referring to Dan and Levi's secret keeping of Levi's proposal, while puffing out her chest, making the glitter on her cropped long-sleeved pink top sparkle under the open light bulb.

'Ahh, you might be able to keep secrets Louisa,' Dan started, winking at Louisa and titling his head towards Amanda in lieu of finishing his sentence. He brought Amanda's hand up to his lips and kissed her palm softly. Amanda prodded him in the chest with her other hand, knowing full well what he was attesting to and stuck out her tongue. Mature, she was not.

Everyone was seated around the table, wine glasses filled to the top, juice for Francesca's kids, plates brimming with food, laughter and chatter in the air. Amanda stood up, bringing her glass with her.

'First and foremost, can we please *salute* to the newly engaged.' Cue clapping, cheers, hollers and wolf whistles from James and Tyler – who was in town for a few more days before he had to be back in LA to begin recording his next album. 'Levi and Sabrina, we are all so happy for you both. You make such a beautiful

233

couple, an amazing team and we all wish you an abundance of love and happiness and a whole lot of fun going forward.' More cheers and congratulations made their way around the table. 'Secondly, I just wanted to raise a glass to our amazing baby sister. Louisa you are making us so proud. In a few short months you have busted out of your comfort zone, brought some absolutely stunning pieces to life and admittingly have made us a teeny bit jealous with your Italian adventures. We love you and I am so grateful that you are here today.' Amanda's eyes grew a tad misty – how could she possibly have any more tears left?

'Thank you to you all for being here. I can't quite believe that you are all here.' Amanda laughed, shaking her head at Dan. 'There wouldn't even be a here if it wasn't for all your love, support, help and belief in me and my dreams. Thank you all for everything. I love each and every one of you. *Buona appetito e salute,*' Amanda finished to a round of glasses clinking and a chorus of, '*Salute!*'.

She took her seat. Plates were passed around the table. Salami, prosciutto, *caciocavallo*, provolone picante and olives all whizzed past her eyes. For a moment she simply sat back and watched her family digging in. Then she turned to her side to find Dan gazing at her, his deep brown eyes studying her. She grabbed his hand and tugged it a little, standing up and indicating that she wished for him to do the same. '*Scusaci.*' She nodded in the direction of the table, though everyone was far too engrossed in the divine spread of fresh breads and meats before them to notice her quick march into the kitchen. Dan came in at a much slower pace a few seconds after. His movements sure and calm, their discussion this morning lending itself to his more Dan-like demeanour throughout today.

Amanda squinted at him. Her eyes wandered over his blue jeans and loose printed shirt. He had his sleeves scrunched up so she could see his toned forearms and inked skin. He ran a hand through his curly locks. His hair was longer than he'd ever had it since she met him four years ago and it only accentuated his chiseled features and beauty.

'You're not like anyone I've ever met, you know,' Amanda said, putting her hand through his hair and tracing his jawline with her fingertips.

His tongue appeared; he ran it over his bottom lip, stopping at the corner of his lips where that side smile of his took over; sexy came effortlessly to him and it made Amanda's knees buckle. He held her up by catching her hips. She bit down on her bottom lip and a smirk played on his for a teasing second before he kissed her. It was a deep, hungry kiss, filled with not only passion and want, but a need, a vulnerability and tenderness that deepened her connection to him. Amanda had always felt that strong pull towards Dan, since the day they met. She saw beneath his cool exterior and he saw through her stubborn heart. Four years they had known each other, but it had only been a little under four months now that she could kiss his lips and feel that surge of love for him in an entirely different way; in a way that she didn't believe could be more powerful, but it was. How could she possibly love him more than she already did? But she did. Since they began dating, every kiss was like a new experience that unlocked more pieces of her soul. And when she felt Dan's soul reach out to hers, she felt drunk, dizzy and yet an unexplainable sense of calm.

'When you kiss me like that, all the craziness vanishes,' Amanda said, pulling away from his kiss a little breathlessly, resting her head on his forehead. In heels she could match his height. "Are we good now? No more secrets? Unless, you know it's the likes of marriage proposals." Amanda added with a playful roll of her eyes; she couldn't believe the thought of Dan helping Levi with something as wonderful as a marriage proposal hadn't crossed her mind. Some secrets weren't exactly terrible.

'Is that a proposition for me to never stop kissing you? Because that works for me,' he said, rubbing his nose against hers. "And yes, we're more than good and no more secrets unless …" Dan's voice trailed off, his lips finding hers once more. There was no need for more words, they were on the same page and it made Amanda's insides flutter with excitement and possibilities for their future together. Amanda's hands were on Dan's neck, his hands strong yet gentle in her hair, holding her head to where he needed her, to keep her, to kiss her.

'I'm pretty sure this kitchen's for making food in, man, not babies.' Levi's smooth voice dragged Amanda unwillingly out of the other world Dan's kiss had transported her to. She took a stumbling step back, bumping into the kitchen island, making Levi laugh. Dan wasn't fazed, his hands simply dropped to her lower back, keeping her steady, before he took his time to turn around and address his best friend.

'Can we help you?' Dan asked Levi, as he flipped his unruly curls over his head. This action didn't do a thing to Levi but caused Amanda's breath to hitch.

'Just wanted to say thanks dude, is all,' Levi started, walking closer to Dan and reaching out his hand. 'Thanks for last night. I couldn't have pulled it off without you.' Dan shook Levi's hand and pulled him in for a hug. Amanda watched them both, her heart bursting with love for her boyfriend and now soon to be brother-in-law.

'Come here you,' Levi said turning to Amanda once Dan had released him. She stepped forward into his embrace. 'Sorry if I hogged your boyfriend a little too much these past few months and made you worry. He's been like my personal assistant trying to pull off arranging trips and getting our moms here. I know it wasn't easy for him keeping it all a secret from you, but I promise, he's all yours now and thank you for this gorgeous celebration today,' Levi added, giving her a squeeze and sending Dan a wink, no doubt teasing him about the personal assistant part.

Amanda chuckled at Levi's use of the word gorgeous but appreciated his sentiment about Dan; everyone had been aware of the tension. She felt grateful to have friends who she could feel open with and who loved her and Dan enough to care. And there was a part of her that was relieved to know that part of Dan's distant behavior was due to him keeping such a beautiful secret and helping Levi. 'Well, I never could have predicted this four years ago,' she said with a laugh.

'What's that?' Levi asked, as they stood huddled up by the kitchen island.

'Us three standing in my very own café. Dan and I an actual couple and you and Sabrina on the road to marriage,' Amanda replied, leaning back on the counter, her stomach rumbling. She was ready to tuck into the feast that she had lovingly prepared.

Levi and Dan both shrugged, matching each other with their handsome smiles. 'It's been a pretty rad year so far,' Levi noted. He wasn't wrong and Amanda nodded in agreement. Then she threw one arm around Dan's shoulder and the other around Levi's. 'Come on, everyone will wonder where we got to,' she said, leading the march to the door.

'I can just tell them you were getting busy trying to put a bun in the oven,' Levi teased. Amanda shoved him with her hip as the door swung open. 'Behave or I'll sign you and your fiancée up for dance lessons,' Amanda said with wink as they stepped into the café. The sight before her took her breath away all over again. Mum was fussing over Nanna. Emma and Joanne were chatting happily to her zias and Louisa. Luca, James and Tyler were talking loudly, god help Luca trying to understand those two boisterous wonders. Dylan was engaged in play with Francesca's children and the girls' dad was speaking merrily with Francesca's husband and her papa, while Francesca herself was laughing heartily with Kate and Liam. It was a beautiful site to be hold.

'Ooh dance lessons. We should take dance lessons for the wedding maybe, that's a good idea, Amanda. I mean, there's no rush in having a wedding anytime soon, but we could practice, be prepared, it would be fun,' Sabrina said bouncing over to Amanda, Dan and Levi, having overheard their conversation.

Levi glanced at Amanda with a twinkle in his eye, then turned to Sabrina and took her hands in his. 'Anything you want, baby,' he said. Amanda relaxed her arm from around Levi's neck, allowing him to wander off and talk all things wedding related with his new fiancée.

'Hungry?' She felt Dan's lips brush her ear as his gravelly voice sent her stomach swirling.

'Aren't I always?' she replied, mimicking the line he so often used on her whenever she asked if he wanted food or was subtly hinting at him to be her guinea pig for a new recipe. He winked at her and lead her back to their seats at the table.

They took their seats at the table and helped themselves to lamb and roast potatoes, breadsticks and *mortadella* and joined in with the flowing wine and conversations. The café was toasty, warm from the buzzing bodies and high spirits. Amanda chewed thoughtfully on a lemon-stuffed olive. Her family was growing. Friends old and new had become family. Her grandpa had been right; she had never felt richer.

Chapter 24

Lemon Cupcakes

Ingredients:

For the cupcakes:

Eggs
Butter
Sugar
Flour
Pinch of salt
Lemon rind
Lemon juice

For the frosting:

Limoncello
Butter
Icing sugar

What to do:

For the cupcakes:

Cream the butter and sugar together.
Add eggs one at a time and mix.

Add in the dry ingredients and combine, before stirring in lemon juice and lemon rind.
Bake at 180 degrees for 20–25 minutes.

For the frosting:

Using a mixer or an electric whisk, beat butter and icing sugar, adding a few drops of limoncello at a time, to taste.
Once cupcakes have cooled, spread frosting over the top. (Drizzle more limoncello over the top if desired. Almost always desired.)

It felt like no sooner had Louisa delivered the three time-consuming and extravagant dresses to Giulia, she found herself under a billow of lace once more. It had been a flying visit to the UK over Easter, two months ago, and she still felt as though she was on Aladdin's magic carpet, whizzing through the clouds. *Torta per Tutti* had been a fairytale come to life. Amanda had created a piece of Italy in the Northern Quarter and, even though it might appear biased, Louisa thought every corner of it – from the lush, potted herbs and violets, dainty ceramic cups, pops of blues and yellows, to the exquisite pastries themselves – was perfection.

San Francisco Beat had torn the roof down with their intimate Easter show and Levi's surprise proposal had been the most grand and romantic gesture Louisa had had the pleasure of witnessing; she could still hear his speech in her head and felt thrilled for her sister. She had been able to take Luca on a tour of Manchester's finest – that being Old Trafford, which had been the top of Luca's list – and show him a token of what Manchester had to offer. She hoped she could return soon and explore more of the UK with him, though he had been content seeing where she had grown up and she had been grateful to Levi for keeping her in the loop and getting her home for such a momentous occasion in her sister's life.

Now, tucked away at the back of Giulia's boutique on the mountain side of the Amalfi Coast, Louisa was veiled with a super special secret project. Her fingers tingled and her heart beat an overexcited, joyous beat every time she got to work on this. Louisa took every job seriously and respected every design and alteration she had to do, but this one – this one needed triple the care, time and patience. Every detail, every lace thread and pearl bead would be a piece of art. Five months from now it would be revealed, and it had to be exemplary. It wasn't like the dress's recipient was some demanding, monstrous client – in fact, she was everything but. She was laidback, sweet and totally giddy about letting Louisa have full creative control over what she was making. The pressure Louisa felt, she had put on herself.

Louisa looked the fabric up and down. She had the frame and the base material, but it was time to nip, tuck, tweak and sew to bring her idea off the page and on to the mannequin before her. She scanned her desk for her sketchbook to go over the final design specs but couldn't place it. Where was her book? A lump grew in her throat as she rummaged around her workshop, moving tape measures and pin cushions and lifting boxes of lemon cupcakes to find her prized possession. Where was the darn thing? She had it just yesterday when she was sneaking in minutes away from her work for Milan Fashion Week, coming up in autumn, to add more intricate bits and pieces to her super special secret project whenever she could.

Small beads of sweat started tickling Louisa's forehead, her pulse beating quicker and quicker. She looked under the worktop, peeked under the dress. She needed her notebook. More importantly she needed to know where her notebook was. Her eyes were the only ones allowed to see its contents.

When the front bell chimed, letting Louisa know a customer had left and the shop was clear, she dashed out to speak to Giulia.

'Giulia, have you seen my notebook? The white one? It only

had sketches and notes for one design in it, but it is *molto* important,' Louisa asked, shifting her weight from foot to foot, unable to calm her nerves.

Giulia's gorgeous fuscia lips curved into a delighted grin, her hands began clapping.

'I want to surprise you. I see the design *e* it is like a princess, no? I pass it on to someone very special.' Giulia's excitement was evident in her childlike singsong voice, meanwhile Louisa knew her face had turned a wonderful shade of green. She felt faint. She had to burst Giulia's happy bubble right now. There was no way around this, she was going to hurt Giulia's feelings, but it had to be done.

'Giulia, I need my book back right now.' Louisa spoke calmly, doing her utmost to ignore her clammy state and fix this disaster without too much drama.

'You do not need to worry, Louisa. Your work, they love it. It is one of your best. Giulia takes care of it. *Non preoccuparti,*' Giulia said, dismissing Louisa with a happy wave of her hands.

'No, no, no Giulia. Whoever it is, they can't have that design. They absolutely, one million per cent cannot have that design,' Louisa said, her voice building with exasperation as panic rose in her chest.

'*Ma cara, per che? E bellisima, e* Viola Donatella!' Giulia protested, cheekily dropping such a name into the conversation, like she had let the cat out of the bag when she shouldn't have. Louisa nearly choked on the air she breathed next. Viola Donatella. Oh god! Louisa understood how crazy she must sound to Giulia. This was Viola Donatella. How had Giulia managed to get her work into the hands of such fashion royalty? The magnitude of Viola Donatella looking at one of her designs was not lost on her, but she couldn't do it, she couldn't possibly give it away. Not to her, not to anyone. But Viola Donatella? All eyes had been on this Italian fashion mogul for the past two years running. Her dresses were like nothing else Louisa had ever laid her eyes on before; they were haute couture, bewitching and absolutely flawless in both design and creation.

'*Ma* Giulia, it is not for sale. It is not for the catwalk or for magazines.' Like every Italian conversation, this was escalating quickly; Louisa couldn't curb her rising and slightly high-pitched voice. Both women were now waving frantically and pacing the shop, shouting over each other. Over the past six months their bond had been well and truly tied and, between work and family affairs, they had become like sisters.

'*Per che, per che*, I do not understand,' Giulia yelled, frustration in her blue eyes at Louisa being so ungrateful for this opportunity. 'She like it. I say it is hers. You will be happy *per che,* this make your dreams come true. *Ma* now I tell you, you are not happy.' Giulia sounded like Louisa's mum and nanna whenever they told the girls off when they were kids. The guilt in Louisa's stomach was real.

'I know, I know, I know,' Louisa shouted back. 'I am happy. Thank you. You are incredible and I can't believe it.'

'Then you not be silly or nervous. We wait for what she says next,' Giulia said with a wave and a defiant nod, mirroring Louisa's nanna when Louisa said she wasn't hungry, but her nanna insisted on cooking, telling her she was hungry and needed to eat anyway. But this wasn't as simple as taking a few bites of *melanzane* to appease her nanna or was it? Louisa tugged at her bottom lip, one hand twirling around her high ponytail in thought. She took a deep breath, grateful that there were no customers in the shop or waiting to be seen to. No, if there was one thing the girls had learnt from their new ventures this year was that recognition, success, fame and fortune all came second to family and remembering who you were. Sabrina had faltered finding her feet once more in the world of entertainment, but Levi had got her back on track showing her that love was more important than record sales and that he would always choose her over the latter. Amanda had feared renowned critics and reviewers but came to realize that those who truly mattered were the customers that kept coming back, whom she gave a home to. While at the same time she and Dan learnt that though outside interference and events can affect a relationship, it was the two people in it and how they treated each other and loved each other that made all the difference. Of course, having one of her designs gracing the cover of *Donatella Designs* would be a dream come true for Louisa, but she could not do it at the expense of her client.

'Giulia, no. I can't. I need it back. Can you get it back, please?' Louisa said, her voice mellowing out, out of shock and fear.

There was no denying the disappointed look on Giulia's face. Louisa feared Giulia would not likely be doing her any such favours again. What with this and not winning the showcase, Louisa was zero for two. She would seriously have to make up for it come Milan Fashion week.

'*Per che, per che?*' Giulia yelled, her thumb and forefingers pressed together angrily pointing in Louisa's direction; her one final attempt at understanding Louisa's crazy request.

'Because … because it's Sabrina's wedding dress,' Louisa shouted back, her arms rising at her sides and flopping back down. She felt ashamed that she had let it out of her sight in the first place now.

Giulia's eyes bulged out of her head. Her pacing immediately picked back up. '*Mamma mia,*' she exclaimed. 'You not tell me this. Ehhhh, *mamma mia,*' she added under her breath, pushing past Louisa and picking up the boutique's phone. She dialed while shaking her head at Louisa and uttering, '*Mamma mia*' for the tenth time. Louisa stared at her until Giulia gave her a stern glare and nodded towards the back of the shop. Louisa shuffled back into her office, her feet dragging behind her.

Was she being insane? Couldn't she just design another dress for Sabrina? But this had been *the* dress; the dress where every line drawn, every idea thought, and every embellishment made, was made with Sabrina in mind. The look on Sabrina's face when

Louisa had presented it to her had been something Louisa would never forget. It had been the recognition and success she wanted to achieve; getting to design something so special for a person so special to her and them love it with all their heart; she couldn't possibly give Sabrina second best now. But was Giulia going to be able to get her design back? Too distracted to concentrate on the rack of work next to her, Louisa picked up a lemon cupcake and stuffed it in her mouth. Lemon cupcakes were the real deal when made with lemons from Amalfi.

As she licked her fingers, savouring every morsel, Giulia walked into the back. Louisa stood to attention, wiping her hands on her pink slimline trousers; instantly regretting the decision. She would have to put the washing on as soon as she got home. Giulia followed her movements, her face a little less sparkly than it had been earlier when she thought she had done a wonderful surprise for Louisa. Guilt churned in Louisa's stomach once more. Giulia's intention had been pure of heart. Louisa couldn't be mad, but she could be more careful in future where she put her notebooks when filled with super special secret projects.

Louisa raised her eyebrows to urge Giulia to speak. Giulia sighed, but smiled a hopeful smile.

'I did my best, *ma* she would like to know if her magazine can cover the wedding of your sister? This dress, she believes, is special.'

Louisa felt her jaw hit the floor with a hard knock. She was speechless, stunned, completely taken aback. She had to lean back against her desk to keep herself upright. Was it just her or was the room spinning? She felt a touch woozy. Viola Donatella wanted to feature *her* dress in her bridal magazine and cover Sabrina and Levi's wedding? Louisa was both thrilled and jealous. Her brain ran away with images of how unbelievably beautiful shots of Levi and her sister would be in such an elegant publication. The thing was, that while this sounded like an absolute dream for her, one that she would happily sign herself and Luca up for anytime, Sabrina and Levi were not her and Luca. Keeping their private life private was an everyday battle for them; would they really want it to be in print for the world to witness? Would Sabrina recognize the opportunity it bore for Louisa? Would she maybe take one for the team? There was only one way to find out …

Crashing cymbals and a solid bass line filled the screen first, followed by a whirring of a kitchen mixer, before both her sisters came into view looking slightly harassed.

'Sup Lou.' Amanda greeted her from a distance, waving with dough between her fingers, her phone propped up on the counter away from the food.

'Hey Lou, everything alright?' Sabrina asked next, clipboard in one hand, bright eyes and glossy lips taking up most of the screen. Louisa smiled, nerves causing her question to get lodged in her throat. How could she put this so Sabrina didn't feel pressured?

'Sabrina what would your publicist say …' Louisa started, then shook her head. 'Sorry, what would you say or how would you feel if there was a small, smidgen of a chance that your dress could feature in *Donatella Designs* with maybe a wee possibility of you being in it and them doing a feature on you and Levi? I know the wedding is a family affair and I understand privacy being an issue, but just throwing it out there on the off-chance that Viola Donatella saw my design and loved it, you know, on the off-chance and like in another universe? And then I just got thinking about how magical it would be to share some pictures in a tasteful way rather than them being leaked and I think it would be a wonderful way to show the boys in such a light with this new album and how special and from the heart it is.' Louisa was out of breath rushing to get everything off her chest and her idea out in the open, the rambling just kept coming. She scrunched up her nose, terrified of her sister's response. She considered she had a fifty-fifty shot at a yes. Sabrina loved fashion and all things floaty and elegant, but at the same time she was all about her band and keeping herself out of the limelight. If

246

Sabrina said yes it could bode well for both of them; Louisa being taken seriously as a fashion designer and getting her foot in the door and Sabrina and Levi being seen as team and a pairing to be reckoned with.

When Louisa stopped talking Sabrina's mouth flew open; her hazel eyes sparkled. 'Are you serious Lou?' That sounded like an excited, 'Are you serious?' to Louisa but she needed to be a million per cent certain.

'It's just an idea I was thinking about, that's all. So, you, hypothetically, would be fine with it and like the idea?' she asked nonchalantly, swiping frosting off a lemon cupcake. How many lemon cupcakes should one eat in a single sitting?

'Are you kidding me? I'd wear that dress everywhere, every day for the rest of my life if I could. Of course I'd show it off in that beautiful magazine. My goodness, oh wow. That would be too weird though, wouldn't it? I'm not a model,' Sabrina said, her eyes glazing over as if dreaming about what it would be like.

Louisa felt bad for shouting at Giulia earlier. She could make this work, couldn't she? Sabrina was naturally stunning; her airy nature came through her features often giving her a radiant glow. Louisa could picture her on any cover, but in her one-of-a-kind wedding dress and with natural makeup, *Donatella Designs* would be lucky to have her. Not to mention getting to feature one of the world's hottest drummers alongside her. Put Levi in a tux and the magazine would fly off the shelves. The shots of them both would be utterly gorgeous. Furthermore, one of the reasons Louisa adored *Donatella Designs* was that it featured models and people of all different shapes and sizes and ethnicities; everyone could be a model and rightly so.

'Just to clarify, you'd be totally cool with it?' Louisa asked once more, aware that she was going to start hyperventilating soon. Just then Giulia poked her head in front of her phone screen and in rapid fire Italian gave Sabrina the run down on what she had been discussing on the phone. Louisa stared at her feisty Italian boss with a mixture of awe in her eyes while doing an impeccable impression of a goldfish.

'You didn't tell me all that,' Louisa noted to Giulia, trying to process the new information that Giulia had just shared with her sisters. Apparently, Viola had spoken of envisioning the dress amongst a winter fairytale. Now, either Viola had some sort of crystal ball, could read minds or she was just really, really good at her job (being that she was Italy's number one designer for wedding dresses, Louisa would bet on the latter), but a winter fairytale matched Sabrina's wedding plan already. Sabrina had talked of getting married at a Duomo in Ravello and holding a reception at Hotel Caruso after falling in love with its Neapolitan style and tradition and its lush gardens. Twinkling lights, garden candles and a touch of Christmas would make it a photographer's dream and the most divine backdrop for Louisa's design. Excitement bubbled inside Louisa; it felt like this was all meant to be.

'*Ma*, we need Sabrina's blessing first,' Giulia responded innocently with a shrug. Sabrina was currently rendered speechless – even Amanda had put down the dough and come closer to her phone to take everything in. Louisa shrugged. 'I think we have her blessing,' she said with a chuckle.

A few moments passed where everyone simply stared at each other. The music had since silenced, as had Amanda's kitchen mixer. There was an electricity in the air, a sort of magic that only the power of celebrating love could induce.

'Sup ladies?' Levi's voice interrupted the calm as he appeared on screen to give Sabrina a kiss. Sabrina didn't skip a beat and got straight to it.

'How would you feel about having our wedding covered by a prestigious bridal publication? It wouldn't be too invasive, more about the dress and the reception, nothing at the church,' Sabrina asked with a giddiness in her tone.

'Is it something you would like? Would that be good for Lou and her design?' Levi replied casually, saluting the screen to say hi to everyone.

'I think it would be beautiful,' Sabrina expressed. Levi kissed her forehead. 'Then let's do it,' he said, simple as that. Louisa could feel Giulia melt beside her, having not been accustomed to the charm of the members of San Francisco Beat. Though they were always swoon-worthy on camera, it was dialed up by about three thousand per cent in person. Oh, Giulia was in for a treat come the wedding when she would get to meet them.

'Thank you both, I appreciate this with all my heart. I love you,' Louisa gushed as the reality of this conversation started to hit her. Amanda had remained quiet throughout the exchange and was back to prodding and poking dough only now with an even bigger grin on her face than before; it was not often she cooked without a smile on her face, even when frazzled it was there.

'Is that okay with you Amanda?' Sabrina asked. This affected everyone. Amanda was of course in charge of the wedding cake and Louisa knew that the nerves that came with making something for someone special was one thing but then to have it under scrutiny in a magazine was another.

'Ooh I don't know, I was thinking of phoning it in; now this seems like a big deal it might be too much like hard work,' Amanda said, appearing up close again, a teasing side smirk creasing her face.

Levi promptly burst out laughing while Sabrina and Louisa rolled their eyes.

'Are you behaving, baby girl?' Dan's voice crept up behind Levi. Louisa watched Giulia take a seat and start fanning herself with papers. Louisa laughed at the 'Dan effect'. Amanda chuckled, 'Don't I always?'

'Right, well this is awesome.' Louisa said, shaking her head in disbelief. Not only was she going to have one of her designs in a high-end magazine, but it had now become a family affair; she was getting to do it with her sisters.

'I feel like *The Avengers* have assembled,' Amanda noted, her eyes on Dan.

'*Mamma mia*,' Giulia chuckled, taking in the sisters talking and Levi and Dan's handsome faces squeezed onto Sabrina's screen.

'Right, well we best get back to it, everyone has a whole lot of work to do,' Sabrina said, gently waving her boys away to find their instruments. The band were currently doing rehearsals for their tour that would be kicking off in Manchester in July and take them all around the world over the summer. Louisa was incredibly excited that they would be making a stop in Italy. She couldn't wait to hear their new album live and get to fit her sister for her wedding dress while she was at it.

There certainly was something to be said for stepping out of your comfort zone and learning balance and patience in both life and work. Sure, she had failed in scoring the magazine spread from the Young Designers Fashion Showcase and she had missed Amanda's grand opening, but fate would have it that Louisa was able to attend Sabrina's engagement, spend Easter with her family and visit *Torta per Tutti* and now she was getting to work with Viola Donatella. Louisa had learnt over the past few months that there would be hits and there would be misses. The road to your dreams was not a straight path. The dream itself came with a life that needed to be lived; with ups and downs, twists and turns, happy chapters and sad ones. It's who you share the moments with and how you cope with those turns that matter the most.

ACKNOWLEDGEMENTS

I want to start by saying a massive thank you to the entire team at HarperCollins and HQ Digital UK for believing in me and allowing me the opportunity to write more books. To Nia Beynon for your support and initial thoughts on *The Ingredients for Happiness* and for getting me on the right track with where I wanted the story to go. To Cara Chimirri for always being there to advise, guide and encourage me – emails from you always motivate me and make me smile. To Suzy Clarke, thank you for pushing me and making sense of my mind, and helping me to tell the story I wanted to tell. I can't express how much I appreciate all your input and how much it helped me to get the story out of my head and onto the page when I felt a bit lost. You are amazing. Thank you also to the wonderful design team for creating such a gorgeous cover that I can't stop staring at and fills my heart with so much joy. And thank you to Helen Williams for your edits, input and for catching my (sometimes amusing) spelling mistakes.

Thank you to all the readers, book bloggers, book reviewers, awesome persons of social media and lovely humans who shared, tweeted, messaged, liked, read, talked about and championed *How to Bake a New Beginning* and joined in with my excitement to bring you this book you are now holding: *The Ingredients for Happiness*. I honestly wish I could hug you all. Since last summer you have filled my life with such light, love and joy and it means the world to me. To know my book connected with you, made you smile and that you enjoyed it is everything to me. I appreciate every single one of you and can't thank you enough. You are truly incredible. Please know that I appreciate the time it takes you to read, review, tweet, take pictures and all the other wonderful ways you support authors.

To Maxine Morrey, Katie Ginger, Victoria Cooke, Jennifer Joyce, Rebecca Raisin, Belinda Missen, Lindsey Kelk and Zoe May – I adore you all and thank you with all my heart for your love and support, and for being there for me every step of the way. I am beyond grateful to be able to turn to each of you for words of wisdom and inspiration. Your support has been invaluable and has meant the world to me. There are so many amazing authors who I get to engage with on social media and meet at events, and to you all I want to say thank you too. I'm afraid of missing anyone out if I start a list, but you all inspire me daily and I am grateful to each and every one of you for continuing to make me feel so welcomed within the world of books.

Thank you, Harry Styles, for just being so lovely and keeping the inspiration of love alive in this book when I really needed it. (This book has been fueled on Harry Styles 'being cute for 30 minutes' videos and lots of coffee.) Thank you Heidi Swain for the endless Chris Evans gifs, Katie for the Sebastian Stan gif game that got me to the end of this book and Kelly, Jen, Shelby and Amanda for the Zachary Levi pictures and gifs that injected my life with so much happiness and made writing romance fun again when I was feeling down.

Thank you to all my lovely friends, especially Jamin, Brittany, Katherine, Michael, Sam, Kayleigh and Negin, for being pure awesomeness and for being there for me. Thank you for our talks, that so often helped to clear my head so I could write better and get this book finished. I hope you all know how much you mean to me and how grateful I am to you all.

Thank you to my incredible family. There were some unexpected plot twists in my life during the release of *How to Bake a New Beginning* and during the writing and editing process of this book that made writing a touch difficult. Your love and support have always gone above and beyond but this time it left me pretty speechless. Mum and Dad, again I struggle to fully express how much I love you both (it's a heck of a lot) and how grateful I am for all you do. Kelly, Chris and Jen – I have the best sisters and brother in the entire world. I love you with all my heart and then some. Chris, Kate and Ashley – I don't think anyone could have a more wonderful, supportive and inspiring set of sisters- and brother-in-law than me. I love you. Nanna, it's hard for me to write without getting teary but you are my world and the absolute strongest person I know. You and Grandad are the heart of these books and I am forever grateful for the love you fill my heart with. I love you both with every piece of me. To all the Knotts, Gentiles and Sharpes, I love you tons.

Lastly, I do have to just take an extra sentence or two to thank my Kelly again. From tweeting, taking endless pictures, Instagramming, overseeing blog tours and cover reveals, to keeping me on track, organized and positive, you have been the absolute best and most amazing cheerleader in the world. I know you're my twin and it sometimes goes without saying that we are there for each other, but honestly, I never want to take for granted all you do. Thank you for everything!!! Oh, and Jen: Aces!!

Dear Reader,

I feel incredibly blessed that I am getting to write to you again, at the back of my second book. It still feels very surreal to me that I am getting to do this. It's an absolute dream come true.

Thank you so very much for picking up this book and for giving me a chance. I truly hope you enjoy diving into the worlds of Amanda, Sabrina and Louisa once more. I have been extremely excited to bring you along on the next part of their adventure and hope that they will inspire you to go after your own dreams and passions in life.

Just like with the sister's, there will be bumps in the road, be it outside critics, life changing events, doubts in your own mind, good days and bad but I truly believe you can do it. Please know that you are awesome, worth it and so amazing and the world needs your love, your voice, your creativity and talent.

I hope this book makes you smile, provides you with a little escapism or connects with you in some way. Thank you again for giving it a read.

All my love.
Lucy xx

Dear Reader,

Thank you so much for taking the time to read this book – we hope you enjoyed it! If you did, we'd be so appreciative if you left a review.

Here at HQ Digital we are dedicated to publishing fiction that will keep you turning the pages into the early hours. We publish a variety of genres, from heartwarming romance, to thrilling crime and sweeping historical fiction.

To find out more about our books, enter competitions and discover exclusive content, please join our community of readers by following us at:

🐦 *@HQDigitalUK*

🅕 *facebook.com/HQDigitalUK*

Are you a budding writer? We're also looking for authors to join the HQ Digital family! Please submit your manuscript to:

HQDigital@harpercollins.co.uk.

Hope to hear from you soon!

ONE PLACE. MANY STORIES

Turn the page for an extract from
How to Bake a New Beginning by Lucy Knott ...

How
to Bake
a New
Beginning

Three sisters. One Christmas.
A whole lot of pastries.

LUCY KNOTT

Chapter 1

Beans on Toast

Ingredients:

Bread
Butter
Heinz baked beans (Always stock up when you go to Target)

What to do:

Toast bread and heat up beans in a saucepan or microwave. (Never tell Amanda you use the microwave.)

Butter toast and drizzle beans over the top. (Doesn't taste quite like home, but it will do, I suppose. Don't get sad, you're living your dream and don't be ungrateful, the boys are awesome, and you've worked so hard to get to this point. Mmm beans, I wonder what Levi is up to? Why does England have to be six hours ahead when you're spending another night alone and could do with a sister chat? Just eat your beans.)

Sabrina realized that she had been mindlessly shuffling paper for the past fifteen minutes. It was gone five in the afternoon and she needed to go home and pack. Yet, she was sitting at her desk, eyes wide, staring at the mini chandelier that hung from the ceiling. The crystals bounced light off the walls and led to the dreamy state Sabrina found herself in as she daydreamed about the day that Levi first burst into her office.

Why did she always do this to herself? Every Christmas for the past two years she couldn't get him out of her head. Was she really that lonely? Couldn't she fantasize about men who weren't off limits? Better yet, couldn't she stop fantasizing altogether and venture into the real world and meet a non-rock-star man who wasn't way out of her league? She huffed to herself as her phone rang, startling her. Seeing that it was her baby sister, Louisa, she put on an enthusiastic smile and answered with the cheeriest hello she could muster.

'Are you all packed? Do you have everything ready for tomorrow?' her not-quite-as-cheerful-sounding sister asked abruptly.

Sabrina blinked away the dancing crystals of the chandelier that were starting to give her a headache and went back to shuffling papers as she answered her sister's questions. 'Yes, yes, of course, Lou. I have everything organized – you know me, what am I if not organized?' She felt a twinge of guilt for her white lie, but she didn't want her sister to worry. Normally, she was the queen of packing, but with the band's new release approaching and her brain often getting distracted by a certain drummer, she hadn't quite been herself lately.

'OK, so you *will* be on that flight tomorrow?' Louisa asked, her voice a little imperious.

All Sabrina's attempts at bubbliness evaporated. She snatched the band's schedule from the desk and made her way to the door to head to the photocopier room. She was too tired to deal with Louisa's sceptical, patronizing tone.

'Lou, please. It's Grandpa's ninety-sixth birthday; of course I will be on that flight tomorrow. I *am* going to be there,' she said with force. Her heels echoed along the deserted corridor. The cool office interior, bland cream walls and stark white furniture personified elegance and a modern flair in Lydia's eyes, but at this time in the evening when most of the staff had gone home, it screamed cold to Sabrina. It lacked vibrancy in her mind and could do with some fresh flowers and a pop of colour.

'Well, I'm just checking. It's not going to be some glam, flashy party,' Louisa added, a hardness to her voice that stung Sabrina and caused anger to bubble in her stomach.

'I know it's not going to be a bloody glamorous affair and I don't bloody care. You know how much Nanna and Grandpa mean to me. I wouldn't miss this for the world. I miss them, and I miss you all and I will be on that plane tomorrow, so please, give it a rest.' She practically punched the copier to life and let out a frustrated sigh. She was growing tired of her sister's guilt trips over missing family affairs, especially when Louisa knew how hard she worked, and especially as Louisa knew she was busting her butt for their big sister Amanda's best friend and not just some random pop act.

Sabrina made a mental note to start adding pictures of the piles of paperwork and late-night sessions to her Instagram, to break up the once in a blue moon flashy press events – maybe this would appease Louisa.

'We all miss you too and can't wait to see you,' Louisa whispered after a minute or two.

Sabrina collected the photocopies and decided to call it a day. She picked up her pace, wanting to get back to her office and get home to pack. It had been months since she had been home and though she felt nervous about leaving her boys, she could do with the break.

'Look, I'm sorry for getting snappy with you but I'll be there, and it would be nice if you believed me, for once,' she said, softer now. As she walked past Lydia's office she noticed the light was on. It hadn't been on earlier. She had thought Lydia had gone home for the day. Squinting her eyes and sending a quizzical look through the glass, she noticed Lydia was not alone and her breath caught.

'Is everything OK, Brina? I'm going to head to bed now – it's pretty late here,' Louisa said.

Sabrina tiptoed into her office as quickly and quietly as she could and gently closed the door behind her. She steadied her breath to answer Louisa: 'Erm, sorry, yes, Lou. I'm fine and gosh, yes, please get some sleep. It's already morning there. I love you and I'll text you tomorrow.'

'OK, love you, Brina,' Louisa said before putting the phone down.

Sabrina placed her phone in her bag and shook her head. She needed to pull herself together; she was being ridiculous. Tears pricked her eyes as she gathered her belongings and dashed out of her office. Without glancing back at Lydia's window, she took the lift to the ground floor. When the doors opened she marched to the huge glass doors and swung them open with force, letting the cool LA breeze graze her warm cheeks.

She felt ashamed for her dramatic performance and scolded herself for allowing Lydia to get to her so much, but this had been the final straw. Lydia could boss her around, criticize every move she made and talk down to her all she wanted – it was business; it was work – but to mess with her heart in this way was beyond ruthless.

How could she work for such a horrible woman? It was Lydia who had warned Sabrina to stay clear of dating clients. The company didn't tolerate it and Sabrina was asked to promise that she would not date any member of San Francisco Beat. This rule, however, had only come into play after Lydia had heard that Levi and Sabrina had got rather close at the band's album launch party two years ago. Sabrina had never heard of it prior to the event. And Sabrina hadn't intended to be unprofessional, but it just sort of happened.

Naturally, she had pulled away from Levi, worried about being taken seriously, scared that she would get in trouble, that she was breaking rules. How silly had she been to throw away what she and Levi had – and for what? There hadn't been any rules then, but now Lydia had gone and created and enforced those stupid rules. And she'd made it abundantly clear that when one of the boys dated it should be with a fellow star – a model, an actress, someone who could raise their profile, someone who was definitely not Sabrina.

She dragged her feet along the sidewalk towards her apartment. How could she have been so naive? Of course, Lydia had only been jealous – she had wanted Levi for herself. Sabrina realized this, but it was too late. The image from moments ago now burned in her brain: Lydia with her arms wrapped around Levi's neck, falling with him onto the couch in her office.

Sabrina shuddered. She didn't know what hurt more: the fact that this woman hated her so much or that she had thought Levi had felt the same way she had that night they kissed. Who was she kidding? What guy waited two years for someone? She didn't live in a fairy tale; this was real life and in real life she had chosen work. She had stomped on the book of love without turning another page, and in doing so had well and truly placed Levi in the friend zone.

She didn't have a right to be sad. It had worked out well for everyone. The band were doing fantastic and she had progressed tenfold with her job in spite of Lydia. Yet here she was, with another Christmas upon her, daydreaming of Levi. Whether she had the right to or not, she did indeed feel sad. She needed her grandpa's pizza and she needed it now.

Chapter 2

Grandpa's Pizza

Ingredients (I'm sure this makes a lot of mini pizzas; need to check on pizza for one?):

10oz yeast
1lb flour
Olive oil
1oz butter
Mug of water
Cheese and sauce

What to do:

Once yeast dough is formed (thank you, Grandpa), roll it out to fit the trays/baking sheets.
Place trays in clear bags (not Tesco bags like Grandpa did once; they will melt) and leave in warm oven until risen.
Once the base has risen, take the trays out of the bags.
Turn the oven on and when ready, cook one side of the base until golden brown.
Flip over and add sauce and cheese like Grandpa does.
Place back in the oven and allow cheese to melt and edges to turn golden.

With a tear in his eye Grandpa reached out and touched Amanda's arm. He pulled her towards him and gave her a kiss on the cheek. 'Thank you,' he said with so much sincerity that Amanda couldn't stop her eyes from welling up too. She paused for a moment to take in his features. His bright blue eyes glistened, the wrinkles on his round face crinkled up and a small smile developed at the corners of his mouth as he looked at her. If hearts could leap from one's chest, smile and do happy dances, Amanda was certain that's what hers would be doing right now. Her chest felt fit to burst, she loved this man so much.

'Grandpa, *grazie*. I'm so excited. I think I finally have it all up here now,' she said, knocking her knuckles against her forehead. She then wrapped her arms around his waist and squeezed him tight. 'Come on, let's go and sit in the living room and have a break.'

Before they could leave the kitchen, Grandpa did his usual check. Deep down, Amanda knew he didn't doubt her knowledge in the kitchen, but at the same time she was aware that Grandpa liked being thorough. He loved teaching her and repeating the steps to every recipe numerous times and she loved learning from him and could listen to those steps every time he repeated them.

'It will take about ...' Grandpa started.

'... an hour,' Amanda finished. Both were looking at the oven door.

'Ah, you know.' Grandpa's face lit up as he said this. He nodded and walked in the direction of the front room to join the others. He had his arms outstretched, touching the walls as he walked. They were his guide now; he didn't quite trust his failing eyesight. His shoulders were hunched from years bent over the kitchen counters and his legs wobbled delicately with each step he took.

Amanda puffed out her chest. She loved the feeling of making her grandpa proud. Then she subtly walked behind him, his shaking legs making her anxious that he would fall. They had been in the kitchen for the better part of an hour, making pizza dough. At ninety-five years old that was no mean feat. You still couldn't get him out of the kitchen when he had his heart set on cooking. These days, however, he knew when to stop and rest, when his legs couldn't take his weight much longer and no amount of his determination and strong will could hold off the aches and pains.

Grandpa went to sit down beside his youngest granddaughter – Amanda's baby sister, Louisa – on the soft grey couch. Louisa placed a hand on the small of Grandpa's back, guiding him down, aiding him with his balance as his old knees did their best to bend. Then she scooted up to give him some space and make sure he was comfy.

Amanda made for the little blue chair in front of the fireplace. This had been the girls' favourite spot to perch when they were kids. In the cold months, they would run in from school, drop their schoolbags at the foot of the stairs and race to the living room, ready to fight for the chair. With their arms outstretched over the flames they would try to capture the heat, as Grandpa shouted, 'Careful not to roast,' with a chuckle. They would tell their *nonni* about their day and what they had been up to while taking it in turns to sit on the chair, indulging in soft, buttery Bauli cakes as crumbs sprinkled the carpet.

Things hadn't changed much, except these days Amanda had to position herself more carefully in the chair. When she looked up she caught sight of Louisa who was grinning, her brown eyes looking from the chair to Amanda. They weren't kids any more. The precise movement – a twist of the hips and a gentle shuffle to avoid getting stuck between the armrests – was certainly a sight to behold. She couldn't help but reciprocate Louisa's grin. She would not get stuck today; she'd mastered this by now.

'Grandpa, would you like a biscuit?' Louisa asked, picking up the tin and offering it to him.

'Just one?' he questioned, making both girls laugh. Amanda watched him tuck into his chocolate biscotti. Tears threatened her eyes again as she replayed his 'thank you' in her mind. Though

269

Grandpa could be impatient at the best of times, his passion for cooking knew no bounds and it was getting harder for Nanna to help him in the kitchen.

The girls' mum would often tell him that he couldn't start whipping up things left and right and then leaving it for Nanna to finish and clean up. Mum would have to explain to him that Nanna was getting old too. This frustrated Grandpa. He would get bossy and occasionally snap when the girls tried to help him.

Today, hearing him say 'thank you' after Amanda had helped him mix up the pizza dough and prep it to rise in the oven had melted her heart. Not only because in that moment he seemed to acknowledge his sometimes-bad moods and apologize for them, but also because she couldn't imagine not being able to cook whenever she wanted. She understood his need to be in the kitchen; after all, he had passed on that same passion to her. She knew how important cooking was to him. His 'thank you' had been filled with gratitude – all because of the simple act of being there for him, allowing him to do what he loved.

'One for Amanda too,' Nanna said to Louisa, pointing at the gold tin of biscuits on the coffee table. Tins of biscuits were a permanent fixture in the living room. '*Mangia, mangia,*' Nanna continued, as she turned to look at Amanda.

'I am, Nanna, I am, look,' Amanda replied, her nanna's voice snapping her out of her thoughts. She stood up out of the chair, with a ninja-like swivel of her hips, so they wouldn't get caught under the tiny armrests, and took a biscuit from the tin. She smiled at her nanna and stuffed the whole thing in her mouth.

'You're a cheeky girl,' Nanna said, with a tut and a shake of her head.

Amanda took another biscuit and bent down to kiss her nanna on the forehead. 'I love you,' she said, with a mouthful of amaretti.

'God bless you,' Nanna replied, her voice wobbling slightly. '*Grazie, grazie* for helping Grandpa.'

Amanda leant down and kissed the top of her forehead once more, her nanna's rose scent filling her heart with contentment.

'What time is it?' Grandpa asked, squinting through his round glasses, to see the clock above the fireplace better.

'Nearly time, Grandpa,' Louisa answered. Both sisters knew all too well why he was asking. Amanda and Louisa's sister, Sabrina, was due any minute and Grandpa had spent the better part of the morning looking at the clock. It had been a while since he'd had all three of his granddaughters together. His excitement was clear from the sparkle in his eyes.

'Ahh, I ask you too many times,' Grandpa said, shrugging his shoulders and placing his hand on top of Louisa's biscuit-free hand.

'No, no, it's OK, Grandpa – we're excited too. We understand,' Louisa replied, chewing a crunchy Pirouette thoughtfully.

'But what more is there for me to think about?' he continued, turning to face Louisa.

Amanda smiled, knowing this action meant Grandpa was about to impart some wisdom.

'At my age, what is more important than family? What do I have to think about? To make sure they are fed, me and Nanna have food for them. I must think about you girls being safe. Your mamma, yes, she looks after you and well, yes, your daddy can provide for you, but me and Nanna, we can only do so much. We can help too. We are always thinking like you are our own daughters.'

Her grandpa's broken English made Amanda's heart soar. The girls were fluent in Italian, but they often alternated between the two languages when speaking with their *nonni*. It helped them all: the girls to keep their Italian fresh and their *nonni* to understand English better for when they needed to speak with English family and friends.

At that moment, the doorbell rang. Both girls looked at each other with Cheshire-cat-like grins. Louisa sprang up from her seat. Amanda stood up, less frantic. Both Nanna and Grandpa sat upright, their eyes shining like they had just won the lottery.

'She's here,' squealed Louisa, gently shoving Amanda out of the way and racing to the door. 'I'll get it.'

Amanda merely chuckled and walked behind, allowing her little sister to take the lead. Louisa often got angry with Sabrina for moving away to LA and leaving everyone behind, but it never changed how excited she got when Sabrina came home. Amanda, on the other hand, was a little more reserved. She was pleased her sister had followed her dreams and over the moon that Dan and his band were in good hands, but there remained a part of her that stubbornly missed Sabrina and was mad with her for being so far away too.

'The eagle has landed,' Mum reported as she came through the front door first, arms loaded with birthday balloons and cards, having just picked up 'the eagle' from the airport. 'Safe and sound – she's home,' Mum said. Her eyes shone as she kissed Amanda and Louisa, as they passed each other in the corridor. Mum continued to the living room to say hello to her parents, as Amanda walked leisurely outside, and Louisa practically flew.

Like a local celebrity, Sabrina, the middle child, was standing in the middle of the path, between the cherry trees and the fence. Her sandy blonde hair was blowing in the breeze and she had clearly picked up an LA tan. Amanda noticed her bronzed skin glowing under the soft British sun, as Sabrina waved and said hi to the neighbours.

'All right, Jennifer Lawrence, it's only been an entire year – we all haven't missed you that much,' Amanda shouted into the street, from her position leaning casually against the doorframe.

Sabrina turned to face them at the same time Louisa leapt outside and nearly bowled her sister over with a hug.

'I've missed you, Brina,' Louisa said, sweetly, as Sabrina gasped for air, Louisa's hug choking her. Amanda looked on in amusement.

'I've missed you too, Lou. It's good to see you. It feels good to breathe in this British air.' Sabrina took a big breath in, as Louisa let her go, and then she let out a deep sigh. Amanda knew she loved parts of her life in LA, but it comforted her to know that it hadn't stolen her sister just yet. Watching her hazel eyes soften as she took in the surroundings, she could tell Sabrina was happy to be back and that nothing compared to home.

'You look exhausted. So, what presents did you bring back?' Amanda asked, leaving her position by the front door and wandering over to join the party.

'Always so kind with the compliments, aren't we? I might have gifts for you, but I'll be needing a hug first,' Sabrina said, and waved her arms in the air, dramatically motioning for a hug, while giving her big sister her best puppy dog impression.

'That we are, and it better be an awesome gift. I can't just be giving away free hugs,' Amanda said, rolling her eyes and stepping forward to hug her sister.

'Come on, Brina, Nanna and Grandpa are so excited to see you. You know what Grandpa's like – he hasn't stopped asking about you all day. Plus, we've held off with the birthday celebrations till you got here,' Louisa said, grabbing her sister by the arm and pulling her towards the house. Amanda strolled calmly behind them. Though she didn't quite display her emotions on her sleeve like Louisa did, there was no hiding the bright smile that was now etched on Amanda's face.

* * *

The dining room was full of colour. Red, green and white balloons were bunched up – dangling from the doorframes and curtains – and wrapping paper had been strewn across the table, as had bags of pasta and vibrant Italian cake boxes.

Sabrina's eyes drifted round the table. She took in everyone's features, everyone's movements: her mother's chocolate eyes sparkled with pure delight; Dad had his hands resting on his stomach as he leant back in his chair, stuffed and happy from all the food; Grandpa's eyes twinkled; Nanna's smile reached all the way to her ears, making her look twenty-one and carefree again; Amanda's green eyes focused intently on the food in front of her and Louisa simply watched her grandpa, making sure he had everything he needed.

Everyone talked over one another, laughing uncontrollably in between devouring each piece of pizza quicker than the speed of light. In that moment, she felt content, like there truly was no place on earth she would rather be. All the stress and drama of work melted away like the mouth-watering mozzarella she was chewing; it was heaven on earth.

'Grandpa, I sure have missed this,' she said, holding her piece of pizza in the air, like it was a trophy.

'You can get pizza in America, no?' Grandpa replied with a cheeky grin.

'Ha, you know as well as I do, Grandpa, that no pizza on the planet tastes as good as this. No one will ever be able to make it taste as amazing as you do,' Amanda said.

Sabrina loved the passion her sister had for their grandpa's food. It made her laugh hearing Amanda's voice rise with pride when talking about his pizza.

'It's crisp, yet chewy, with the perfect amount of crunch, and it's as light as air,' her big sister continued.

Sabrina watched as Grandpa's gaze met Amanda's and he gave her a small wink. They were like two peas in a pod.

'Hear, hear,' Sabrina chanted, raising her wineglass now that her pizza had been demolished. She felt dizzy on love and Lambrusco, but her eyes threatened to roll back in her head. Amanda had been right: she not only looked exhausted, she absolutely felt it too. Her bones were heavy, her neck tight. She rolled her head from side to side, hoping it would loosen up.

'It's good to have you home, sweetheart,' Dad said, raising his glass and clinking it against hers.

'It feels great to be home, Dad.' Sabrina smiled softly. It really did feel wonderful to be home. Her shoulders relaxed at the thought of not having to deal with her wouldn't go amiss in a Disney villain line-up, Cruella de Vil of a boss, Lydia, for the next few days.

The warmth of the room and the bubbles from the Lambrusco made her feel a world away from LA. Tonight she was surrounded by the people she loved more than she could say, and who genuinely loved and cared for her. '*Buon compleanno*, Grandpa,' she shouted, raising her glass to the room once more. Seeing her grandpa's face light up would keep jet lag at bay for a while longer.

'*Mamma mia, grazie, grazie*. How many girls have I got here now?' Grandpa said. His voice filled the small dining room, his happiness radiating to each of them.

'*Buon compleanno*,' Nanna shouted, clapping her hands together. 'Louisa, get the *pandoro*. Come on, come on.' Nanna too was thrilled to have all her girls round the table together. Any time this happened was cause for cake and celebrations, but when it came to birthdays and special times like Christmas, Nanna looked like a child, her face etched with glee. She looked to her husband and whispered, '*Buon compleanno*, my dear,' before cutting a huge slice of *pandoro* and placing it in front of him. She then went back to cutting more big chunks of cake and passed everyone a piece. 'Be happy, happy,' Nanna continued. 'Ahh *grazie*, God.'

Sabrina wasn't sure her stomach could handle the mountain of *pandoro* in front of her, after eating so much pizza and drinking a fair bit of wine, in addition to jet lag that had now kicked in, but it smelt so buttery and delicious and Nanna was staring at her expectantly. Not eating it was not an option – it was never an option. Plus, she was only in town for a week. She had to eat all her favourites while she could get them, and it was Grandpa's ninety-sixth birthday after all.

With these thoughts sloshing round her brain, she laughed to herself and took a huge bite. No sooner had the vanilla flavour hit her taste buds than her slice had gone. So much for not having any room left.

'*Grazie*, Nanna,' she whispered, with a chuckle.

The next book from Lucy Knott is coming
later in 2019!

ONE PLACE. MANY STORIES

If you enjoyed The Ingredients for Happiness, then why not try another delightfully uplifting romance from HQ Digital?